I0589343

THE RETURN OF WHAT'S BEEN LOST
Stories and Poems

PETER WELTNER

MARROWSTONE PRESS

SEATTLE

For Atticus Carr,
again and again

Table of Contents

The Return of What's Been Lost

His feet drag along the river's ford. His ears throb from too much song. "I baptize you, I baptize you, I baptize you in the name of the Lord." The congregation gathers around him, thigh-or waist-deep in the sand-colored river, its bottom stirred by recent storms. Stumbling on a rock, he splashes into the water before his father shoves him all the way under. His legs buckling, Leith slips on the slick bottom. No one's holding on to him anymore. His father's hands have ceased to grasp his shoulders. He feels as if he's being washed away.

There's no air, only river in his nostrils and mouth. He tries not to breathe, not to swallow. Baptism is our first death, his father preaches, killing sin in us so that at our second birth, that's no death at all, we'll fly to heaven. Wrapping his arms back around him, his father hauls him up from drowning. Water drips off Leith's face. He can't see. Everyone looks blurred. Everyone presses too close. His mother offers him a towel.

He feels nothing. Nothing's changed. The Lord's face does not shine upon him. His eyes follow a jay, not a dove, flying not down like a heavenly spirit but further and further away.

"Glory," his father intones in his singsong voice, separating the word into its two syllables as if each by itself were an incantation. "Glory."

Leith's eighteen, arriving late to the river and its rites. The next morning, a titmouse lands on a persimmon branch and, bobbing, cracks a seed, a flicker stares at him from a tulip tree, a hawk spirals over an old oak stand, all laughing him awake. Go now, they seem to say, it's time to quit your daddy's world. There's a war on. Be like us. Find a god elsewhere who'll set you free and bring you to glory.

Kasserine Pass. Snow-like drifts of sand cover dead men's faces. Sooner or later the desert will bury them all under dunes fierce winds shape into graveyard mounds that never stay still more than an hour. As after a late summer thunderstorm back home, when the winds quiet, the sun throbs hotter, rippling the air until it seems to bend and break and splinter like glass.

The sky is blindingly white. Even the pass where they'd just fought glares back at him with eyes as blank as plain white paper though unburied bodies, shredded uniforms, metal shards splotch it like ink stains. He stares harder, trying to read the marks they'd left in the desert as if they were holy writ. Rubbing his eyes, he turns away, not wanting to see more ruin and waste. He would like to sleep, but never can.

At their sergeant's command, the men pick up their weapons and drag themselves forward toward the invisible line in the sand they'd been told the Germans and some Italians have recently drawn a few miles east, somewhere so empty, Leith guesses, it's long past worth fighting for. Past where birds can fly and still find food. Close to where his father's God might have been born. The last place on earth.

Home again. Through the church's milky windows, the noontime August light is sand-colored like the cypress-rich, gritty Mayodan River's banks fifty feet away. The church is bare-plank floors, white-washed walls from which spare, bodiless crosses hang, a lectern, a tiered choir loft behind it.

As his father is preaching that man is born of blood corrupted by the heat of desire and the fires of lust, two deacons open the rattling church windows to let in some air. As his voice rises to a higher pitch, his father gazes out at the summer thunderheads, grackle black and iridescent. "God rides on the wings of the wind in chariots of cloud," he preaches. "Thunder sounds his wrathful warning. Lightning's his sure messenger. Behold and beware."

Around the church's cemetery where Leith's family has buried its dead for more than a century, wild datura thrives, columbine, phlox, salvia patches, red and black sumac, and honeysuckle vines dusted with yellow powder. Invariably dressed like a notions salesman traveling from town to town by train, his father is wearing his favorite electric blue suit. He wipes his brow with the oversized handkerchief that throughout his sermons he waves as if forever saying goodbye. He flourishes it like a flag.

"For the Lord to enter us, we must become wise enough to despise ourselves. Be small to yourselves, my children," he admonishes, "to be greatly with God."

Leith steps outside. Near the church, the river grows lazily fat. A black bull ambles through an opened gate in a tall picket fence and gazes at him with the disdain of a pagan god who knows far more than most men do about wisdom and its uselessness.

Back inside, his father is preaching again about how baptism is our first death. It's not a good day to risk the river and the boy has refused to wait. No more than thirteen, garbed in a white robe, he's standing in the pool, holding his nose. Leith's father lays his hands on his head and gently immerses him, but holds him down almost too long. Throwing his arms around the boy, he hauls him back to life. The boy sputters and coughs but is smiling, wide-eyed. The people of the town, the devoted members of his father's church, all except Leith applaud.

His father shakes the boy's hand and returns to his lectern. His face is gray as he prophesies the doom soon to come to too many others. "The hour is upon us." He heartily slaps the boy's back as he walks, still dripping, down the aisle and out the door where three deacons await him with towels and dry clothes. "Welcome to paradise, my son," he calls after him. From the back of the church, two elderly women begin to mop the floor.

His mother's faith belongs not to her husband's church, but to the land around it, the twists in the river, fresh mown hay, fresh cut corn, crows cawing, squirrels hurrying through underbrush, a spider's web, wet from dew, drawn tight as a cat's cradle between the spindly fingers of two shrubs.

On Saturdays, she works in her garden dressed in heavy, manly shoes, jeans rolled above her ankles, a checkered shirt and embroidered vest, and cloth gloves with rubber palms and fingers to protect her hands from thorns. A blue bandanna knotted over each ear grips her long red hair as she prunes and nurses her roses. Behind her, black columns of hickory, pine, tulip poplars, and oak reach higher than the church's roof, as if soaring toward the heights of the sun, of a gold leaf sky.

Leith sits on the stone wall of an ancient bridge across the Mayodan. Leaves bristle or rustle in the breeze. The river's stream trickles over broken stones. As he watches his mother work, the rhododendron and laurel bushes tangled together at the end of the woods smell burnt, like the change in the air before a storm or after a savage battle.

He hears a cry from his parents' bedroom window. His mother drops her gardening tools. Leith runs in behind her.

Wearing only his skivvies, his father's fallen onto the hardwood floor. Blood seeps like spittle out of a corner of his mouth. His limbs squirm and jerk. "It's come so sudden and so welcome. Cover me up, son. Don't let strangers see me unclothed like this."

The ambulance is slow to arrive. The hospital is far away. "Nakedness pours water on the Lord's oil and puts out His light," his father says, barely audible, between heaving breaths. "The grave's our common shame. Pray for me. I must go to my Lord disrobed."

Leith wipes a fold of tissue across his father's mouth, wanting to comfort, eager to quiet him, to spare him the effort of speech. It fast turns red. He dies in his arms. He tries to, but cannot mourn him who has done him no harm that was not well-meant.

A boy's belly button, shiny and pink, the tufts of hair below, the thighs, the knees. The burned butter color of his skin, china doll eyes set in a tough guy's head, the shock of their two bodies coming as one.

Outside his room in the motel on the two-lane blacktop, a motorcycle sputters and stalls. With a corner of the sheet, Leith wipes the beads of sweat off the boy's forehead.

His muscles ache. His gut's sore. Yet his skin's delighted in every touch, every finger strolling over it, the boy's tracing the name he won't tell him on his flesh. Leith watches him dress and leave. The silence afterward is all that remains of the absurd brevity of their love. All that he'll be able to save.

He's buying some aspirin for his mother in the small town's one drugstore when he hears a voice from somewhere else. "Leith. Leith Elliston. As I leave and breathe, I thought you were dead."

It's strange, more than strange, it's uncanny and disquieting to have friends, pals, fellow soldiers he knows have died, some in the war, some at home, confront him almost daily, as if he should be numbered among them, buried in sand or a grave somewhere without a name or a place whose name's on a map only strategists read.

The return of those he's lost. Two days ago it was Kip Holloran on a bike. Yesterday, Mark Antonacci turning the corner at Smith's Store, chomping on a bear claw out of a plastic wrapper. From nowhere, nothing they appear, greet him, and vanish. Now it's Steve Brandt, smiling his toothy grin.

As Leith settles into the seat of his mother's pre-war car, an orange light pierces the breaking mist. Slick as enamel, the wet sidewalk steams. The whole county feels as oppressively humid as a crowded North African port, bits of it clinging to him like grass or dirt to his sweaty skin. A bird, confused, almost flies into a window. Inside the car feels hot as a tank.

He dreams of the last day he heard his father preach. He sits in his white oak chair in front of the choir, his right foot rising and falling in a slow, steady tapping motion. While he sings the hymns as lustily as ever, his black robe hangs askew off his hunched shoulders.

Laying her palm fan across her lap, his mother turns to her son in their pew, her face glistening through its veil of powder. In a raspy voice, she whispers, "I love it here. You think it's still spring. Then suddenly it's blazing summer."

He throws the covers off his too warm body. Why does he stay?

The rain stops before dawn when the birds start to chatter. He wanders across a field through woods to the river where, sitting on a boulder, he watches the water from a late storm overflow its banks. Grabbing a branch of a sycamore that had collapsed during the night, he climbs down its fallen moss covered trunk to where the branches sink into the flow.

The sun glares through low clouds. Two crows cling to a pine limb and caw at squirrels shinnying up its trunk. Far off, nearer the church, a hound brays at the last sliver of the moon. Leith tosses a clay clod into the river to test its strength as it rushes west through thick brush banked by forest.

In the parlor, his mother's untying the green velvet ribbons that bind her red hair and lets it down over her shoulders. The soft light of a cloudy day colors her skin pale as the white lace round her wrists or the old maid's collar of her dress.

She glances past a neighbor's barn toward the church and its cemetery. "I saw your father last night. In our bedroom. He looked so peaceful. Like he did the day we were married."

She removes a picture of him from her skirt's pocket. A stray dog, maybe wild, rustles through bushes outside. She lets it in. It licks her hand.

"Wide is the road that leads to death," she sings, "and thousands walk together there."

Leith tries not to cry. The world is beautiful, but there's a desert of lives lost within him. He misses them all. Pins of sunlight prick his eyes. Far off, as if in the next county, he hears a train, the Southerner bound for New York. Its whistle blows two long blasts, a short one, another long. He'll soon be going. He won't return.

The Wild Waters in This Roar

It's too early for the sun to have risen,
though first light's breaking over
Mount Davidson. The dying night
grips the dark tighter, a depth
to the sky like a bottomless lake's
unplumbed mysteries.

The ocean's at its fiercest, its roar
brawling, tsunami-like
and menacing, as if many jets
were on a mission climbing higher,
faster, or thunder were rumbling
ever louder, encroaching closer.

I wake to the sound on the Pacific side,
the rear of our house. Fear
can be thrilling, like lightning storms
in my childhood in Carolina, the hail
pelting windows, ripping twigs
and leaves, toppling weakened trees.

I step outside. The breeze
smells of seaweed, sand, and smoke
from the last of Sunday's beach
bonfires. High tide's slapping
the sea wall, its cold foam
prickling my face and hands.

The pelicans, gulls, plovers,
crows have flown someplace
inland, hiding in safety
from the force of the sea. The wind's piled
sand on the highway in mounds
as high as the smaller dunes.

A car with its headlights off
drives by, gets stuck. I recall
a man, his mule who tilled his field
at night, a sight I saw
when I couldn't sleep. What reason
or need made him farm at night?

They walked up and down in a pounding
rain, storm wailing, roaring
as I stared from a screened-in
porch bad dreams had sent
me to, man, mule sinking
in mud, unwavering in their plowing.

On the road, the car's wheels buzz
in the sand, drive free. Dawn's
like a scrim dimly backlit,
a soft yellow white.   Day
returns calmly. The winds have died.
The sea's his worked field, the furrows of waves.

Movietone: Detour

Gulls strut on the dock. His fresh blue shirt spangling in sunlight, Sayler sweats as he coils hawser around bollard. If his crotch itches, he stops to scratch it. While he works, a tug nudges a sludge barge up river. Train-flats, two freighters, and a fireboat glide past. Chain pulleys carrying supplies clatter shipside as swarming men on the deck funnel down planks to the pier and race toward shore. Back on board, his crew the last done, almost alone, Sayler tries to rest in his bunk. His mind sinks into a sleep like the sea.

Dead eyes are as lusterless as scratched marbles. On oil-slicked water, burning hair and skin crackle. As you hook them out of the drink, their stiff bodies squeak like wet rubber. Blood seeps from their noses and ears. When in her small garden Sayler's mother, clipping roses, pricked her thumb on a thorn, her blood did not gush but trickled. Just before the crash, his father threw his body across Sayler to keep his son's head from smashing into the windshield. Afterwards, all Sayler heard were tires whirling, the wind, and his father's voice rasping, "May God work more miracles through this boy." When he looked at the gash across his thigh, his blood was barely oozing out of the wound. He wakes in his bunk sweating.

An old guy sitting on the crapper to his right whistles "Jingle, Jangle, Jingle" to himself. In the shower, a fog-like steam veils the men's bodies and clears only once they've left the room. Alone, Sayler stands in the corner prodigious and alert, like a boy hidden by a wall of bushes and woods, scrubbing himself in a clearing under heavy rains. No undertaker has laved a body more carefully, no sea washed one more clean.

He spit shines his shoes to a bootblack's pride. His fresh whites stick to his skin. With a small steel mirror, Sayler checks the tilt of his hat on his head. He flips open his wallet and counts the bills. If he is careful, they will last until the end of his leave.

He smartly salutes four more times before he steps back on land. His watch says it's already half past nine. When he stares beyond the reach of the city's lights into the sea-dark sky, he finds neither moon nor stars. Their absence twitches a nerve in his groin.

Times Square lures him like a pulp book cover. His lips shape the names spelled out on a dimmed marquee. A barker wearing a weather-worn, snap-brim fedora pulled down to his ears tugs on the sleeves of the two marines who peek into the crack between the doors to a peep show. At the end of the block, another calls to the crowd and points to where the jazz band's playing some Dixieland. Globes hanging in a triad draw Sayler's eyes to the front of a honky-tonk bar where soldiers huddle singing "Who Wouldn't Love You," slurring the words. At each mistake they make, they laugh harder.

Sayler claims a surveyor's patch of vacant pavement and tries to count the pinpoints of the skyscrapers. He needs to find a place to sleep. Across the street, GIs fire rifles at metal targets in a shooting gallery. Two whores wearing short yellow skirts stroll past him, their arms linked, their heels clicking on the sidewalk.

The hot night sky sweats. Heading uptown, Sayler reaches a street as black as the sea, the air sharp with the smell of brine, and turns away from the piers. Close to Third Avenue, he stops where the sidewalk and part of the street are slashed by slats of light from a window in which a sign reads, Cheap Rates. By Day, By Week. On the El, a train screams past.

The desk clerk is as thin as light at dusk. When he speaks, his voice bat-squeaks. He studies the blocks pencilled in on a large torn paper sheet, deliberates, and slips Sayler a key to six fifteen, saying, "You tell 'em yours is the cot." Sayler looks at the clock that ticks above three rows of empty pigeonholes and slides the key toward him under the grate.

The elevator doesn't work. From the sixth floor stairwell landing, he hears some shouts, a few curses, laughter. When he reaches his room, the door is wide open but, though he knocks loudly, no one bothers to answer. Two sailors are playing cards. Smoke fogs the room. Sayler drops his sack in a spare corner and leans against the wall near an unmade bed where a guy, wearing only his skivvies, lies smoking a cigar, a round glass ashtray nestled in the black mat of his chest hair. He glares at Sayler and blows three perfect smoke rings. "You gotta be kidding. Where you supposed to sack?"

Sayler scratches the back of his neck. "Desk clerk said that cot."

"Tough luck." A fourth ring drifts toward the ceiling. "It's taken."

The card dealer twists around to take a look at the newcomer. "Aw, let him have it, Doc."

"Yeah," a red-haired kid winks. "Better this than that stinking spic. Where'd he go to anyhow?"

The dealer throws down another card. "Ben spooked him. Scared him shitless with that knife of his."

"Hell, Atkins," the red-haired kid complains, "another humping deuce. Next time, let me cut those fucking cards."

"Your first night back on shore?" Atkins asks Sayler without taking his eyes off the deck.

"Yeah."

"Which ship?"

When Sayler tells them the name, the guy on the bed snickers. Sayler sees he likes to show his body off, his sinews pulled tight, his thews taut. "Where's the head?" Sayler asks. "I got to pee."

The guy in his skivvies crushes out his cigar and sets the ashtray down on the bare floor. "Down the hall." He studies Sayler like a cop a suspect. "What do you think, Chuck?"

"He looks okay to me," Atkins says, reshuffling the deck. "What do you think, T.K.?"

The red-haired kid shrugs. "Sure. Hit me, Chuck."

"Ben'll have to talk to you, too," the guy on the bed explains.

"What is this?" Sayler says. "The third degree?"

Doc's tongue probes the inside of his cheek. He spits. "We're going crawling later. Before the bars close. Maybe find us some girls. We're particular about who we get drunk with, that's all. Ain't that right, Chuck?"

"Damn," T.K. snorts. "A lousy trey."

"Want to come along?" Chuck invites Sayler.

"Not tonight, guys. Too tired. Maybe tomorrow," Sayler says. Outside in the corridor, Sayler passes two soldiers, both drunk, each barely supporting the other. In the john, as his piss floods the urinal, he reads the numbers and names etched or scrawled on the crumbling wall and studies the crude pencil sketches. But he wants mostly to sleep.

He waits downstairs in a corner of the crowded lobby for the others to leave. After they've gone, back up in the room, he opens the window, strips, and stretches out on the cot. Hours later, when Sayler wakes as if startled from another bad dream, the red-haired kid is spewing vomit out the window as Atkins clutches the boy's waist to keep him from falling. The wall across the alley is a black backdrop to the struggle of a four-legged man.

"Jesus, T.K.," Atkins pleads, "take it easy, buddy. Keep still."

A big guy Sayler hasn't seen before leans back against the closed door and wolf whistles. "Ain't they cute?" he says to Doc.

"Shut up," Atkins hollers, "and give me a hand, damn you, Ben."

"Not a chance," Ben says. "I'd like to see him fall."

"Get a hold of yourself, T.K.," Atkins orders. "I mean it now."

"Fuck him. The fruit can't hold his liquor," Ben says, sneering at Doc who upends a nearly empty bottle and drinks it dry. "Who's the new girl in the cot?" he asks Doc, grabbing the bottle from him and tossing it across the room toward the window where it shatters only a few feet from Atkins and T.K.

"Damn it, Ben," Atkins yelps.

"Okay. He's okay," Doc says, his speech slurred.

Ben's nostrils widen. "Sure he is."

"No, really."

"What's your name, sailor?" Ben commands, officer-like. His voice sounds as if it means to stalk him.

When Sayler tells him, the big guy whoops and slaps his hands together. "My mother's maiden name," Sayler explains fast and spells it twice.

"Oh, Christ," T.K. moans and staggers toward his bed.

"Let's go," Ben nudges Doc. "We've got better things to do than play nursemaid to these old ladies. The night's still young and there's money to be had and whores to lay, right, Doc?"

"You better believe it, Ben," Doc says, racing him out.

When Sayler finds sleep again, he hears his mother crying and he wants to tell her there's no need. He'll be all right. But she continues to rock in her chair like someone beyond comforting. A torpedo hits below the waterline. After the last blast, the ship slowly sinks. Then the sea is calm and empty again. Sayler sees a distant shoal and feels less frightened as he swims toward it. But no one is there. Nothing is ever there.

When he wakes at dawn, the shade blows in from the open window, and a single bar of light crosses Atkins's and T.K.'s heads where they lie sleeping side by side in a narrow bed. The big guy sprawls on an uncovered mattress laid out on the floor and snores like a horse snorting. Doc has bunched his sheets into a corner of his bed and lies on his back, his stub cock flopping through the fly of his shorts. The room smells like a drying pond.

2.

Before the others wake, Sayler showers in a rusted stall, dresses, and escapes, though it is already nearly noon. Under the shadows of the tracks of the elevated railway, he slowly eats an orange he's just bought at a stand and cut open with a penknife he carries in his pocket, picking out the seeds with the blade. An ancient Chinese woman in slip-slop slippers passes. A young girl wearing a blue cotton frock and Minnie Mouse white high heel shoes strolls by, then turns around to stare and wink. In the air, he sniffs grease, smoke, malt.

Already the bars are as packed as troop trains. He walks west, then north toward the park he remembers from his last leave. Down narrow streets, delivery trucks rumble and reverberate. Fleshy women sit on the stoops of smoky brownstones, sipping the sun, their lips thick and wet. All around him, tall buildings shine bottle-bright.

Sayler reaches the park at the circle. Paradise, his father had preached, was the park which the Lord had built for Adam in Persia or Mesopotamia. No other will ever be like it. On the plains where Sayler grew up there were only dust and wind. Every day he had to sweep the dirt out of the white clapboard church and the small frame house where they lived across the road. When the winds stilled, his father would point to the clouds, "White as a good man's grave clothes," and to the sun which he said coursed through the sky like a burning and a shining light to all the gentiles. As they mopped the church one April close to Easter, his father, seized by the spirit, laid both hands on Sayler's head and, re-baptizing him Jonah, delivered him to the Lord.

Sayler stops at the streetlight and watches the driver in the wing-fendered Checker cab curse the stooped driver of an old hansom. The sky sparkles quiet as the sky over the sea. In the park, children are flying kites. A solitary man dressed all in green sets up croquet hoops near the boating pool. On the other side of the path, four fat and grizzled men toss horseshoes. Sayler squats on a hump of basalt rock. A heart-shaped leaf spirals down onto his lap, its broad blade tough and shiny. Sayler jumps up, brushes off the seat of his bell-bottoms, and exits from the park onto the street where everyone he sees looks wrinkled and rich.

He starts up the steps to the museum where he senses he doesn't belong. Once inside, he imagines himself in a mansion or palace, himself its lord or prince. He passes quickly through the chambers filled with gloomy religious pictures or portraits until he finds the room he remembers liking best in his first visit here, where the paintings' colors are billboard-bright and the surfaces thick with juicy gobs of paint as tempting as the candy buttons he used to scratch off paper to eat.

He approaches one in which lilies flicker where they float on turquoise water, checks both doors for guards, leans into the painting to squeeze a bubble of pale yellow to see if it will ooze like a popped pimple onto his thumb and fingers.

He escapes fast, almost running down both flights of stairs, laughing so hard he can barely breathe. At the park wall, he slows down and leans against it, rubbing his thumb against his forefinger, darkening the yellow pigment with his skin's own oils.

"Hey you. Sailor," he hears.

Sayler stuffs his hands between his armpits and glances over his shoulder. The man is dressed in a white suit like those men wear in hot places in the movies, his face angular and ax-head thin like an actor whose name Sayler can't remember. "You talking to me?"

His sharp chin juts out as he jangles change in his pocket. "Don't you realize that Monet is a masterpiece? Irreplaceable?"

Sayler eyes him nervously. "So what?"

"So what?" the man burbles. "So what? I should have you arrested is what."

Sayler arches his back and yawns. "Anyone ever tell you you look like that actor? You know, the one in all those shoot-'em-ups."

"What?" The man smiles like a child still half asleep. "Oh, I see. You're flattering me. For a price, I imagine. Well, then. How much?"

Sayler grins back boyishly. "Not much."

"Why is it I doubt that? Boys like you are all expensive." The man steps closer. "Let me take you to the Hotel Lexington first. We can go to the Hawaiian Room and drink out of coconut shells and talk. Would you like that?"

"I don't drink," Sayler says.

"What a pity." The man's right eyebrow crooks suspiciously. "But I won't insist."

Two boys dash past them on their bikes. A young woman leads a band of children up the museum's steps, each child holding the hand of another, all of them chattering. A taxi stops at the curb and lets out a man whose gold watch flashes in the sun. The man in white stands next to Sayler and whispers, "I can't resist blonds. Do you understand me? They'll be my downfall, no doubt. But who would mind sinking in eyes so blue?"

Sayler shrugs and rubs a little of the yellow paint onto the man's sleeve. "I got to meet a buddy down at the Midtown Bus Terminal in a couple of hours."

"I don't live far from here. There's time."

The building is only five blocks away. Its façade shines like gilt in the noon sun. Sayler pauses to notice the bowed iron window grates and the iron scrolled glass door. As they pass through it, the doorman pretends not to see Sayler and acknowledges only the man in white linen with a salute to the brim of his cap. As they enter the apartment, Sayler observes the pictures as dark as those in the museum's darkest rooms, the closed curtains, and the gloomy wood panels and walls. When they reach the bedroom, the man is trembling and nuzzles Sayler's offered neck. Like blind men's, their fingers read each other's bodies. They undress slowly, but move swiftly once naked, rushing into each other like water into a ruptured hull.

"Would you mind telling me your name?" the man asks Sayler as he dresses. "I like knowing names. Mine is Bill. Bill Blake, in fact." He finds his wallet in his suit pants and hands Sayler a fifty. "You were very sweet. Really. And I adore foreskins. Some of my friends think they're nasty. But not me."

"Thanks," Sayler says, blushing slightly, and stuffs the fifty in his pocket.

"Bill Blake," the man repeats. "Please, sailor," he pleads.

"'Sayler.' Just call me 'Sayler,'" Sayler says, laughs, and leaves.

When he steps back outside into the light, the blaring sun burns his eyes. His brain feels shackled. He breathes deep but the world under his feet buckles like the earth after he's been months at sea. He fixes his bucket hat on his head and tugs on his neckerchief.

The air feels wet and salty. He checks his watch. There's plenty of time. And that fifty makes him rich. Yet as he approaches Times Square his heart pounds and his lungs struggle for air. Like a swimmer who's gone out too far, he finds himself caught in currents which sweep him further and further from shore. Which should he try next, the Pink Elephant or the Astor bar?

3.

The night is stubborn, the stars like pins. Sayler squats by the shore-end of the pier and watches his day's second lover disappear behind the stacks of crates and boxes that had hid them from the streetlight on the other side. A police boat churns the dark river. Water slaps at the piles. Flecks of black clouds smudge the sky lit by the new moon's thin crescent. He refastens the buttons on his bell-bottoms and wipes his lips with a corner of his neckerchief. Near the ocean, a ship's siren sounds. He brushes himself off and heads back toward the cheap hotel where he's bunking.

Its lobby is jammed with men in uniform gathered in groups. Shoving his way through, he drops the gum he's been chewing into the encrusted maw of a brass spittoon. He climbs the stairs with exhausted legs, enters the room, tosses his hat onto a dresser, and flops down on his cot. The red-haired kid is opening a beer with a church key.

Doc regards Sayler with a toothy leer. "Look who's back. Hey, Sayler. You know what the definition of dancing is?"

"An old one, Doc," Atkins complains from across the room where he's pouring whiskey into the big guy's paper cup. The bed springs sag under their weight.

"A navel engagement without the loss of seamen," Doc says and guffaws. "Where you been, kid? Out getting your morale boosted?" He whiffs the air. "Only I don't smell no pussy. Do you smell any pussy, Ben?"

The big guy scratches his head with a sweaty, paw-like hand. "It all depends upon what you mean by 'pussy.'"

Doc opens another beer and chug-a-lugs. "Let's make him drop his flap and see if there's shit on his stick."

"Why, he's blushing, Doc," Ben hoots. "Blondie's blushing. I think you may be right, lookee there."

Atkins leans over and pulls a bottle out from under the bed. "You want a beer?" he offers Sayler.

Sayler shakes his head. Ben crushes his empty cup and tosses it out the window. "I bet the pussy don't even drink."

"Leave him alone, Ben," Atkins says. "He's okay. He's one of us."

"Yeah, he's okay," T.K. agrees. "Listen, we're going out drinking and looking for girls," he tells Sayler. "Ben knows this place where we can drink just about for free, he says. Get us some pocket money too, didn't you say so, Ben?"

"Shut up, jerk," Ben warns.

"I need my rest, guys," Sayler says.

"Fucker thinks he's too good to drink with us," Doc says, reddening.

"Preacher's son," Sayler says to explain and yawns.

Ben lumbers off the bed and grabs Sayler by his sleeve. "We're all in the same navy, bub. Understand?"

"Okay, okay," Sayler says. "I'll go."

"Nice ass," Doc says, following him out the door.

Ben grabs his crotch and wolf whistles. "Ain't it though?"

The strip joint Ben leads them to is back closer to Broadway. As he walks down the steps first, Sayler feels almost safe in the press of men at the door. A blue light beams on the dancer doing her bump and grind to the accompaniment of a three-piece band on a narrow stage across from the bar. The fringe on her halter and g-string shimmers like tinsel. The five sailors wedge their way through the crowd to the end of the bar. Ben steps up to the brass rail and orders them all beer. When he's handed his, Sayler says a silent prayer and drinks it down.

"Sayler's okay," Atkins says.

"Sure he is," Ben say. "Did I ever say different?"

"Our kind have got to stick together," Atkins drawls.

"Damn straight," Doc says.

"Wrong kind's taking over," Atkins says. "Sayler's all right."

"Besides," Ben grins. "Blondie here's our best bait."

The beer tastes bitter and stings his throat. "What?" Sayler says.

Ben sucks on the space between two teeth as on a chunk of hard candy. "You know what I mean. Look," he calls over to Doc. "He's blushing again, just like a fucking virgin. Ain't that sweet?"

"This place sucks," Doc complains after their third round.

"Screw you," Ben says. "Fuck-face."

"Where'd that stripper go?" T.K. asks as he settles onto a just vacated bar stool. "Where are all the dames, Ben? You said there'd be plenty of good looking dames."

"I said later, asshole," Ben says. "First we got to get some dough."

"I like that tune," Sayler says woozily. "Nice tune. 'Who Wouldn't Love You.'" Sayler reaches in his pocket for a nickel. "Gonna play it again." He hops off the stool and zig-zags toward the juke. He watches the record spin and the colored lights flash as a man's firm hand grips his right shoulder.

"My God, it is you. After this afternoon, I never thought in my fondest dreams I'd ever see you again. But see? Fate is sometimes kind. Here you are."

Sayler does not budge. "Go away, Bill," he says, his eyes still intent on the turning record.

"You can't be worried about your friends over there. Surely they know what kind of bar this really is. Why ever else would you have brought them here?"

"I didn't," Sayler says between clenched teeth.

"Well there you are then. I was watching him from across the room. That big one certainly does look menacing. Not my type at all, I'm afraid. Too rough. Too dangerous."

"He is dangerous, Bill. Leave me alone. Please."

"Oh no, baby. I think I fell in love today. Oh my," he says, twisting around. "Who do we have here. How's every little thing?" He holds his hand to be shaken but jabs it back into the pocket of his linen jacket when he sees the gesture is to be ignored.

"Are you a friend of my friend here?" Ben inquires in a voice lacking his usual growl.

"Why, yes. I am. In a way."

"He's not. I swear he's not," Sayler says. "Get him away from me, Ben."

"I think he is. I think he is a friend of yours. A good friend. A rich friend. And so he's a friend of mine. Why don't you come join us for a drink. You'll be buying, of course?"

"Of course," Bill Blake agrees amiably.

When the bar closes, Ben talks Bill Blake into buying them a couple of bottles to take back with them to the room. "I told him to leave me alone," Sayler drunkenly whines as he follows Atkins and T.K. up the steps.

Blake glances back at Sayler uncertainly. "I think perhaps I should say goodnight here," he says as he starts to walk away.

Ben crushes his cigar on the top of the stairs and grabs Blake by the collar of his jacket. "What was that, faggot? You're coming with us."

"Watch it, Ben," Doc warns. "S.P.'s at three o'clock." Ben claps a hand over Bill Blake's mouth.

Back in the room, Sayler collapses on his cot and props his head on his pillow, trying to see what is happening in the midst of the whirl. He labors to focus his eyes on a rust-colored water stain or on the lightbulb dangling from a cord that won't stop quivering. His old pocketknife is digging into his skin. He pulls it out and drops it on the floor. Ben forces him to drink some more, pouring in straight whiskey as Doc holds his nose. Sayler fights for breath to keep from drowning.

The first blows sound far away, like distant gunfire. He tries to get out of bed, he wants at least to raise his hand to stop it or to cry out, but he can't. Not even Blake screams. All Sayler hears is a steady pounding and something being slowly torn, like grass or weeds being uprooted.

4.

Bile and phlegm clog his throat. His stomach feels clotted with rot from harbor stews. Save for the distant roar of waves fading in his ears, the room is as quiet as if he were waking there alone. He holds his breath and hears no other breath, but on his tongue he tastes brass and acidic, slightly rotten tomatoes. When he breathes again, he smells blood. His cock swells from fear. In the hall, a body falls against the door and starts to puke. Sayler's stomach churns. Blood rains in his closed eyes.

When Sayler opens them, the light on the ceiling from the window is gun barrel gray. He needs to piss and rolls onto his side, but his vomit erupts and splatters on the floor before he is certain what he has seen. He steps out of his cot and wipes his mouth on a towel that reeks of sweat and mold.

Blake's body lies on the floor between the beds. Drool has trickled down the chin and dried like snail slick. Rust-colored stains streak the sheet which binds his naked body. His ears have been sliced off, his fingers and toes have been severed, his penis has been sliced down the shaft by a blade as broad as a bayonet's. From Blake's heart rises the handle of Sayler's penknife, its mother-of-pearl almost lustrous against the pool of blood.

Sayler recoils to the darkest corner of the room where his clothes have been tossed over his bag. He fumbles for his wallet and finds all his money still there, but it won't be enough. His eyes blur as if the room were suddenly filled with death-mist or fog. With the corner of a pillow case, he tires to wipe away the lick spittle from Blake's face and to close his bulging eyes. His stomach heaves again. He hurriedly cleans himself off, dresses, grabs his bag, and darts panting out of the room like prey from a lie of weasels.

Trying not to run, he heads for Times Square, too frightened to think for long of Blake. He sees the doorman point his finger at him at the line-up. Blood throbs in his brain. The sky is lambent, though bleached and sunless. Footsteps on the sidewalk behind him scare him, and he hears someone closing doors down a narrow hall. He needs more money. Two tricks, maybe three, should be enough, a day's work. Then an early evening visit to that locker room to check his uniform and rent himself some civvies. By nightfall, he is standing on line at the bus depot, his wallet full.

5.

Two days later, at dawn, he sits near the back of the bus and watches the country slide past him, the summer dry grass acrid in the hot breeze. At night, the stars swarm as at sea. The fourth morning, he wakes to a train's whistle filling the sky like the sun at daybreak while the bus waits at a rest stop somewhere in the plains for the last passengers to return from breakfast.

He stretches and turns his head to look at the little copse of spindly, silvery trees. Beside them, a four-door Nash with sidewall tires and wheel shields idles empty, puffs of smoke spiraling up from the muffler. Sayler feels the hand of providence grasp his shoulder and reaches for his pack from the rack above. He rushes up the aisle and jumps down on the hard packed dirt. "We'll be leaving in a jiffy," the driver warns, stifling a yawn.

Sayler dashes around the gas pumps and past an ochre hut and hides in the trees' shadows, waiting. Slowly, he walks up to the Nash. The driver's door is open. He checks around him, sees no one, hops in, and tosses his few belongings into the back seat. Even as he drives off, nobody rushes out from the restaurant to chase him. In the rearview mirror, he watches the motionless bus fade into the distance. The seat beside him is covered with maps. God, his father would declare, is marvelous to his saints. Sayler breathes more easily. The wind dries the sweat off his face.

When he can, he keeps to back roads and sleeps as he slept at sea, in the breaks between boredom and fear. His memory tests the latches on all the rooms he's left behind him now that he's AWOL and finds them all locked. He buys food at a village general store which feels to him as safe as the shoreline seen from deck. Near the desert, the first rains begin, the lightning like sheets of foil unrolling in the sky.

He pulls off at a diner. He sits in a booth beneath a row of buzzing lights, his drained coffee cup shoved aside, and rests his elbows on a red tabletop too shiny for his eyes. Rain splatters the plate glass window to his right. When he glances out into the dark, he does not recognize himself in the reflection but sees instead a grainy snapshot of another boy, yellowed and faded, eyes bleached to white slits by the steady wear of too much light.

The guy with a broom picks a nickel off the floor and slips it into a slot of the jukebox as the cook presses the flat of the turner onto the hissing meat and stirs the mess of frying onions. Winds slap the roadside sign and streak through the roof. When the cops stomp in, dripping wet, they hook their hats and jackets onto the rack beneath which tiny pools of water slowly form like splashes of light that he watches sparkle in a corner. He reaches for his change and places a quarter under the saucer. As he drives off, no one notices him leaving. All the way through the desert, the windshield wipers go click clack, click clack.

He crosses a mountain pass barely able to see through the rain to the edge of the road. At one sharp curve, with his brights on, he sees the guard rail's red reflectors flare, brakes, and skidding quickly turns. On the other side, close to the border, barricades have been set up, but he does not really believe that they are searching for him. It is only a detour, directing him a different way. Because it is so late when he gets to the town, the streets feel deserted, though the sky is now clear and the moon shines bright.

At the plain hotel, he must pay in advance before a room is made available to him. Having locked the door, he rests on a bed too soft for his body but blessed with a view of the river from where his head lies, the shade pulled up so that he can almost see the water rushing over rocks and the dark woods where owl, wildcat, shrew, mouse, and bat perform their nightly rites. In the morning, he sits on the porch, eating eggs and ham, and watches a groggy lizard slither across stones.

6.

Before he leaves, he reads another map. In less than a day he could be at the ocean. As he whistles the tune to "Who Wouldn't Love You," his muscles relax. He steers the Nash like a sailboat driven by strong winds. Green fields flow past. At a roadside stand, he stops to buy oranges. When he reaches in his pocket for his knife, panic scratches at his heart. He tears at the orange's skin and sucks it dry.

He would drive faster but the car balks and through the sleepy towns he must slow to a crawl though the billboards prod him on. In a valley of flowers, a boy stands by a eucalyptus, a straw hat tipped on his head, his dungarees too big for him, his thumb held out. Sayler brakes for him. As the boy runs toward the car, Sayler mutters to himself. That could be me almost, a few years ago. His father's sweaty palm presses down on his forehead as he leans across the passenger seat to open the door.

The boy says "Hey," and tosses his canvas bag into the back. "I'm headed for L.A. Where you going?" His neck cords are pulled tight and the smile in his eyes is desperate.

"Same place."

The boy offers his hand. "Terry. Terry Pruett. I've been drafted."

"Sayler. Sayler Watkins," Sayler says without meaning to.

The boy slumps in his seat as Sayler cuts back onto the road. "I ran away."

"Oh," Sayler says, frowning. "So did I." The sun pounds on the dash.

"You look like me," the boy observes and laughs.

"Yeah. I noticed."

They ride in silence through the orchards. The smell of the citrus etches like acid in the air. Sayler wipes his tired eyes and stares where a flock of blackbirds swoops down into a field of trees. Globes of ripe fruit are shining like lanterns. Terry rests the back of his head on the seat and gazes up at the car's ceiling. "I'm going to die. I know I'm going to die."

He swallows the saliva in his mouth. Dogs on the porch of a bungalow bark at them as they pass. "I'm going to get shot. Right here," he says, pointing at his guts. "I know I am."

Sayler looks away. "Yeah. I know what you mean."

Once in the city, Sayler gets directions from an attendant at a parking lot and drives three blocks from Terry's destination to an old hotel the guy had told him was cheap. "You don't have to report until tomorrow you said. How about it, soldier?" Sayler says. "A night on the town?"

Terry shakes his head "No."

The room stinks of fish. Sayler quickly opens the window. Outside, pigeons coo, their coral claws fixed as if snagged on the fire escape. Spider webs weave together in dusty cornices. Cockroaches scurry up the warped wallpaper.

"Stand here, next to me," Sayler directs and together they stare into the yellowed mirror. "You see, I really could pass for you."

"Maybe." The boy tosses his hat onto the bed and looks again. "Maybe you could."

"It's settled then. Tomorrow I'll go instead of you."

"Why?"

"Why not?" It seems a way out is all. For both of us. Listen, Terry. That car out there is stolen. I'm running from something terrible that happened. I need to disappear."

The boy chews his cheek. "What'll I do? Where'll I go?"

Sayler steps back from the mirror and sits on the edge of the bed. "You'll have to figure that one out for yourself, kid."

In the morning, Sayler wakes first and slips on Terry's briefs, socks, shirt, and dungarees. Even the boy's shoes fit him. He shakes Terry awake. The boy's muscles ripple as he stretches and yawns. Sayler smiles grimly. "How do I look?"

Terry rubs his eyes. "You wouldn't fool my mom."

"I don't need to fool her. Just some dumb sergeant who's seen you only once or twice before. It might work. It just might work."

"You're going to die."

"Yeah," Sayler says. "I know."

"You want to die?" the boy says, puzzled.

Sayler fixes the boy's straw hat on his head, getting the angle exactly right. "No." He chucks the boy's chin. "It was a swell night. Will I see you again?"

The boy stares back at him, uncomprehending. "I don't know."

7.

Angaur. Peleliu, honey-combed with natural caves that face each other across sheer gorges, their entrances sealed by concrete blast walls or oil drums filled with coral. Mangled corpses spew out across shallows. Leyte. Ormoc Valley where storms turn day into night. He slithers and slips from one steep muddy slope to another, from ridge to ridge where mountain meets sea. Men are bled white. Like bread or bits of cracker scattered for birds, they lie on the ground, soggy and bloated from rain. A bridge explodes. Howling men, their bodies already blackened by fire, scramble out of bunkers along a front no wider than an end zone and tumble, silenced, into a pit-like ravine. Flames billow from pillboxes as from a funeral pyre. Luzon. Each bend of the trail they cut through exposes more jungle. They march higher into the mountains. Here the thunder is manmade. At times, afraid, they hide in empty caves. His stools are bleached as bones. Though dizzy from disease, he sees the trigger wire concealed in an overgrown path to an old stone bridge and safely guides his men around it to the bank where they rest by a stream. Overhead, flocks of birds flap their wings and squawk like sullen gulls.

Missa

Playful seals, otters, a surfer riding waves alone,
a jam jar tossed intact on the beach, driftwood,
a soaked scarlet scarf, a polished, iridescent stone:
random things, each in its way enough, each good.

The wind's changing. A few close shutters against
new cold. Far off, crab boats resemble small islands.
The sea stays calm, though pelicans have sensed
shifting weather, flying as a flock over drifting sands.

I walk in the park past vines and brush, a pathless
thicket dense as a forest's. Migratory birds
rest by a lake that raccoons slip in through a mess
of algae and ferns. The sun's testing the edge of words

as it rises higher over hills, past clouds, a radiant
dawn widening the sky, filling the blessed country
of morning with a light that leaves nothing to recant
or regret. How speak idly of 'peace'? How talk of 'glory'?

Whose Woods, Their Silence

My story or sketch, call it what you will, is an attempt to tell you, many decades later, how the elderly man I am remembers my one brief sighting of him, never to see him again. It's a moment that has stayed with me throughout my life, that has made me, more than anything or anyone else ever has, the person I became or, better said, revealed to me who I was and would be throughout my many years. Or perhaps more candidly I should say it was him, the soldier, who revealed myself to me and still does. I have made his story, what little I know or suspect is true of it, into words because it is mine. Believe it or not, it's a summing up.

For the first time in my life, seeing him, I felt love in the way that would lead me to search for it later over and over, an unnameable desire, I suppose, a yearning for someone, something whose origin has remained always a mystery to me. Every person is a mystery to him- or herself in almost every respect, of course. We all acknowledge that.

But love is even stranger, more elusive. Why this man and not that or this woman and not that one? How and where does it all begin? Psychology's no use. No theories explain it. No science. One day it starts, even if you are surely too young for it, even if seems to begin in little more than a trivial incident, a chance meeting. Thereafter the course of your life is set forever. It makes no sense. It is wonderful and painful and makes no sense.

However inadequately, I can say or at least attempt to describe here what happened in my instance. It's the why and wherefore of love and all that flows from it that elude me, the longing for an unrealizable vision that you were given out of the blue one day. It's beyond the reach of your arms. You want to embrace it, to hold it tightly to your heart. But you can't. It's too far away, too long ago.

No words were ever exchanged between us, me and the solider who was a year or two late coming back from the war when those who hadn't fought were already beginning to put it out of their thoughts. It was all too quick, the encounter, if that is the right word for it, and I was just a boy, just thirteen.

Thus, there's no dialogue in this story because we didn't speak. And it will be told in the third person, though it happened to me, because the boy I was then and the old man I am now, though the same in a manner of speaking, bearing the identical name and all that, live in worlds so far apart, so different from one another, that we two are almost foreigners, speaking different languages.

Yet it's a single world we live in, isn't it? The past and the present co-exist in the realm of the soul. Now and then are, in a way, despite eternal arguments about progress and decline, despite the apparent differences between hope and nostalgia, mostly the same in all the ways that matter in the end. I find, don't you, that as I grow old my memory seems ever more eager to bring together its disparate parts, to tie together what's frayed, to make out of endings beginnings, out of beginnings your inevitable end, even the one you rue most and must finally face.

The first part of this story is largely true, the second part mostly, necessarily imagined, but never false. The two parts to me are equally real, if you see what I mean from what I've just written. Or meant to write anyway. Written out of desire, how could they be otherwise?

1.

He just turned thirteen, free to walk deep into the woods behind his family's home on his own during the long summer of the first polio quarantine. The dogwood had bloomed late that year but when it arrived it came in full May glory. Pink and white, its flowers tickled his nose with the woody smell of hearth logs drying. Wet rhododendron leaves shone with an olive green as dark as a pop bottle. Heavy with dew, laurel, pine, hickory, and oak, all the trees' limbs and branches dripped onto the forest's floor. The trail he used was slick from decayed needles and last fall's leaves, leaves mired in red clay and dark gray mud.

Black beetles, ants, a few white grubs and milky caterpillars, and foot long blood red worms crawled or squirmed over rocks or through dead tree trunks, hollowed out by rot. A spider had knit its web among ferns that shimmered, glinting in a shaft of sunlight. Wild ivy and honeysuckle vines threaded in and out of brush, their gnarly roots thick and tight as a strong man's fingers meshed together, impossible for him to make let go, no matter how hard he tried to break through.

He squeezed through scrub to the sandy clay bank where a shallow creek emptied into the lake. Jagged pebbles and round, slick stones were scattered over the water's bed. He took off his shoes and socks, briefs, t-shirt and, naked, slowly waded into a chilly stream that trickled round his ankles. The lake's water was as calm as a pool's. No ripples disturbed it on a windless Monday morning, save for where the skaters darted, zig-zagging crazily over the surface. Near the bank, a solitary backswimmer, lurking, waited for its prey.

Threads of cloud, winding their slow, sinuous way up, dissolved into a clear blue sky. He tugged on some mayweed and queen anne's lace growing along the shore, examined the green stains they'd left in the palm of his hand, waded deeper into the lake's chilly water, and swam to the two logs that formed a bridge of sorts to a narrow, overgrown island. He sat cross-legged on the trunks' water-smoothed bark, lay back and basked in the morning's warmth and comfort.

When, bothered by a fly, he looked up and around, he noticed on the bank a man who looked to be no older than in his early twenties or so, tow-headed, still in uniform. He seemed, like a ghost, to have come from nowhere, without the boy's having seen or sensed him emerging from the woods.

The war had been over for two years. His khaki clothes were wrin-kled and dusty. His duffel bag rested behind him on the ground. Hun-kering, hunched over, the soldier stared into the water, shook his head, spat, and struggled up. His face was the same as the teenage boy's in the photograph he'd taken, no, stolen a year before from an abandoned farm house on the woods' other side. The boy wanted to cry out. He waved wildly at the soldier, flapping his arms, as he turned around. Had he seen him? He retreated back into the thicket of trees.

Having swum back to shore, the boy walked through the tall grass to where the soldier had stooped, where he'd crouched, hunkered, and bent down to drink just moments before. The boy could have sworn he saw his body floating just below the water, his blond hair gently swaying in the current. But no. It was only his face, his eyes, pale green like his own, that lingered on the lake's glassy surface, as a drowned man's features are rumored to do, glossy and wet, hazy at first until like a photograph dipped in its bath a clear image appeared, resolved. It might have been his own eyes he was staring into.

In late spring of the first year after the end of the war, the abandoned cabin sat nearly forgotten and hidden on one side by a thicket of honeysuckle, brush, and young pine. Nearby were untilled cotton and tobacco fields. No one had lived in it, rumor had it, since both sons had gone off to fight. Few knew it was there even before the war had started. It was too isolated, though close to the lake, and belonged to a small family that kept to itself and was rarely seen in town.

On one of his hikes, the sort of solitary, worry-free trek possible for a boy then, he discovered it. It was early June of 1946. He felt as if he'd been invited in, the family having just stepped out for a while, not locking the doors. Nothing about it had been disturbed yet. Even the beds, though a little musty, were neatly made, four places were set at the kitchen table, as if arranged just a few minutes before.

A bluebottle vase stood on the mantel next to a propped calendar for 1941 of Christ knocking at the door. Another calendar, for '42, pinned to a kitchen wall, advertised Coke with a picture of Santa Claus drinking a frosty bottle. Magazines lay arranged in rows across a big wooden box. A jelly glass held darning needles, paper clip chains, sharpened pencils, erasers, a pen. Pipes rested in a pipe stand next to a conch ashtray. A small spiral notebook was open, waiting to be written in, by the sink where a glass and a speckled kettle waited, half filled.

Almost a month or so after his first visit—or was it a break-in, he wasn't sure what he should call what he'd done—the house had been violated. The mess they'd made scared him. The bedding in the brothers' room was ripped to shreds and the mattress stuffing tossed all through the house. Boys had scrawled girls' names in crayon on the walls and broken most of the windows. Beer cans and broken bottles littered the floor. One morning, the boy found three rubbers lying proudly stretched out, lined up and newly filled on the steps to the porch. It was being used for orgies. The thought aroused him and dismayed him for his being aroused when he should have been furious.

He began to spread stories among his and his sisters' friends about how the house was haunted. He wanted to frighten people away. By then, he'd learned more about it, about the family who lived in it, from a friend's father. One of the brothers had been killed in North Africa, near the Kasserine Pass. The other had been fighting in the Pacific somewhere. No one knew whether he was alive or buried on some island. Their father had died, their mother had died. The boy thought: Why shouldn't it be protected by angry sprits? Why wouldn't people believe that?

Yet no one did believe him until a friend reported his older brother had also seen something out there, by that old abandoned farmhouse, and refused to go back. Some talked of hearing wild dogs howling in the woods—maybe at ghosts, it might be true out there, so far from town after all—others of seeing the apparition of an old woman without any eyes in the house's kitchen, stirring a pot. The older brother was report-ed to be lurking like a disembodied spirit close by. Most people want to believe in ghosts. The boy believed in them himself. But inside himself he knew it was all claptrap. Some people, like him, just wanted to keep the house for themselves, to use as they liked.

Yet the rumors scared him away nonetheless. On his last look around, he'd stolen a photograph, just the one he'd been admiring each time he went there. Though he knew he should, he couldn't put it back, return it to its frame, even if it hadn't been smashed, since he'd become fearful of the place himself. He couldn't decide what to do with it, the picture of the brother he'd wanted to save to stare at, the younger brother with the light green eyes, lighter than his, and tow blond hair.

Each time he'd tried to put a match to the photo over his bathroom sink, the flame blew out, so he kept it folded and hidden in a drawer. He didn't want anyone to know he'd stolen it. He didn't want anyone to try to figure out why. He didn't know himself, why it had become so import-ant to him, why he would stare at it for half an hour at least before falling asleep, though he suspected the reason must be something important.

The day after he'd seen him in the flesh, the boy returned to the lake, hoping to see him again, wanting to make certain it had been really him. But no one was there. The banks were deserted, the lake and the woods empty of other people.

Back home, he removed the photograph from its secret place in a chest of drawers below his underclothes, but it tore along creases that had become fragile from his unfolding and refolding them too often late at night or early in the morning. A strong wind through his bedroom door blew the several fragments high into the air and out his window, the pieces floating in the air like an uncontrolled kite, descending, darting this way and that. The boy watched them fall. Outside, as he searched, he could not find them. How could they have been so easily blown away? No more dreams. No more hopes. No more fantasies. He'd lost him.

At dinner that night, his father told his family that he'd heard that the old abandoned cabin way off Rt. 440 which had been the subject of so many rumors and so much gossip in town had burned to the ground. A vagrant probably, his father said.

A hobo building himself a fire or having himself a smoke that got out of hand.

But the boy knew better. He'd seen him. He knew who'd set it and why. He'd felt a thrill inside as he imagined the smoke from the house on fire rising higher and higher, slowly changing from black into white, from white into the clear blue sky of a cloudless summery day, the best kind for a swim in the lake.

2.

After four days of walking in the heat from where he'd been left off miles outside of Cherith, he was eager for a swim, to immerse himself again in the clear, pure waters of the lake which he meant to hike to even before he'd gone home, deliberately bypassing the house on his trek through the woods. The lake was more his home than the old house anyway, his and his brother's private place, though his father occasionally would join them on a bank, sitting on a flat rock to fish while observing them swimming.

He badly needed to wash off the grime and sweat from a long, arduous, exhausting journey that had started at Letterman Hospital in San Francisco. The lake was where he'd always felt cleanest, he and his brother diving in after a day's work or early in the morning before their work began. But the boy, the naked boy sitting on the logs so innocently, so peacefully, had stopped him, made him want to retreat back into the trees. He hadn't expected to see anyone. He didn't want to be seen, especially not by a kid who was still almost a child.

Once he'd left the islands, he'd hoped that he might never be dirty again. He had dug shallow graves for friends with a bayonet and his bare hands and for weeks thereafter confused the dead men's blood with the mud caked on his skin. On Luzon, after he had fought all the way up from Lae and Hollandia, he'd shoveled up a human skull to which shredded flesh still clung.

The worst was the cave where some Japs had been incinerated. When he tripped and the mine exploded, he might been buried alive with them. Only after he'd loosed himself and tried to stand up did he feel any pain, his buddies standing over him in a warped, broken circle, strangely smiling, their heads drifting and bobbing like balloons. From a place as far away as the farm, he'd heard himself scream.

Having fled the boy, his curious gaze, the intense way he looked at him, he raced through the woods until he reached the gravel cut-off that quit at his family's land. He began to breathe easier. The grasses beside the black top highway he'd hiked on so long had baked in the heat. He knew what they felt like. He was as parched as they must have been.

His pants' were filthy. His feet hurt. His duffel bag sagged so heavily on his shoulder that he held it like an old woman grasping a cumbersome bundle of laundry.

His family's house waited for him on the other side of the woods, sitting alone in a corner of the fields where neither tobacco nor cotton had been planted for more than five years, not since he and his brother had enlisted to fight. His grandfather had built the house himself before his own father had been born.

It was his all right. All this land was his. He could live here forever alone and be safe if he wanted, in the peace solitude promised. He doubled his pace.

He sat on a stump while he caught his breath. Once more he had to catch his breath. His wounds, his scars, still hurt.

The house's discolored white clapboard had blistered and peeled. The windows that had looked out from the two front rooms onto the woods were only broken, jagged pieces of glass jutting from the frames. Dry mud coated the house's eastern side where it must have been slung time after time as if at a bull's eye. Who would do that? Why? Chips have been knocked out of the cement blocks on which the house stood. Milk and pop and liquor bottles, most shattered into bits and pieces, littered the smooth, damp reddish gray clay of the earth.

As he climbed the steps, the air stank of the piss-like odor of cardboard boxes and the acrid smell of the piles of decayed cotton they'd held. He shoved the door open. So much was missing or destroyed. The porcelain trinkets his mother had displayed on a three-tiered stand lay on the floor as if they'd been stomped on. His stomach churned with disgust. He searched for the picture of him in his uniform that she had placed on the mantel beside the one of his brother, each photographed on a visit home after they'd finished bootcamp, but both were gone or, like so many other things that were part of him, tossed into a pile like garbage or ripped or thrown apart. Everything was in ruins, the house a shambles, fetid and rank, abused and violated

The mirror in the lyre frame had been smashed, too. With black crayons, someone had scrawled lewd words on the Santa Claus calendar his mother had hung up in her little kitchen. The stuffing from the cushions of two chairs had been tossed around the room, leaving the springs twisted and exposed. The back door's panes were broken. The sinks and counters reeked of rotten food and booze the intruders had spilled and left to fester and decay.

Everything was covered with dust, dirt, and human grime. The wooden wireless. The china pot. The chipped enamel basins. The wicker rocker. The iron stand-up lamp. The stacks of "The Upper Room" his mother stored in a corner. The olive drab sofa. The straight back chairs. Their beds had been taken apart, the bedding strewn about, cum- and blood-stained mattresses thrown haphazardly onto the floor.

In a tall chest of drawers his father had built, he discovered a slew of unused prophylactics still in their silver-colored packages. In foot high letters on the white washed plaster, someone had scrawled LUCY-BECKYWANDAJOALICE. There were other words, far worse, scribbled everywhere, obscene and violent.

He stood on a stool, grabbed a pair of striped, ripped, sagging boxer shorts off an exposed light fixture, dropped them on the floor, stumbled, coughing from the dust, rushed out the back door, and vomited into a patch of scrub grass.

The pump worked, though unsurprisingly the water alternated between dark brown and rusty at first. He tried to wash his hands. Unclean, unclean. All was unclean and impure. Balancing it between his knees, he searched in his duffel bag for a wooden box the size of a cigarette pack that held needles, thread, razor blades, buttons, a tube of petroleum jelly, and a thin tin of wooden matches.

He lit the first fire in the pile of sheets in his parents' bedroom, the second in the clumps of stuffing and excelsior scattered over the living room floor and in the remaining upholstery from two emaciated chairs, and the third, the fastest to catch, in the lacework curtains his mother had sewn. Black bits of burned thread fell like dead flies onto crumpled sheets.

The dead are not still in their bodies, he whispered to himself. They live somewhere else. In fire. In water. But not here. Not in this filth.

Heat drove him outside. Flames at last leaped through the roof and charred a blossoming mimosa that drooped over it. A morning breeze rose and thrust the fire toward a pine grove. A few low grasses, briars and brambles and other weeds growing in scattered clumps took flame and burned, turning into black or gray ash. When the house was consumed, nothing left of it but embers and a single pillar of smoke spiraling like a sign from the smoldering timber, climbing as if to heaven, he breathed with relief. No more squalor. No more war. No more harm.

He squatted near his duffel bag and removed his shoes and socks. His feet were tender from days of walking but he didn't wince from the pebbles and small rocks that lay scattered on a creek bed. He peered into the run-off water in a gully. Again he saw his face staring back at him. Bending over, he struck it with a stick, as if to crack the mirror, not worried that it might bring bad luck.

He hunkered on a sandy clay bank of the creek that eventually flowed into the lake, the stream he used to wade in, splashing, with his brother. His dead brother whom he missed most. Swimming with him, fishing, gigging frogs, though he couldn't kill anything anymore, not even with him, not even for food. His dead family. The meaning of alone. The dark peace.

He'd never wanted to leave. The war came to the U.S.A. after Pearl Harbor. His brother joined the army. His father died. Seeing the misery in his mother's eyes, he'd waited a few months to sign up. The military promised they'd end up together in the same company and screwed up. He and his brother were shipped to opposite ends of the earth.

He trekked back to the lake. The boy was gone. He was glad. He swam across it and sat on the same old gnarled root of a cypress where he'd spied the kid sunning himself. Lazily, he counted the skaters as they darted and zigzagged over the surface. A solitary backswimmer stabbed its prey.

Only one. Always alone. As if always the same one. To survive is to kill. An empty shell drifted past him in the quiet water.

His brother told him backswimmers were solitary hunters. Since they ate immature mosquitos, he'd said, they were good to have around, but they ate almost any small prey including one another, the old eating the young, even their own offspring. By early summer, they're all cannibals. A backswimmer seldom survives long enough to be threatened by starvation. Each backswimmer either is eaten or remains alone, the last survivor, his brother had said. So it must be true, true even of him. How many men had he killed or seen killed? The last survivor.

The dead are not still in their bodies. He swam and floated on his back. Slightly more than two hundred yards away, threads of smoke were still winding their slow, sinuous way upward and disappearing, dissolving into the purer air above. After a short while, the air, the sky, the clouds were clear again. The fire was out. For the first time in almost five years, he felt safe. The dead are not still in their bodies.

Yet sleeping on the naked ground that night, in fresh air, not in the shed or the curing barn, he could taste ash in his mouth. Gunpowder. The aftermath of grenades.

He woke thirsty, swallowed water that tasted of tin from his canteen, gargled and spat. An hour or so later—he could not know the exact duration because he was asleep all the while—his demons returned, the great gray monsters that lurked in the backs of closets, in bootcamp tents, in jungles and swamps. Many wore the faces of friends in his platoon, those who were killed, those who survived alike. They'd pick hungrily at his bony carcass and beckon him to join them.

He lay on his back, his blank eyes enough alive to plead with dumb speech to the eyes of the hungry ones for a quick end to the life, to the horror they'd shared. One night on his way home, not so long ago, they'd told him they'd never leave him altogether because they alone could take care of him now since there was no one else who would.

Although he slept badly his first night home, he knew from experience his demons had not meant only to harm him but, like angels, intended to minister to him as well. A wave of fear had passed through his sleeping body like a sudden, brief change in the weather that had left behind, like a fading memory, his mother's voice in the break between storms calling him from the fields to come eat and the sound of his fyce dog barking at the rumble of thunder from the east.

It was not until twilight of the next day that he realized how much he'd enjoyed the work, clearing a site of cockleburs and coffee weeds for the new cabin he planned to build, cutting down the first trees he'd use to erect most of it. Often he'd worked without wearing clothes, to protect them from rips or tears since he had no others yet, careful not to expose his hospital gray skin too long to the strong July-like heat of the sun.

Late in the afternoon, he'd taken a break to rest his scarred body in the sandy creek, the clear, black waters of the stream trickling pleasingly over him. After sunset, he was hungry, almost famished. He'd finished his one remaining can of vienna sausages, eaten the last of the peanut butter from the jar. Only a can of peaches was unopened.

For the first time since the war'd been over, he'd wished he could still bear to carry a gun and shoot it, as he and his brother used to do back in the days before everyone had died. Often his dad had roasted a duck he'd shot on a spit. But merely the thought of it nauseated him now. The sight of more blood. The realities of death, any death.

It was during the last year of the war that he knew that God had abandoned him forever. What he could believe in thereafter was only abandonment. It was all he had left. It was the most he could hope for.

He'd become unable to separate friend from enemy. One night, after a banzai attack the previous afternoon, he'd woken up believing he had opened fire on his own troops. He started to cry and couldn't stop even when some of his men shook him violently. He quieted only when he remembered pine woods and home, the clear, clean air, the fragrant sandy rust of the tobacco leaves he'd helped cure, the rain clouds sailing in from the Atlantic.

The next dawn, as the sun rose over the trees, it challenged him like the eye of a dead Jap, black as the barrel of a rifle. The war had led him into a new dimension of time, the dimension of darkness, the sunless demons. He'd seen them again, though changed, transformed when, after he been declared well enough to go out for walks, he'd stood on the Golden Gate Bridge looking north while, in the near distance, a youth, luminous, clear-eyed, tall, skinny crossed from the other side to greet him.

He tried to signal the boy to let him be, waving his arms. The youth only quickened his pace, beckoning him to join him with a smile that seemed to promise an end to all torment. But as the kid ran forward he'd lost his balance, fell over the rail, and vanished into the waters of the Golden Gate. A fantasy. A ghost. A phantasm. What desire is. What love was. He could never have stopped him from toppling over the bridge. He could not have prevented his dying.

Had he returned home only to go to war again over and over in his mind? The time of combat, for demon, for angel, who knew which, was a fight he could never win, a war that was perhaps only just beginning. Recalling the bridge and the boy, the mirage of their meeting, the sad boy smiling in the flower of his youth, he told himself, "I could die and remain in the world forever. So I've got to stay alive if I want to leave it."

He meant to remember everything, no matter whom he belonged to, the demons of war or the angel across the bridge. Maybe they were the same. He knew he might have cared for many of the Japs he'd killed, hate them though he did as passionately as any soldier would who had seen what they had done to his friends. He might have loved one in a different world where a man could let himself love and be loved by his enemy.

He was uprooting mayweed and queen anne's lace near a wide strip of cecil clay where he hoped to plant a small new cotton field close to his family's old tobacco acreage when he began to feel almost at home. He was good at it, good at farming, what he could recall of it. Could he still plow straight, remember the trick of tying a bowline or clove hitch, the right time to transplant young tobacco plants, the sure sign of where to dig for water? His mother had taught him and his brother to ask themselves each day, "Do I belong to Satan or to Jesus?" He broke his dead man's stare, glowered at the silt black sun overhead, and knew he no longer could answer her question, once so easy. He no longer cared what the right answer was.

What if his life ahead should be nothing except trees, leaves, weeds, the abundant, prolific Southern foliage? He leaned over and ripped out a vine. The kudzu had taken over, claimed the earth in a rampage of green. And the pine, the deep rich green assault of its needles. The thick, dense brush behind had grown into jungle, impossible to penetrate, to enter without a machete.

If green could be evil, how would he resist its attack? How arm himself if he could? Saw, axe, plow? Cut down all the pine, oak, hickory? Burn all the grass, the ivy, the vines with a flamethrower? Poison the kudzu? The green he'd seen in the Philippine jungles, the green of sunlight that was so strong it managed to shine through the impenetrable tangle of growth and rot. That burned his skin and made him sweat with fever and thirst for what water could not quench. It was the same green here, at home. Everything had turned green. The color he had fought in. The terror of what might be lurking, hiding behind it, inside it.

He was shaking so badly he had to quit working and ran as fast as he could along the weed tangled path to the lake. A chink opened in the cloud-covered sky. The sun, pouring through, transformed the water from black tin to gleaming copper. The air bristled. Half-blinded by the sun, the water's dazzling brightness, he squinted and cupped his hands over his eyes.

Waving to him with one hand, the same boy he'd seen days before stood at the end of the bridge built by two fallen trees. But clouds sealed the crack and hid the sun. The abrupt change in the light startled the boy. He slipped off the slick logs and fell over the swamp grass head first into the shallow water. Having angrily picked himself up, he swam toward shore, his hair and face, chest, stomach, cock, and legs dripping with black mud and silt as he trudged along the lake's edge.

The soldier grimaced and turned away. Not again. He couldn't trust his eyes anymore. He was back on Tarawa, watching with horror as his best buddy, his face shot off, bloody from head to toe, stepped out of the ocean to fall dead on the beachhead. It was only a vision, a moment's delusion. There was no boy.

He hunkered on the shore of the lake, gazing for the last time into the water's glassy mirror. His pale green eyes stared back at him as at an enemy. Behind him, a tree cracked and crashed to the ground for no reason on a windless day. The sky bearing down on his body felt not oppressive but as soft as feathers, as dew, the air sharp as an ocean breeze, washing everything clean.

The earth blossoms in spring. The land's renewed. Green purifies, too. What to do? Go? Stay? In the west, nothing but fallow fields laid out before it, the treeless horizon was brighter than mere daylight. Here was home. Everywhere, the sharp, resiny scent of pine. He could no longer endure it, the endless passing of days, the drifting white clouds cleansing the sky into a blue so pure it promised a peace he knew he'd never see again as lovely as at that moment.

The boy, of course, has grown into the man I am. When I was old enough to leave home, I moved to a northern state where I could be more free to be myself. I have a lover, younger than I am but old now, too. I became a nurse and a part time, though unpublished and unread writer.

I'm often happy, I guess I could say with some misgivings, happiness being a state too difficult to discern in anyone, least of all yourself. Because it depends on comparisons with others, it has no real meaning in itself. Anyway, happiness, Flaubert wrote, is a concern only of adolescents. I was too greedy for it when I was thirteen.

Sometimes, not just in dreams, I find myself watching as smoke suddenly starts to rise from what I presume for a moment is a real burning house. One of our neighbor's, perhaps.

It is of course only a dream of a sort. His farm house on fire and smoke billowing above a high wall of heavily leaved trees. If I look around for signs of a fire close by, sniff the air, listen for sirens, I know better right away.

My tow-headed soldier with the pale green eyes, even lighter than mine, disappeared just a few days after he'd returned. No one in the county knew where he'd gone or why. No one really cared. I hadn't tried to find him either. Or I did search. It's just that I couldn't admit it to anyone how hard I had looked. They might have asked me why. His family's land was sold at auction, though there was no one to pay for what little it brought.

He'd left no sign of where he'd gone and nothing behind except for the ashes of the abused house the town's officials had ruled he'd burned down himself. That and some cut trees and logs and sawed boards, the tools he'd used they'd found in a shed, and a note he'd written on the blank back of a small calendar from '44 with dates crossed out on the other side. He'd nailed it to the trunk of a giant longleaf pine. The local newspaper printed it as if it were news. "These woods are mine."

Empathy

1.

Fifty two years ago, a young woman
is murdered in Queens. Her brother, a vet,
a double amputee in Vietnam,
makes a documentary to learn why—
what, stabbed, she felt as her dying began.
He hires an actress he'd never met
to scream like her. It's not the same,
he knows, sobbing as he hears her cry.

2.

This painting's your woods, the moon
sun-bright, a gray, curvy lane
rising like smoke, thin-
nest near the forest. Soon
it'll be dark. Tall pine, stripped cane
line the way. Go in. Walk deeper in.

Gift Givers

The earth's steaming. Dark clouds are rumbling. A new storm's on its way. Cicada chirr, flies and bees buzz, lake frogs croak, tree frogs throb, birds twitter, chirp, spin, pipe melodies in a boisterous choir. Jeff's playing in the yard outside his house built from soil-colored weathered clapboard with a tin roof and an open hall leading through it, in one door and out the other. His mother darns or sews throughout the morning. If they should hunger, the Lord will take care of them. Their tears will be pearls some day. As Jesus suffered for all, so must they as willingly for each other.

Early heavy with ripe fruit, a cherry tree is ready for picking. Jeff digs a hole for his box turtles, paints a slat chair leaf green, reties the strings in an old hammock. A jug to store water from rain has a hair line crack across its rim from a cold snap late last winter. The drink he takes from it tastes as good as what he brings up fresh in a bucket from their well. Birds perch on its stone edge sometimes as if they were looking for a birdbath, orioles, redwings, grackles, starlings, and jays. He wonders how they hear the nearly silent snap of a twig as he steps on it that scares them away. There's no breeze. Some days he feels so strange in the world he almost can't breathe.

A friend from another farm crosses a slate path toward him carrying a paper bag in one hand. Jeff helps him pick cherries from his mother's tree. His bag overflowing, the boy studies the branches he's stripped. He's proud of his work and pours from his bag into Jeff's cupped hands enough for them both to enjoy without getting sick. Cherries are Jeff's second favorite fruit, after peaches. His mother might be angry he's given so many away. He's only six but his father whips him when he's been bad or smacks him with the back of his hand.

The northeast corner of the county is a solitary, impoverished place. Most make do with what they grow for themselves or sell at market in town for a few dollars to spend. Bad times make life not hard but harder. Tribulation is what folks expect from life and little more. Tribulation is a test of faith many wonder if they'll be able to pass.

Jeff's mother cooks for everyone she can, often shares more than she can spare. The word 'poor' means those poorer than you are. Jeff's mother's father's father built their house. It could use much repairing. The roof tilts east, the porch west. Butterfly bushes darken most of its windows. Wild ivy has sunk its roots in the infertile ground and looks painted on the clapboard or pasted on like storm borne leaves.

It's early in the year of Nineteen Hundred and Forty Two. Jeff's just turned eighteen. The New Deal still hasn't reached them yet. Few know or question why except to acknowledge the will of the Lord.

Jeff's been a good boy growing up. At high school, he'd sometimes give his lunch away to a Merridale or a Singletary child if his or her stomach was empty. Sooner or later, some sickly kid would be writing with Jeff's pen or wearing his scarf, cap, gloves, or galoshes. Sometimes he got them back, more often he didn't. He'd given his rifle away, a fishing pole, a dowsing stick he'd found. He sleeps with his dog and feeds him sufficiently with scraps from his plate. His mother loves him for it. His father sometimes gets angry at the waste of good food.

In March, his daddy sometimes has trouble catching his breath for fear of what might happen to his boy. He drives his son into town to meet the bus that will deliver him to bootcamp. Jeff waves back and mouths words Amos Carter cannot hear but reads as if his son's promising him he won't let himself get killed. His mother makes such a display she's trembling. She's been ruining his day by embarrassing her boy in front of others.

As the days, months, years pass they hear from him seldom, though he writes when he can. He's in battle after battle, on island after island. Charlie Ebert lost his son Gary on Guadalcanal, Buster Coombs Buster Jr. on Kwajalein. "How long did Jesus mourn for Lazarus?" Amos asks his wife who weeps without needing to, what little news about Jeff they get no reason for tears yet. That's how Amos feels. It scorns the Lord to mourn before you ought to or too long when you should. Rebecca looks at him with eyes that are fiercer than he's ever seen her use to glare at him when he's done or said something she feels is wrong.

Five months after the Japs surrendered, Jeff finds himself in Frisco on his way home, a soldier for only a short while longer. He meets Ray in a bar popular with the Presidio quartermaster's corps Ray's served in throughout the war. It's too noisy to talk and so crowded they have to sit at a table with seven other soldiers.

When Ray asks to bum a smoke, Jeff offers him the whole pack. When Ray admires his lighter, a silver plated one a bullet had dented on Luzon, Jeff asks him to keep it since Ray likes it so much. Ray demurs, slides it toward him across the beer-slicked table, but Jeff refuses to accept it back.

"My gift," he says. "I'm quitting anyway."

Ray's car's parked outside, two blocks away. Inside his apartment off base, the first floor of a rickety old building starting to decay high on the west slope of Telegraph Hill, Jeff touches things he's never seen before: burnished copper urns, Chinese porcelain vases, carved jade, velvet curtains, stained glass lampshades. A college lacrosse stick hangs on a wall over Ray's bed. A model sailboat decorates an opened roll top desk.

"You o.k.?" Ray says. "You seem nervous. Worried. I'm harmless, you know. You're safe with me."

"Farm kid," Jeff says. "Redneck. My folks are tobacco croppers mostly. A little corn. Some chickens. Dirt poor, but we were better off than most of our neighbors. Not used to this. Not used to the world, really. The war taught me a lot. I'm still new to life, really, I guess I can say. This one, at least."

"You mean my things?"

"Yeah. Those too."

"And me, you mean? What we're about to do?"

Jeff turns his eyes away, no longer faces Ray but looks out a window that opens to the bay and the rotating lights of Alcatraz. "It's a beautiful view."

"Thanks. I was lucky to find this place."

"I couldn't have. Before the war." He moves close enough to Ray to touch his arm. "I couldn't have done this."

"'See the world,'" Ray says. "Remember that?"

Jeff shakes his head. "Sure."

"It doesn't matter. You can change your mind if you want to. Anytime."

"I don't want to."

"You've had a rough time of it, haven't you?"

"A bad enough one to make me think about what I believe, if that's what you're asking.

About a lot of things. Things I learned aren't so from what I've seen." He glances over at a framed oil painting resting on an easel. "You do this?"

Ray smiles. "No, I bought it. When I was in college at a show in Washington Square."

"New York, right? That must be the Hudson then, and a tug boat on the river. Nice. Whose work is it?"

"A minor unknown artist who had a scruffy beard and wore a beret. DeTirefort, his name was. You can see his signature there on the bottom left. I just liked it. Sort of Ash Can school, wouldn't you say?"

"I wouldn't know. All most people had hanging on their walls back home were some pages cut from old calendars and a picture of Jesus knocking at the door. Sorry."

"Don't apologize. I should be asking for your forgiveness. I'm a bit of a snob, I bet you're thinking. And I've assumed way too much about you. You really have never done this before? Gone home with a guy for sex?"

"No, not really. I've touched a guy and he touched me till we came together. Twice. Once over in the Philippines. Once here in Frisco in the dark in the back of a bar last week."

"You like it?"

"Yeah. Sort of. It scared me, though. My people say if something makes you feel good, especially that way, it probably means you're going to hell."

"You barely drank any of your beer in the bar."

"I'm not supposed to drink alcohol. We're backwoods Baptists."

"Sleeping with guys must be the worst sin of all, right?"

"Yep. Worse than murdering your own daddy. No one talked about it. You just knew." Jeff grimaces. "Some Baptists are heavy secret drinkers. Preachers even. But not my dad. He's strict. Not deliberately mean. Not most of the time anyway. Just strict. He wouldn't allow a bottle of the stuff in his house. Moonshine, of course. Prohibition's still the rule in Carolina."

Ray pours them both some whiskey. "To us," he says, clinking his glass against Jeff's. "And your love life? When you get back home? What'll you do?"

"Nothing. It'll be over before it's really begun," Jeff says. "Just like the war was supposed to be but wasn't. Or so my daddy hoped and said so often until not even he believed it anymore. This is it maybe." He glances around the room. "I'm catching the train back soon, day after tomorrow."

"I suddenly feel a truly heavy burden being placed on our night together, Jeff. I'm not that good, I'm afraid. I'm fairly clumsy myself in bed. You sure you want to do this?" Ray asks again while unbuttoning his shirt.

"Yes." Jeff leans over, unties his laces, sits on the floor, tugs off his boots and socks, stands back up, unbuckles his belt, and lets his pants drop. "My first time in bed with another guy. Maybe it'll have to last a lifetime. I'm going to remember you, Ray, no matter what."

"Jesus, Jeff. Don't count on it," Ray says, lighting him a cigarette and placing it, wet from his own lips, between Jeff's. "Chastity's no good, you know. No way to live a life. It turns the brain into mush. Consider all the idiots who advocate it."

"Uh-huh." Jeff takes a puff without inhaling and blows it out. "That's awful, Ray. What is it?"

"Gauloises. They're French. Strong. You'll learn to like it. Become addicted just like me." He takes his hand. "Come on, now. No more talk. The bedroom's down this hall. I want you to spend the night. I want to wake up with you in my arms."

In the early dawn light, Ray's black mat of chest hairs sparkle from lingering sweat, like dew on a spider web or the back of a beetle crawling out of grass to warm itself on a rock in the sun, Jeff thinks, blinking at the sight of him, at how thoughts of boyhood mornings at home come back to him at the strangest times. He's wondering about his life ahead. Of what he might do with the rest of his days living where no one must know who he really is.

The war's destroyed all he'd thought he was before, taken it all away, except for his fear. He doesn't believe in God anymore but can't free himself from belief in damnation. Without wanting to wake him, he lets his fingers skim over Ray's skin. His chest feels like wet moss on slate, like a horse's flank after it's run hard, its muscles taut and strong. His mind's running wild with images from home. He's confused by what he feels. He doesn't want to leave.

A cigarette Ray'd dropped in the night had burned a small hole in his carpet. With a folded piece of paper, Jeff tries to scoop up the ashes to toss into a wastebasket. With a pen he finds by the phone, he prints in caps his address in Carolina on the last sheet of a pad. He rips it off and places it beside Ray's sleeping body, next to the man's skivvies that lie crumpled in his sheets tangled with his own that he's decided to let Ray keep as a souvenir.

He takes a last look. For the first time, he feels deep inside him, like a religious conviction, that the war's actually over. Jeff knows enough about the way things are, of how the world works, of what love must be, to know he'll never see Ray again. Tribulation is what life is

Home less than a week, after only one try, Jeff lands a good job. He doesn't mind the early hours. In bootcamp, in the fighting army later he liked to wake first, listening to the men breathing in the dark. He rarely sleeps much these nights anyhow. He'd lost his enjoyment of it on the islands. It seemed a waste of the little life left him, the pleasure he could find in night sounds that might frighten others.

He lives in his old house with his parents. His dad's made a few improvements, though not nearly enough. New screens on the doors in front and back and two windows. Some paint on the porch. Fresh bricks on the hearth. Salvia recently planted by the steps.

His route covers half of his small hometown along with Zion Bible College on the east side. When his buddy Ted's wife gets sick or his kids keep him home, Jeff substitutes for him and doubles his day's work with no extra pay. He makes sure to store enough ice in his truck to keep the milk, butter, and eggs cool. At the first annual picnic he attends, Jeff and Ted win the three-legged race.

They beat all the rest three years in a row. At pickup baseball, he's a decent hitter, though better at left field. Every Sunday at church, he places a ten in the collection plate and passes it to his father who's embarrassed by how little he can give and tries to hide his crumpled dollar bill under the coins. Jeff wonders why he ever did believe in God or why He seems to matter so little to him now that he's lost his faith. So long, of course, as he keeps quiet about it. No one must know that secret about him either.

When a deacon catches Jeff's father fondling the choir leader's wife's breasts in the Bible School parking lot after a rehearsal, his mother decides her life is over. They give their house to Jeff and move two counties west where, they futilely hope, no one will know them or have heard of the scandal.

Whenever Jeff visits them in their shabby boarding house, in their unkempt rooms above a thrift dress shop, his dad won't look at him. His mother hides in the kitchen, worrying over a lunch or a supper neither her son nor her husband will feel like eating. His parents pick at their food without saying a word while Jeff tries his best to report what little news he has from work.

It's always the same. His mother'll look at him across the table and say, "You're looking well," and he'll say, "I'm feeling fine, thanks," and so it will continue for the rest of the visit. Niceties. Platitudes. Awkward pauses. Uncomfortable glances. His father saying nothing at all. And Jeff himself talking too much without mentioning anything worth breaking the silence among them for.

At least once a week he drives the hour it takes to get there on country roads and is rarely home before bedtime. Otherwise, he's alone with no one to talk to. Really to talk to. Every time he leaves, his mother cries, rubs a rough, calloused palm across his cheek, and thanks him for his kindness.

On the last Sunday that Jeff spends with them, more worried than usual, while he climbs the steps of Sweet Redeemer Baptist Church, his father grabs his head like God's wrath at last has struck him—as his mother will later in her misery say—topples over, and tumbles down the wide, formidable cement steps to the curb. He'd been unsteady on his feet for at least a year. Some whisper, "Drink," but Rebecca knows better. It was the Lord's justice, His reward for her affliction, as if His grace involved a woman's vindication. When his mother tells him what she thinks, Jeff is heart sick that she's grown so hard.

"He slid on slick steps and hit his head," Jeff fibs. He feels like a fool. They both know it was a stroke that felled him, not slippery cement. She'd seen it coming. Jeff tried to convince his father to see a doctor. But Amos wouldn't budge, wouldn't emerge from his rooms to face the world. His mother kept her peace, thinking, she said, it was pointless to try. The man knew he was being punished. Let him be, his mother would say. Tribulation can also cure.

His father had been afraid to die. Jeff had witnessed such fear many times before. It made some of his buddies, at least one or two, maybe more, take risks they shouldn't have. Death was preferable to terror, wasn't it? Or being bored beyond belief as endless horror will sometimes do, wrecking the soul, emptying it of everything worth living for. Jeff had seen too many men lost in despair.

His father was among them. For what? For an instant's indiscretion? At her husband's grave, his mother begs Jeff to forgive her for her hating the man so deeply in her heart. He takes her hand in his and says, to comfort her, "You loved him, too. Maybe a lot more than you think," and held her in his arms as she cried.

At the Baptist Home, Rebecca enjoys the company of other widows and rarely complains, not even after she's broken her hip. She shares her room with a bald, toothless, emaciated woman who curls naked in her bed like a starving baby. When he visits her, the women's bodies smell like a pungent mixture of rose water and urine. Every time, he offers each a bauble or a broach, cheap trinkets really, he's bought at the Five and Dime. The clerk there likes to tease him about how lucky a girl his sweetheart must be whom he's buying all the pretty jewelry for.

His mother dies in her sleep. Near the end, she requested she be buried in the plot next to his father's. No one attends the funeral except Jeff and a few of his fellow workers from the dairy and their wives, but no children. He can't cry. He can't even feel free. Obligations he's long ago wanted to untie still bind him. He has trouble remembering whatever a hope for freedom meant to him during the war, the promise of it or something like it after it was over. He grieves for his parents. For himself, too, since he has no one now, no one to love, to comfort, to hold. He loses himself in work as he always has, by pretending to be someone he isn't and never was. Jeff's a good guy. A good friend. A man you can count on if you're ever in a jam. He knows or suspects it's only a role he's playing to survive.

Ted pats him on the back. "I'm so sorry, Jeff. You've been having a really rough time lately. Both your parents in less than a year. It's got to be tough."

"Yeah. I guess. It all depends," Jeff says.

Ted looks surprised. "On what?"

"On what you measure it by," Jeff says.

It's winter again. And again. It feels as if it's been winter for a very long spell. An ice age. Snow flurries are falling as Jeff walks to his milk truck. A kitchen light in the school dims behind him. The wind howls. A door slams. As he reaches where he's parked, he sees him, a boy it looks like, too tall to hide though he's obviously trying to do so by bending and squeezing in behind Jeff's empty crates. Jeff shuts the truck's back doors, leaving him inside. Despite the cold, the motor turns over quick. The truck skids on the ice of the unlit road.

His route done for the morning, he drives fast as he can safely on icy roads the rest of the way to the dairy where his pickup's waiting. Jeff swings the truck's back doors open, slides down the ramp, orders the kid out, removes all the empty crates, and piles them where they go in rows on the platform. The kid's hands and face are scarlet from the cold.

"O.K. Truth time, kid. Who are you hiding from? You rob someone or something at the college? You a fugitive? What's your name?"

"Mark."

"Right. Mark what?"

"Mark Wales. I haven't stolen anything. I'm not hiding. I'm no thief. I was freezing."

"So you slip into the back of a milk truck? That's dumb, don't you think?"

"I wasn't thinking."

"O.K. We agree. What you were doing out by the school?"

"Looking for something to eat."

"How did you get there, that far from town?"

"Hitchhiking. It's where I got left off."

"Where you from?"

"Outside Goldsboro. A town no one's heard of. Or needs to."

"All right. Go get in that pickup. I'm taking you home. You're a runaway, aren't you?"

"I guess so."

"Guess so? You either are or you're not. Why'd you run? Who from?"

"Everything. Everybody." Mark shrugs. "My dad's quick with the back of his hand. A whip, too. Here, I'll show you." He unzips his jacket and pulls up his shirt. "See?"

"Jesus Christ. How often did he do that?"

"Since I told him, a lot. Every night, almost. He'd lock me in my room."

"Told him what?"

"I don't know. Something bad."

"You don't know?"

"I mean I can't say."

"Or you won't."

"Maybe. Do I have to?"

"No. It's probably better if you don't. Probably better if I don't know. I'm taking you to my place. It's a ways out. You can sleep there for a while. I can spare the food, I reckon. You always been that skinny?"

Mark folds his arms across his chest. "Yeah. So what?"

"So nothing," Jeff says.

At his house, Jeff gives Mark his parents' former bedroom and makes the bed with new sheets and a blanket he'd bought just to have something to buy. Looking at him closer in a stronger light, he decides his own clothes will fit the boy well enough, at least for a start, even if he's a lot thinner. He's about Jeff's height, probably ten years younger or so. He fries them both a chuck burger with cheese, places them on buns, loads them with lettuce and ketchup, opens a bag of chips, and serves Mark and himself a meal they both greedily devour, a lunch or supper not a breakfast they eat less than an hour past dawn.

Jeff went to school with the guy who inherited Moser's General Store from his father two years ago. On Jeff's recommendation, he immediately hires Mark for odd jobs, cleaning, moving boxes and wares, sorting nails and ribbons and fabrics, sometimes working behind the counter, whatever he needs him to do whenever he asks him to do it. The salary's a pittance, but it's better than nothing, and his hours are flexible enough for Jeff to drive him to work after he's finished his deliveries.

As Mark is being shown what his duties at the store will be, Jeff buys five white shirts, two pair of khaki slacks, a belt, some socks, some shorts, pretending they're for him. He gives them to Mark after supper. "You need to make a good impression," he says.

One evening, weeks later, before they start to head out of town and drive back to his small plot of land, all that's left after his father's disaster sent his parents into exile, Jeff hears a pained mewing from a garbage bin behind Moser's. Rescued, the cat purrs in Mark's arms all the way home. After they've fed it some milk, it escapes through an open screen. Somewhere in the woods, it's chased by wild dogs they hear barking viciously after it. Mark finds it after dark shivering in an oak bough, soaked from the recent storm.

Though Jeff attempts to nurse it in his bed, the wounds the cat's suffered from the dogs are incurable. It dies before dawn. A male or a female? In the morning, Jeff buries it without knowing which in what's left of his mother's potato patch while Mark watches, struggling to hold back tears.

Seeming happy, content, not restless at all, not even at work, Cal Moser says, Mark stays with him until summer approaches. "It's time for me to hit the road again," Mark says to him out of the blue while Jeff's pruning some bushes. "I've got plans."

"Really? What plans?"

Mark shrugs as if he doesn't truly know what plans or much care to. "I can't live here all my life, can I?"

"Can't you? I guess not."

"But you can? You like it here, don't you? A lot."

"Sure. Well, sort of. Besides, even if I didn't, I've nowhere else to go. It's my home here, isn't it? It's where I belong. Born and raised, as they say. I've traveled enough for one lifetime, I reckon, not having meant to."

"I should apologize for saying so, Jeff. You've been good to me. Generous. Never asked for anything back. But that sounds sad to me."

"Does it? I suppose," Jeff says, standing up, leaning against a side of the shed, mopping his brow with a rag. "But I'm not sad. Not often anyhow. Mostly I'm glad just to be breathing. Alive, I mean, in this world. It's enough. Right here."

"I want more. What I've had so far's not enough. Not by a long shot."

"I can understand that."

"Can I ask you a question?"

"Sure. Ask away. Anything," Jeff says, snipping the brown leaves off some too tall wild boxwood.

"No." Mark shakes his head. "Another day maybe, in another world." He strolls back onto the porch. From the way he slumps on the swing, Jeff thinks he looks, all of a sudden, much older, older than Jeff even.

"You need someone to love, Jeff," Mark says.

"Like who?"

"I don't know. Just someone."

The day before Mark intends to leave, Jeff coaxes him into one last swim. At the edge of the woods behind his house, the lake is at its widest from the two creeks that feed it. Often in spring during heavy rains, it spills over its banks and floods the shore. Their feet and ankles are wet even before they reach the lake. Dipping his hand into its rippling waters, Jeff smiles. "It's warm enough finally. No shivering afterwards this time, Mark. No need to race back to the house to be the first one in the shower."

They strip to their shorts and carefully wade in, pushing away the water willows and lily pads and sticky splotches of algae. They swim for almost an hour, occasionally floating or sitting on a log to rest. Afterwards, home, they rinse off, first Mark, then Jeff in the outdoor shower Jeff built early in April. At sunset, Jeff cooks them both a special dinner, thick steaks, collard greens with bacon, creamy mashed potatoes. After they've eaten, Jeff says, "Look, I have to tell you this. I want to. I want you to know it. I want you to know how sorry I am that you're leaving, Mark. I think you know that already. I'm not on the make or anything. Don't get the wrong idea. But I care for you. I care about you and I'll miss you. That's all."

"I'm sorry, too, Jeff."

"Then why go?"

"Because I've been living with you for more than four months. Because though I've been working I don't earn enough to pay my fair share. I can't impose on you any longer. It wouldn't be right. I've been here too long already. It's way past time for me to head out. I need to be my own man. To be something more than I am right now. To grow up, maybe. Isn't that what we're told to do? Isn't that what's beaten into us? Grow up? Grow up?"

"If you had some real home to go to, some place better than this," Jeff says, "I'd understand."

"Home's the last place I want to be. God, Jeff. Don't you get it?"

"It seems I don't. But, if not home, where? Where else is there?"

"Don't be mad. Please. Please don't think I'm just some kid anymore, the kid you found trying to hide like an idiot in your delivery truck, some near child with stupid, infantile dreams. Crazy fantasies."

"I'm not angry. You're a man now, Mark. You're a man, not a boy anymore. You've changed in such a short time. I don't how it happened or why, but I can see that. I can see it clearly. Don't you believe I accept that?"

"So I'm a man now? So what? Maybe you've been too respectful, Jeff, too giving. You don't need me here. You give me everything, but I've got nothing to give back to you, nothing that you'll let me give you. Not really. Don't you see? I've wanted to, but you won't let me."

"I don't know what you mean."

"That's just it," Mark says.

Jeff's aware he's sweating. Why? Why is heart beating fast? Is he trying to hold onto something he knows he can't ever have? He knows it's wrong of him to want Mark to stay. But he does.

He takes a deep breath just as the army had taught him to do when danger was so close it might confuse his judgment. "No, I don't see. But I'll shut up. Go if you have to, if it's what you want. End of story." Jeff's face is reddening even more. He can feel it grow flush. He's frightened that he might unintentionally reveal himself. "I think I've gotten life figured out all wrong," he says quietly, as if to himself. "Completely wrong. I don't know what any of it is all about. I guess I never did."

As Jeff stares at him, his eyes narrowing into slits, he scares Mark some. "Maybe it's my fault for not dreaming enough, Mark, for not letting my fantasies run wild. But here's where I stay. I've thought about asking if I could go with you. But I can't. My soul tells me not to. My past, I guess I mean." He opens the refrigerator and removes a carton of chocolate ice cream from the freezer. They eat it straight from the carton with two long spoons. "You have enough money, hard cash, to get you wherever you're going?"

"Yes. Thanks. What I've saved. What you given me. It'll get me to California on a bus and keep a roof over my head for a while when I get there. That's enough. I can work. I can do shit if someone will pay me for it. I'll find a job."

"So it's California, is it? 'California here I come.' That's a long, long way from the fields of Carolina, Mark. I've been there.   For a while. After the war."

"In L.A.?"

"San Francisco."

"Well, it's L.A. for me," Mark says. "Movie stars. Beaches. Sunshine every day. Freedom."

"Tomorrow's the day then? You'll be on your way?"

"Yeah, tomorrow, Jeff." Mark lays his hand on Jeff's and gently squeezes it. Jeff pulls his back. It's the first time they've touched. He's afraid of what he might say if their touch were to linger a second more. The first and last time the same. As it was, in a sense, with Ray. The beginning and the end.

In the morning, Jeff watches through his bedroom's window as Mark clomps back and forth across the porch, working in his new boots whose soles hit the planks as loud as hammers. Jeff tastes metal on his tongue, iron sharp, blood salty, and tries to swallow it, but the taste of Mark's departure won't go away. He's known how their story would end from the first moment he spotted him. Now it's coming to its completion, the one the world had written in his head before he was born. He's unable to change it. He's unable to change anything.

He goes back to bed, to cover himself like a man who's sick. The sheet barely hides his nakedness as he tries to think what to do next. Rolling out of the swaybacked mattress, he removes his other watch, the good one he hasn't worn since he quit trying to be a soldier, from his dad's old dresser. Wearing only his jeans, Jeff enters Mark's room as if to say goodbye, without saying it reaches for his left arm, straps the watch on Mark's wrist, and fastens its clasp. It's a good fit. A good match, watch to arm. The right thing to do.

"It's time," Jeff says. The pun's absurd. "I mean, I want you to have it. A going away present."

"I can't accept this. It's too much." Mark starts to unfasten the leather band.

"I never wear it," Jeff says. "Not since I came home from the Pacific. I have another. The one I always wear. Look, here it is," he says, pointing to his arm. "See? Who needs two watches? Take it. It's yours. I want you to have it. You might need it."

"For what?"

Jeff looks at him, surprised, mystified by what Mark doesn't seem to realize, hasn't yet learned is true for everyone, isn't it? "It's something we have to know, that's all. What time it is. This one tells the day and the month, too. The right order of things. There's not always a clock around when you might need to know what time it is, that's all. It's part of being grown up, owning a watch."

"I've never worn a watch before."

"And that's why you're always early or late."

"Am I? Maybe so. Thanks, Jeff. It's the best gift anyone has ever given me. I mean that." Mark polishes the watch's glass face with a sleeve of his shirt. "I'll miss you, too. Really. You're a great guy. Helped me out when I needed it most when no one else would."

"No tears."

"No, of course not," Mark says. He grabs the bag Jeff gave him with the few things he's taking with him in it. Jeff drives him into town where the bus will stop to pick him up in half an hour or so, waits with him in his pickup for it to arrive, but does not follow him as he strides off like a young man eager for his next adventure. He wonders if he looked like Mark when he sauntered off to the bus on his way to the war. Was it cockiness or fear that speeded up his pace, that made him not glance back as the bus' door opened for him, not wave at his parents as they hoped he would do?

After Mark's gone, for forever he's sure, Jeff wanders the woods, picking berry sprigs for luck as his mother would do on hard days. The trees' canopy's enough shelter for him to weather the downpour that falls shortly after noon. As a snake slithers from under a big rock he's disturbed, he tosses a heavy stone at it, meaning to chase the moccasin back into the lake where it belongs. As if it wouldn't have gone there on its own. "Snake, snake," he shouts after it, enraged. It stops moving. Has he shattered its spine?

My lord, he thinks. What have I done? Pine resin is bleeding from an ancient tree's bark. High over his head, its needles and the intertwined leaves of an oak and a giant poplar permit only a soft light to seep through, comforting him, less blinding than the sun in a cloudless sky shining on an open field. The snake resumes its sinuous movement toward the water. A sign of forgiveness, of God's grace, his mother might have said, the world in perpetual need of redemption.

He's alone again. Does it matter? He'd always been alone, even when a little boy, even when playing with his few friends back then. "A lonely soul," his mother had said once, meaning herself but intending to describe him as well.

No one can alter the way things are. It helps no one to complain, least of all to a God whom Jeff couldn't understand or conceive of even if he existed. It would be like objecting to the sky or the sun or the lake or the woods round his house. To his past. To his parents. To the ground on which he stood. To fate. To the war he hated. He's missing him more than he'd have imagined was possible.

At work, Ted asks him daily how he's feeling. Jeff replies, "Fine." For a few weeks, he visits his parents' graves almost every afternoon and lays a bouquet he's made from wild roses by their headstones. May heaven reconcile them, he prays once and shakes his head. He pities himself as if he were an orphan. Loss makes fools out of everyone. He quits going.

He doesn't like it when he loses a customer on his route or one moves away. He needs patterns, he knows that, something regular, orderly, some plan to follow every day. Change upsets him more than it used to.

But he welcomes every new customer with a gift of a pound of butter that he pays for out of his pocket.

In June of the year after Mark had gone, he buys a new used pickup to replace the old one that had conked out on his way to work early one morning, but the radiator's acting up. He's draining it on the driveway when he sees him walking down the gravel road past the big curve in it about a hundred feet off.

Mark's not looking good, too thin, carrying a battered paper sack instead of the bag Jeff had given him for his trip. As he steps closer, Jeff notices that his face has been badly scratched, maybe by briars in the gullies and fields where he might have slept hitching back. Or maybe someone's worked him over. A quarrel turned mean. A fight over food. Who knows?

In the kitchen, Jeff ladles hot beef stock into a big bowl and breaks bread he's just baked onto a plate. "Go ahead. Take it. Eat," he says. He tries not to show how happy he is that he's back. "But not too much too fast, all right?"

"Yes. I'm trying. Not too fast."

"Do you want to talk about it?"

"Nope. I sure don't. Not any of it."

"Later, maybe?"

Mark smiles at him, just as he used to, thank goodness. "Maybe," he says. "It depends on how long you'll let me stay. I shouldn't have gone, Jeff. I was hurt. Worse than my dad had hurt me. That's all I can say. For now. O.K.?"

On Mark's wrist is the band of the watch Jeff had gifted him with on his last day, though nothing remains of the watch itself. Only rubber bands and a bit of twine hold it securely around his wrist. Mark removes what's left of it from his arm and ties it round Jeff's wrist.

The battered leather band is so oily from Mark's skin it almost glistens in the sharp sun pouring through the kitchen window. For a moment, shining in the light, it looks to Jeff almost like a gold colored band or chain, some trinket Jeff might have bought for his mother at the Five and Dime. Or it might have been the prize bauble he won as a little boy at the county fair, trying again and again to succeed without any luck until he risked everything he had in his pockets on one last throw of the ring. On his arm, now, in this strong light, he feels as if he's wearing the much nicer bracelet he couldn't afford and gave to his mother for her fortieth birthday. Stay, he silently prays. Please stay. Mark. The gift of him.

His daddy is teaching Jeff how to swim in the lake. Near the shore, he throws a stone in to measure where it's shallow enough for his boy. Jeff watches it sink and disappear into the water, vanishing as birds do into the sky. Where do they go? The small boy releases himself from his father's grip, darts to the lake's edge, leaps in. Free, he is sinking too, just like the stone his father threw in. Reach for the falling thing. Wherever it is, find it, grab it. Where's bottom? Swim, swim. But he doesn't know how.

The water's cold. Struggling to breathe, he sees only black, like night inside his room whenever his mother clicks off the light. It's like not wanting to sleep, fighting it off, until it comes anyway and everything is right after that. That's all he can remember, or what he recalls best, the darkness of it, of almost drowning. Then his daddy's wrapping him in a towel, gently holding him, patting him dry, repeating his name like a cry, "Jeff, Jeff." Pencil dots, ink spots splotch the sky. The sun's too yellow in his eyes. He must squint to look, to make out anything in the glare. He's a little boy, happy to be alive.

What does Jeff want? To feel like that boy again. He's trying to sleep in his room while Mark rests in his. To lie in a creek once more, as he'd do as a kid, the water lapping over him, keeping him safe in its shallow bed. Or impetuously, recklessly, foolishly to dive after a stone his father's thrown in the lake to plumb the water's depth and so be saved.

What had made Jeff brave enough to make that crazy leap? As his father rescued him, he was holding on to the stone he'd somehow, unknowingly retrieved underwater, grasping it tightly in his hand, refusing to let it go. Why couldn't he remember that? Why had he had to be told about it afterward, after he'd dropped the stone, his amazement even greater than his dad's?

Is it a sign, this waking dream, this memory that's just come back to him of his almost dying from a dive he didn't mean to make? Did it intend to show him that he can both save and be saved at the same time? Dive in, the boy he was dares him. Follow me. Do what I did.

Wearing only his skivvies, Jeff gets out of bed. Everything that follows will happen as it must, by grace. Or nothing will come of it. Blessed or not blessed. He taps on the jamb of Mark's open door.

First Love: August

1.
Behind the library, the names that are chiseled
into the granite gravestones are the pale gray
of faded tattoos. Sunlight climbs easily

up ancient trees that are bent, grizzled
with moss, gray caterpillar tents, rai-
ded by borers. The air's too hot to breathe, yet breezy.

2.
Jays hide in shadows like bats in the back
of caves. His day's a promise he's made
to be broken. He's a long wait for the mail

or his voice on the phone. He sees a sack
of kittens thrown in the Yadkin. Should he wade
in to save them? Crud crusts one tabby's tail.

3.
A can of chicken soup, egg whipped in,
poured over bread. A Dr. Pepper.
A hunk of cheese. Honeysuckle

sticks to the house. A yellow, thin-
ly painted, colors the blistering plaster.
Two beams and a rafter look ready to buckle.

4.
An orange tastes sweeter than honey on
his tongue. Summer's thick with salt
on his skin, the bitter sweet sweat

of his body's responding to the heat, the sun
in August. The dry thunder's at fault
for bringing no relief, no rain yet.

5.

The morning air is rippling. Sun-white
soil, the sky a blue glaze. Sharp, tall
grass, frazzled leaves. Cooling

shade, shadows, shutters. The fight
to find comfort. The heat hitting like a wall,
like strong waves, a storm at last incoming.

6.

Drifting past, new clouds are white as smoke,
dead cinders, furnace ashes. The sky's
gunmetal gray. The cleansed air gleams

like light off copper. Twigs from oak,
sycamore, pine litter the water rising in gutters, the rain-filled streams.

7.

The earth's steaming, as after a fire's
put out. Porch swings creak. Moths cling
to screens. Tires splatter the road's shoulder.

He moves his bed near the window. Choirs
of tree frogs, mosquitoes that sting,
howling dogs, the smell of mice left to moulder.

8.

Bat cry, owl cry. The buzz of insects
against the windows. Leaves rustling
in the spare night breeze. A pickup, four

on the floor, parks off the road. They have sex
deep in the woods. Locust rasping.
His black hair. His jeans on the forest floor.

9.

Jesse and him shooting the breeze
after, playing cards, listening to '45s,
smoking, talking about plans after school,

bragging about the future, distant seas,
foreign cities, what their lives
would feel like if other guys weren't cruel.

10.

He sees two suns by shutting his eyes.
When one descends, the second rises.
He lies alone on his drooping mattress.

He's happy. The cloudless night's sky's
on fire with stars. August hypnotizes.
Jesse and him. Him and Jess.

Return of the Fallen

Gerald is at the high school ten blocks away, his shirt off, shooting baskets with his friend Zack on the outdoor court behind the boys' gym. Somehow he will step on the loose laces of one of his sneakers, tripping, toppling face forward off the cement court and into the hard packed dirt. He breaks his fall badly, arms stiff and fingers spread wide, but comes away unhurt except for a cut across his left palm, a shallow gash zigzagging down his skin. Probably once the top of a tin can, the piece of rusty metal almost crumbled as he fell on it. It was still sharp and mean enough to have done its work on him before disintegrating, more or less, into flakes of rust, which he examines even before he checks out the damage done to his hand.

He tries first simply to wash the cut clean in the water fountain near the gym door, but the pressure is weak and the wads of gum floating in the basin put him off. No matter how hard he pushes the pump, he can produce only a trickle. Zack takes a look at the wound and suggests the infirmary. Summer school is in session after all. But Gerald shakes his head no. When he comes home, I wash and dress it in the bathroom upstairs.

Though I can't see her from where I sit thinking, I know how Mother sits waiting in her small sewing room. Her back erect as always, board-straight and slightly imperial, her legs crossed at her ankles, her arms at rest on the lace-covered arms of her favorite chair. Only her fingers move, playing with the pins that hold the doilies primly in place. Between her thumb and forefinger, she twists the unraveling strands of the fabric into tiny knots. Later, she will take scissors out of her basket to cut them off, tug the piece of cloth a fraction of an inch down the chair's arm, and re-pin it.

By this time of late morning in mid-summer, the sun has reached over the trees across the street and slipped into the room to warm her. Though I can't hear her either, I know that she is almost constantly coughing, as she has coughed all night long, a high-pitched hacking cough that starts near the top of her lungs and which she is barely able to muffle when she is awake. Rarely will she bring her hand to her mouth, as she would trust us to do even when we were alone if we had a cough. Because the gesture would confirm what she knows anyway. She is dying, dying fast, her lungs full of cancer.

Our father, Gerald's and mine, died a few more weeks than nineteen years ago. Though Gerald and I have never been certain of the exact date, I believe Mother knows it well enough. Even if all three of us knew, we would observe it only with our customary silence. We don't talk seriously much, Gerald, our mother, and I. I think about my father a lot lately, now that my mother is dying. I suspect that Gerald and Mother are thinking about him too.

The story is that he might have been killed advancing across the Tanapag plains on Saipan the same day that hundreds of fleeing civilians who had taken refuge on the northern shore and in the caves in the cliffs which faced it killed one another and themselves, thinking something worse than death lay before them at the hands of the invaders. Parents shot or stabbed or strangled their children and threw them over a precipice into the sea, leaping after them. I've read about the whole campaign extensively, hoping to find a clue.

The sick and wounded Japanese, amputees, men wrapped in bandages, even the blind, had earlier helped one another kill Americans, among them perhaps my father, using a few grenades or a bayonet lashed to a pole or a club or whatever was available that would destroy a man for good. (Why do I find it so difficult to accept that my father might have been killed by a dying man?) In their hospital, they killed three hundred of their own people who were too weak to move.

In death there is life. Anyway, that's what General Saito told his troops in his last message. I don't think so. The only truth for me is non voglio morir. Not now, not ever. The general committed hara-kiri. Using a ceremonial sword, he drew his own blood. Then he was shot by his adjutant through the right temple. So much for conviction. Three days later, that campaign was over. Somewhere, sometime during it my father died. He was only one of thousands. I tell myself, a fact is a fact. Nonetheless I regret that his body was never sent back to us.

Now something called tangan-tangan which was imported for the purpose and grows furiously like kudzu here in the South, has done its work and covered most of the wounds and scars of war. For that very reason, I try to see more clearly the moment of my father's death, to imagine him in his death agony, as I try to picture the facies hippocratica of my mother upstairs, or my brother, or myself when our time comes. Because we need to care about how we look when we are about to die.

When Mother was notified by the War Department of Father's death, I was not quite nine years old. Gerald was only four. I hadn't seen much of him since I was six. Needless to say, our lives changed. Mother mostly made believe it had never happened. So in some ways nothing had changed.

She didn't behave as if Father was still alive. She did something almost as crazy. She acted like a jealous woman who in order to protect herself from her jealousy pretends that she has never been in love at all. Mother would never be so literary, so operatic that she should think of death as Father's new lover and her rival. Yet for her it was almost true. I mean that much of the time she talked and acted as if he had never been born, had never courted and married her, had never sired us, had never bought this house and left just enough money and additional real estate to keep our lives comfortable without her or our ever having to worry about an adequate income. She kept no pictures of him, saved none of his letters, none of his medals, none of his clothes, almost never talked or reminisced about him, never slipped and called me or Gerald by his name, never caught herself remarking out loud how either of us was different from or like him.

We learned things about him anyway, of course. One person alone can't eradicate the memory of a man, not without a lot of hard work. His name was Frank, after his own father and his father's father before him. (I've often wondered why I am not a Frank Lassiter too). Members of his side of the family used to drop by occasionally and begin to reminisce, recalling off-hand a characteristic quirk or oddity in his speech or manner which would give his life some dimension and flavor to us. I noticed very early, it's one of my clearest memories of her, how Mother would always frown at the speaker and put a finger to her lips, darting her eyes significantly over at me or Gerald until even Father's closest relatives took their cue from Mother and stopped referring to him even in passing.

Since we've never talked about it, I can only guess why mother chose to keep the memory of our father from us. The second she finished reading the telegram, she decided in the clarity of her inconsolable grief that we must not be allowed to feel any of that loss ourselves. No one should have to bear such pain, especially not her own children. If we never really knew him, we could not miss him. She loved us too much to allow herself or anyone else to hurt us with his memory. Or maybe she just didn't want him to survive. Maybe she never really liked him or maybe he had hurt her in ways time could not heal. Or maybe there just wasn't much about him to remember.

Mother was on the go all the time. She joined all sorts of garden clubs and bridge clubs as well as the PTA, the UDC, and WCTU. She went to every church social and worked on every fund-raising drive Calvary Methodist Church could concoct. She served as a gray lady at the hospital and worked for the YWCA until it started letting colored people into the white folks' branch.

She never worked a day in her life for money. She just couldn't do that. She meant to be known as a lady. She busied herself with volunteer work, I'd guess, because she wanted us to believe that despite appearances nothing really changes in life. She was saying, You see, with a little effort, one can always find something useful and familiar to do. The consequence was that Gerald and I were often alone, and I knew very young that I preferred life that way. Brothers, she lectured us often, should also be best friends.

Over the years, she received numerous awards, tokens of gratitude, certificates of appreciation. She never mentioned any of them to either of us. Once we saw her picture in the paper. She was holding a statuette and shaking a man's hand, a grim smile fixed on her face. When we asked her about it, our delight too apparent on our faces, she told us it was nothing and not to mind what we saw in newspapers because people who were always minding about getting their pictures in the paper were bound to turn out bad. Memory is only the worst kind of sorrow anyway. Why let it hurt you or the children you love? Keep busy, she seemed to be telling us, let nothing matter to you.

This past Sunday, shortly after we'd returned from church, she began to spit blood for the first time. She refuses to go back to the hospital. For the last three days, she has sat alone in that fine maroon wingback chair Gerald moved up there for her and stared into the wall of trees that edges the back of our yard behind the gully, watching the shadows swing from limb to limb, waiting for the tumor she knows has accomplished most of its work to eat through the blood vessel in her lung whose rupture will kill her.

I talk to myself a lot these days. I've always talked to myself. I guess it's why I teach school. It's my way of filling the silence. Sometimes lately when I talk to myself I feel like a man with the horrors politely conversing with his hallucinations and afterwards writing them down in his notebook.

I don't know how any of us bears another person's dying. Because in this one way at least each human being is an image of oneself. When Mother dies, another part of me will be gone for good. Like a double amputee, I'll have to hold on to life with arms that are not there.

Zach drives Gerald home. They used to drive to school together all the time. Now they shoot baskets almost every morning. Some afternoons, they play tennis or go for a swim. Once, a long time ago, when I went for a swim with my brother, I noticed how the moonlight on his swim suit made it look like metal or foil. As the car door slams shut, I look out the living room window as best I can through Mother's thicket.

"Is it his?" I ask when Gerald comes in. He hasn't hurt himself after all.

"Is what his?"

"That new car. The red MG."

"It's a Healey. A new Austin Healey."

"I see. Well?"

"Of course it's his. He's an Elliston, isn't he? He can have anything he wants."

"It's nice."

"It sure is."

Gerald drops the mail he has picked up onto an end table, still fingering a letter from his girlfriend Jan who is going to summer school at Chapel Hill, working to make up the units she lost last semester trying unsuccessfully to keep Gerald from flunking out.

Later this afternoon, when Gerald has once more left with Zack, I'll go to his room, open the bottom drawer of his dresser, fumble through his clothes, slip the perfumed letter from its yellow envelope, and read it. I will try not to pay attention to the cute little creatures and abundant leafy flowers she has drawn in the margins or to the effusive words she writes. I'll forget most of the contents when I return it to its hiding place. But I'll feel fearful some while I'm reading it. I always do.

Because of the difference in our ages, Gerald and I ought not to have been so close when we were little. I think I tried to act younger than I was sometimes just to keep him as a friend. We would explore the woods out back almost every rainless day, even in the cold, until we knew each tree by heart in relation to every other and could never get lost. After they began to bore us, because we knew them too well, we no longer paid attention to the woods and its trees. With increasing boldness, we wandered away from home, trying to discover where and how far those sidewalks would take us, even when they took us much further than Mother would have allowed. Movies were our happiest discovery.

Gerald and I would often play act what we had seen, using sheets and blankets or towels for almost every costume. We could be Sabu or Captain Blood or King Richard the Lionhearted or anyone else who lived far enough away or long enough ago to stir us into making believe we shared their adventures. More than once, I knighted a chair or portioned out the world with my curtain rod sword. We built tents out of our bedspreads and waited to take India for the Queen. Only as we got older did we play cowboys because now we owned water pistols and cap guns with which we could blast our way through. I always wanted to be the Lone Ranger.

Mother worried about me. She thought as a child I was too imaginative and as an adolescent too slow to give up childish games and grow up. I couldn't will away the physical effects of puberty, of course, but I managed to ignore them, or most of them, fairly successfully for a couple of years, hoping that I had arrived at late what Gerald would reach early. I wanted to share all these new mysteries of the body with him. I wanted to discover what he was discovering at the same time he was discovering it.

He was almost thirteen when he broke his right leg falling out of our tree hut while he was clearing the leaves off the roof after a rain. I saw him stand up, begin to slide down it, grab for a branch, and tumble over the edge. Mother said I screamed more than Gerald and cried twice as hard later.

He thought of his crutches as a sort of toy and delighted in using them and showing off. Shortly after the accident while Mother was out, he experimented with them. Stark naked except for the cast on his right leg and a crutch under each arm, he zipped from one end of the upstairs hall to the other and back again almost as fast as he would have managed on his own two feet. He stopped at my bedroom door and held the crutches out to me, supporting and balancing himself against the door frame.

"Do you want to try it? It's fun."

I was sixteen and had never broken a bone. I took his crutches from him, excited at the prospect of trying them out. In part because they were too short for me, I couldn't manage half as well on them as Gerald. Twice I stumbled and had to use my mock broken leg to prevent my falling. Embarrassed at my clumsiness, I gave the crutches back to him. Somehow the cast on his leg had made all the difference. I had become too aware of his body to continue to play.

Downstairs, the house is always dark, even under the summer sun at noon. The shrubs which my mother long ago had planted around the foundation–the euonymous, osmansis, nandina, ligustrum, and boxwood–have grown higher than most of the windows and block out the light. Mother likes it that way. I've offered repeatedly over the years to trim them or cut them back, but she always said that she wanted the shelter they offered.

Our lawn is full of trees. Dogwood and redbud and magnolia, pin oak, loblolly pine, deodar cedar. My mother even allowed the gum trees to stand when all the neighbors were cutting theirs down. She said she liked the devil's pincushions when they drop, littering the ground in late spring and early summer. She said she'd miss them if we destroyed our trees like everybody else. She didn't think they were a nuisance. She enjoyed picking them up and carrying them in a basket to the gully out back.

Wherever there was space she planted something. Pfitzer and creeping juniper line her walls and walks. Pyracantha, forsythia, January jasmine, five or six varieties of camellias, cerise, salmon, and scarlet azalea, pink and white indicas, rhododendron and gardenia all compete with one another for room and air and light. She planted crepe myrtle and lilacs and hydrangea, tulips and iris and roses. She put out seed even in the summer for the birds and made small sketches in ink of the towees, wood thrushes, blue jays, robins, blackbirds, and cardinals that would perch on the feeders or window ledge outside her sewing room.

My study is downstairs, on the south side of the house where the vegetation is thickest. I read there or work on my lecture notes for my history classes at the high school by the light of a modified hurricane lamp which is almost always on. When the daytime dark becomes oppressive, I go outside and stand for a while. Today, look where I will, the afternoon sun glitters and plays on the leaves and needles like light on the surface of a pool, seen from under water.

One day, not so long ago, I found in the woods behind our house the corpse of a dog, partly eaten, whose gray skin the sun had split. At first, I wondered how something so dead could have found its way so close to our property with all its abundance of life. Then I noticed the ants that crawled over the cloudy eyes and out of the nostrils, open as if still alive to the air and sky, and I sensed my father's body in the roots of everything my mother had planted or nourished.

For a long time, Mother spent most of her free nights at home listening to the radio. A dark-stained wooden lyre and heavy brocade cloth covered the speaker. Its veneer long ago had yellowed and split along its base, dust equally long ago had settled into all its crannies. She listened in her chair with an attention neither Gerald nor I could muster. It's in the attic now. She doesn't seem able to remember any of the old programs when I ask her about them, though for a time they had been much of her life.

In the early 'fifties, she bought a TV, one with a round screen which was surrounded by a thin brass ring and which was centered in a cordovan-colored square box dotted with holes to let the sound out. The odd curve of the screen brought out some oblique character, more comic than sinister, in the face of everyone you watched on it. I've never seen another television like it. It took Mother years to notice the distortion, as if she lacked the measure of real life to judge what she saw on the set. Both Gerald and I preferred watching our few programs at a neighbor's house where the people looked more normal. We weren't more perceptive than Mother. Only more wide-eyed and innocent. She never minded our not staying at home.

Three years ago, she bought a new one. Now, since May, when she turns it on, she won't look at it. She sits staring at her hands, as if she were wondering why one of her sons had not yet come to join her, why we were so late, why we hadn't paid more attention to her pain and been on time to share a program she enjoyed. Yesterday, when this look came over her, I cupped my hands around the back of her neck, wanting to promise some comfort.

"Mother."

Tears filled the corners of her eyes. She glanced sideways at me, retreated, and returned to studying her lap, each hand taking turns massaging the other. I started to switch off the set, thinking it merely an annoyance.

"No. Don't. I'm afraid I still need it on. Something to fill in the time."

"What's wrong?"

I could see a sort of hysteria grip her body, tensing it, but she recovered her strength, refusing to let it take control. No more than a minute or two had passed before she slapped her hands hard against the arms of her chair as she used to do all the time when Gerald and I were young and she wished to tell us something that was to her mind particularly firm and clear. Even then I knew she was, despite all her evasions, a pretty tough lady.

"I don't believe in God. I never did. It's too bad. All this wasted time. It would have made life better. I wish for you and Gerald something better. Some faith, perhaps. Some happiness."

This afternoon when I go up to see her, she is already napping where she sits. The television had never been turned on apparently. Her right arm dangles over the side of the chair, thin, blotched, and pale like a sausage in white casing, like an uncooked chicken leg stripped of its meat.

Once there was a Cambridge Platonist who explained to the learned world that his breast smelled like violets. When I leave Mother asleep in her room, I sense an immediate need to move my bowels. I would like to defecate rose petals, sweet gardenias, honeysuckle, and magnolia. I would like to perfume the world with my body. I would like, when I die, so to sweeten the air around me that all who smelled it would recognize this thing of rank earth and meat had in fact been the incorruptible flesh of someone holy, of a saint. Then I grow comfortable once more with my self-disgust. I enjoy the stench I make. Yet I can barely stand to touch the flesh of my dying mother. Whom I say I love. Whom I do love.

I'm working in my study downstairs when Gerald comes home, his tobacco-colored hair still wet from his swim. He holds his swim suit and jock rolled up like some secret in a towel. In his other hand, he carries the evening paper he's picked off the walk on his way in. He tosses the paper onto the corner of the desk where I write.

"How's Earl?"

"Almost done. Another few days or so is all it'll take to finish, I hope."

"Then off it goes."

"Maybe so."

"None of those others ever got published anywhere." He's concentrating on removing an eyelash that's making his eye twitch. "Why do you bother?"

"I learn something. Earl Long was an interesting man, really. Not half so crazy as the newspapers used to suggest. Not crazy in their way."

"Not whacko, huh? So what did he do good?"

"Well, he thought all the race nuts down there in Louisiana were nothing but a bunch of grass-eaters. He said he was in favor of every religion with the possible exception of snake-chunking. He said that anybody who so presumes on how he stands with Providence that he lets a snake bite him deserves what he's got coming to him. Sane, you see?"

"When did he die anyway?"

"Almost three years ago. He'd been hounded by the press. It probably helped kill him."

"That shits. It's fucked up," Gerald says as he starts leaping up the stairs to his room.

"Did Zack teach you to talk like that?" I yell up at him.

He turns on the landing to look at me. "So?" He glances down the hall. "Jesus, I hope Mother didn't hear me."

A professor at Chapel Hill who liked me once suggested that I might try graduate work and see how I took to it. He thought I might have a book or two in me that might emerge some day. I imagine that after Mother dies I'll continue to work at the high school for a few more years and then quit. I'm a decent teacher, fair and clear, but I've begun to lose interest. The same information, the same unoriginal ideas. I'm not even sure how much of it is true.

I'm a teacher because I learned when we were still young that Gerald needed me to get through school. I would tutor him in his room almost every week night, helping him bring up his grades. He isn't dumb. He's quite smart in fact, maybe even smarter than I am. But he needs attention, he needs to believe that he is learning something for someone, for some reason of the flesh. Even now, an idea for Gerald is never a fact to be accepted. If it is true, it's a sort of incarnation. In order to accept it, he needs to be at least a little bit in love with whoever gives it to him.

When I first started college and he was just beginning high school, I told him I'd come back home and share with him the history of the whole world, from Homer to the present. I said I'd teach him everything he would ever need to know, and therefore he'd never need to go to college himself. We could stay home, just the two of us, and master the whole world. From the money we saved from his college education, we could take a trip by boat around the world.

He was still young enough almost to believe me and what I was saying. "Will you teach Mother, too?"

"Sure," I boasted. "I'll teach her everything too."

"Do you think she'll be down for dinner," Gerald asks while I'm fixing supper.

"Probably not. Did you look in on her before you came down?"

"She was sleeping." He's eating green grapes, spitting the seeds into his palm.

"I'll take some dinner up to her later. She's got to eat." I flip the hamburgers and hash browns and stir the peas. "You ought to learn how to cook."

Gerald tosses the grape seeds into the trash. "I hear her."

Mother's clothes were always drab and musty, like the dark brown binding of the books she inherited from her own mother which she kept neatly shelved and unread in her bedroom. Now her whole body smells discarded as if it had been lying too long, slightly damp, in some dim corner of the attic.

"I feel much better now. I just had me a nice long cry."

"That's good," I say.

She almost laughs. "Heavens. I thought I'd already cried enough tears to lay autumn's dust. But I feel fine now. I'm my old self now, praise be." I glance at Gerald who lowers his eyes. Mother has several styles. This is the one she uses when she is most distraught.

Gerald pulls out her chair for her. "Sit here."

The three of us eat in awkward silence which she is the first to interrupt. "I wish it were winter. I would prefer to die in winter. I'd like to drift in the clear night sky, just like the moon." She puts down her fork. "Molly Lathrop told me on the phone yesterday that she believes we become disembodied voices, like what goes out over the telephone wires." She touches my wrist. I try hard not to recoil from the suddenness of it. "Tell me, what did that man you're writing about believe in, Paulie. I've become so interested in what everyone believes."

"Earl Long believed in lots of things. For one thing, he thought that billy goats, tigers, rabbits, and house cats were all going to sleep together one day, if that counts."

She smiles sweetly, her mouth shaped like the mouth on a kewpie doll.

"Oh, I know what that means. I don't think I'd like that." She quivers a little, as if from a slight chill. "No, not at all.

The room becomes uncomfortably, embarrassingly quiet, each of us studying the plate or glass in front of us. "Those houses that are haunted are most still till the devil be up. Grampa used to say that," Mother says.

"I thought it meant that an angel has flown through," Gerald says.

"Both," Mother says firmly.

After dinner, Mother tries to watch television for a while, gives it up, and goes to bed, her cough once more getting worse. She will lie hacking, half asleep, half awake, most of the night.

Gerald writes a letter to his girlfriend Jan, as he has done almost every night since the beginning of summer, then goes for a long walk, much longer than necessary, to mail it. The night is obsidian. The moon, a white onion, slightly ovoid. He will sit for a while on a park bench, a thing of silver in the night, trying to think only of her and failing. When he returns, he makes a point of ignoring me as he rushes past the open door of my study. I can hear him upstairs close his bedroom door behind me with a shove meant for my attention that, had he not been concerned about waking Mother, would have been a slam.

I return to Earl and his troubles with his wife Miz Blanche, a woman whom I've grown to detest. It was she, really, who had him incarcerated in Galveston and then Mandeville Asylum in Louisiana. "They snatched me out without even enough clothes on me to cover up a red bug," he told a reporter, "and a week after I arrived in Texas I was enjoying the same wardrobe. They put me in a room with the door open and crazy people walking in and out all night. One of them thought I was the toilet."

Sometimes he did act crazy, frenetically betting on horse races, buying forty-four cases of cantaloupes off the side of the road or $700 worth of cowboy boots at once, making all those nocturnal telephone calls, acting like a man who didn't ever want to die. His wife betrayed him, all right. That image of him alone in his room in a house of the mad, his door always open, haunts me sometimes at night now that Gerald's door is closed so firmly to me.

Earl Long was a good man as men go. But thinking about his troubles does me no good tonight. I doubt that reading about the troubles of another human being ever really helps us with our own. Hence I don't believe in the medicinal powers of tragedy.

The essay is useless, pretentious. I call it, "Earl Long, or Why Southern Liberals Must Be Crazy." I'd be better off if I directed some of that irony back on myself.

A black, gummy caterpillar inches its way over my manuscript, making for the notes. I flick it with a finger across the room and then get up to go hunt for it somewhere under the floor lamp, hoping to save it and put it back outside. The porch light on, I stand on the stoop and watch an apple-green luna moth flutter over my head.

Gerald doesn't want me in his bed again tonight, I say to myself out loud. And I wonder, is it Jan? Zack? Neither? Both? Or fear of the world and what it would say and do to us, him and me, if it knew?

Zack arrives earlier than usual this morning, the top of his sports car already down. I'm picking up the paper off the lawn, wearing my floppy pajamas and robe which hang off me as if I were an emaciated old man scuffling down hospital halls aimlessly looking for comfort. Yet people who can't see reality in other ways, too, will insist to our faces that I'm the better looking brother.

Gerald runs round me, sleek in his shorts and t-shirt, and eases into the bucket seat of the Healey without opening the door, a beautiful thing into another beautiful thing so beautifully slipping that I feel sure that I have seen him making love to someone else. Inside me, a tightly wound spool unravels like a wide silk ribbon from its bobbin and scoops and leaps and dances frantically in the air. But it's not really jealousy I'm feeling. It's just that I miss him.

After breakfast, I sit at my desk, facing a blank new page. I wait quietly, no words come to me, I thumb through my notes. I seem to have lost all interest in it. I feel I'm not serious enough for it. For anything.

Dying removes everything from the world except pain, as if the fear of death is itself a disease that does not let the body's blood coagulate so it oozes in many spots through the broken skin and seeps internally into the cavities of the body, just as radiation, the right sort and sufficient amount, has done to a man. As the A-bomb did to many. The terror of it, I suppose I must mean.

A reporter once tried to interview Earl in a hotel room when the governor was preoccupied with the fact that the State Legislature Rules Committee had insisted for obvious political reasons that he resign on September fifteenth and thereby risk, among other dismays and troubles, income tax charges from the Feds and the loss of seven months' worth of patronage. The reporter called out from one side of the door that he would like to speak to the governor. Earl's voice responded from the other side. "He's just gone up in a balloon." Well, I'd just gone up in a balloon. My head is full of air.

I look at the blank page in front of me and wonder why I bother. I have little talent and nothing to say. I try to tell myself I'm trying to bear some small witness to that something more in humanity that saves it from a merely clinical exitus letalis. I say it, but I have nothing to say.

I've read that when a man goes truly mad he first loses grammar. Then words fail him. Judged on this criterion, Earl was never close to being really mad. He never stopped talking and talking clearly. I think of that now in a sort of panic to which I'm becoming increasingly accustomed.

For a moment, a split second and no longer, I can find neither words nor an order in which to put them. I go blank. My fears can find no language. I am pure wound. Then I hear Mother slowly making her way down the stairs. I manage at last to forget myself.

"Paulie. Paulie."

I spring up. She's standing on a stair, halfway down, holding on to the banister with both hands, her knuckles white as cartilage. Her pink bathrobe which she has left unbuttoned covers most of her pink silk nightgown. A drop of blood trickles down her chin and neck. Her skin is milk glass, her hair gray down caught in a web of black netting. When she begins to cough again, the sound is violent. The blood oozes out of her mouth onto the fist she brings up to her lips to muffle it.

The coughing stops. "I'm frightened."

"Mother."

"No hospital." Her right hand jabs the air.

"Yes. No hospital."

"Soon." She turns to half walk, half pull her way back up the stairs. She clearly wants no help.

When I return to my desk, the rest of my essay comes to me easily. I finish it by late afternoon.

Oh, my mother whom I say I love. Whom I do love.

Since Gerald is late for dinner, I go ahead and eat. I carry a tray up to Mother who refuses everything except the tea and a warm blueberry muffin which she picks at nervously.

"Where's Gerald? I want him home too. I don't want to see just you all the time."

"I don't know. Off with Zack someplace."

She coughs twice. "That boy will spoil him, make him want things he can't have."

"Yes. How are you feeling now?"

"I wish both you boys were more practical. Gerald's such a little boy still. He doesn't think about the future. Everybody's got to think about the future. Even me right now."

"He'll be fine. Give him time."

She looks at me as if she were looking at the stupidest thing she's ever seen and can't believe her eyes. "Time? What time? I'm done for."

It's already dark long before Gerald gets home. I'm waiting for him lying on a couch in the unlit living room.

"What's wrong?" He slams the door without meaning to. "Why are you here in the living room like this? It's Mother, isn't it?"

"Yes. She's coughing blood again."

"Paul." A little cry stops at the back of his throat.

"She'd like to see more of you. But you're gone all day. She worries about you."

"What for? I'm fine."

"She thinks you have no future."

"I'm only twenty three, for Christ's sake."

"What does Zach know about you? Us? What have you told him?"

"Nothing. Why should I?"

"And Jan?"

He shakes his head. "What could I tell her either, Paul? I can't." He takes a cigarette out of Mother's cigarette box, fools with it, and puts it back. "I shouldn't smoke now, I guess."

"You'll just hurt Jan. You know that. You do understand that, don't you, Gerald?"

"Yes."

"Tell her."

"I can't, Paul. What more do you want from me? We were lonely. We are lonely. But it's not right. It's not…it's not…."

"Natural?"

"Maybe. I don't know about us or anything anymore. It used to be so simple. I wish it could still be. It isn't anymore. Lying seems so much easier. I've gotten too used to it. Sorry, Paul. I have."

"We're not just brothers. There's something strange I don't understand either that binds us together. It's almost as if we're the same, you and I."

"You mean about Dad, don't you?" For the first time since the days after Mother's cancer was diagnosed as incurable, Gerald looks at me as he used to look at me most of the time, with something like love. Something more than love. Maybe better than love since no one on this earth would say yes to it.

Though it's still too early to sleep, I lie in bed anyway, pondering a sentence of Earl's, "I feel like a muley bull coming out of a dipping vat." It took me nearly a whole day to find out that a muley bull was a bull without horns. Frank Lassiter probably would have known that without having to look it up anywhere. But not his son Paul. Well, I feel like that bull, too, though I can't honestly say that I have any clear idea about what Earl meant, about this or about anything else for that matter. I wait, concentrating on the darkness, until I finally no longer have to think, listening to Mother's raspy breathing through our two open doors.

My heart beats so fast I half convince myself I'm fibrillating. To calm down, I roll over onto my stomach, but my body engorges, turning hog-sized and sow-gray and ugly. Children throw rocks at me and beat me with sticks in disgust. I can't keep my balance on anything and I fall off a low brick wall, then a step ladder, then a foot stool. My bones soften, my eyes sting. I curl in bed like a cat. My skin feels as shiny and smooth and hairless as plastic. My dead father, my dying mother. Is this what such loss does to us? Or is it more like fear I am feeling? Inside me, I am nothing but vacancy, absence, salt.

In the morning, Gerald knocks lightly on my door. "Zack'll be here in just a few minutes. I wanted to say goodbye."

"Not today."

"Why not?"

"You stay with Mother. I've got to get out. I need to take a drive."

"All right. Where to?"

"Home," I say.

I drive out the High Point Road past Lake Jenerette and follow the narrow two-lane blacktop most of the way to Bethesda and beyond. Though this was once my father's world, I pursue no real purpose. I am on no sure quest. When I see what I need to see, when I feel what I've driven here to feel, I'll know to turn around and return to Mother and Gerald.

Ever since I got my driver's license, I've liked this stretch of road, its houses built strangely close to the highway on pieces of land crudely cut out of deep pine woods, their sand and gravel and packed dirt driveways randomly placed and rarely used to park a car on anyway, the cars stashed anywhere, it seems, except on a driveway, their nearly identical front porches on which someone–an old woman wearing a yellowing lime-colored apron, say, her stockings rolled over the ankles of her spread legs which are as white and lumpy as mashed potatoes—is always sitting or rocking or standing, staring out toward the passing cars, their eyes glazed with an equal measure of trouble and boredom and patience.

Gables seem to have stuck arbitrarily anywhere on the sharply pitched roofs. Once someone had tried something like landscaping around the house, planting a bush here or a shrub there. But then the plants have been ignored, left to grow and thrive or to die as they will. Those unused driveways are invariably overgrown with the same scattered patches of high grass and weeds which everywhere except on the driveway I'd reckon they'd call a lawn.

Pieces of cinderblock have been strewn, car parts have been discarded, unidentifiable twists of ancient machinery, flower pots and pot shards, a bashed-in wash tub, crumpled cardboard boxes have been tossed aside as randomly as living things are let to fall to rot or decay as they will. Closer to the woods, the picked carcass of a car has been dumped.

Roof trusses sag. The wood houses need paint or repair. The tar paper and sand imitation brick shingles fall to the ground and lie there ignored. Porches sit precariously on chipped cinder blocks or uneven rows of old bricks. The tin roof on the rotting shed out back rusts. The small, bull-frog green pond sits waiting for the algae around its edges to take over.

This is the green world into which my father was born. Another green world has claimed his otherwise unclaimed body. What here is not one shade or another of green either is as rust-colored as dead pine needles or is the pale pinkish orange, the salmon, the Chinese red of the clay, the color deepening as the sun moves west.

After he left here, my father was the first Lassiter to make some real money, real enough anyway for us, my mother and brother and me, to live comfortably in a middle class neighborhood in the city for all these years, with more years to come if any of us lasts. When he went to war, he died from it and promptly faded from sight, maybe because his wife didn't want him to survive her own grief, maybe because there really was no more to remember about him than there is to remember about most of us.

He came from a world of scattered, cast-off things, a world of hard, bright colors whose people long ago learned that nothing is worth the human effort it takes to try to keep it in order after it's fallen apart or to make it go when it won't work or to coax it back to life when it's fixing to die.

The road curves to the south. I slow down to take it. Amazingly, there he is. His rusty hair is scraggly from his sweat. His eyes don't squint in the glare of the sun. His lips, not quite parted, are too proud to have anything to say. He leans his right thigh against the left headlight of his '57 Chevy and folds his strong arms defiantly across his naked chest. The laces of his canvas shorts droop over his crotch. He digs the right toe of his sneakers into the soil. He stares into empty space as if into a camera.

Maybe he's seventeen. His life belongs to his body. He has his car. He is arrogant, he is beautiful, and he will not scare.

I see him for only a few seconds. If I were to drive by here tomorrow or the next day, he would already be gone. So the heart opens to life again. Light filters through dark trees. A scuttling wind blows through me.

I turn around in a driveway two houses further down the road, try to hold him another second or two in the corner of my eye and then in the rear view mirror, and head back for my brother and our house.

He's thumbing through a magazine in the living room when I come in. "That didn't take long," he says.

"I didn't go far. How's Mother?"

"Worse, I think. I'm really afraid for her now, Paul. Scared for her. For us."

"So am I. Very. What would you like for dinner?"

He shrugs. "Ask Mother."

"She just picks at her food. I'll fix what you'd like."

He smiles at me suspiciously, slyly. "Where did you go? You seem in a good mood. What did you see?"

"Us," I say. "You and me."

Gerald and I watch TV alone. Leave It to Beaver. When I watch fathers on television, I can't help being almost glad my own father's not here. Why should I feel nostalgia for the ah-oo-gah of the klaxon, the honk of the bulb horn, the beep or blast on the wheel that tells you daddy's up the drive and home at last? I don't want him in my bedroom, like Ward in Wally's and Beaver's, lecturing me about what to do, how to behave, whom to love, warning me with memories of his own harder childhood, failing to understand, not comprehending his sons at all. My father's dying was a sort of gift, I think sometimes. I feel no need to hate him. But the truth is that, when I think such thoughts, our loss of him feels only that much more grievous to bear.

After the show is over, Gerald flops down onto the leather sofa near the window. I sit in a desk chair, swiveling it toward him.

"I wrote Jan," he says.

"The truth?"

"Most of it. I left out the details about you and me."

"Maybe that was wise."

"Yes. She can't keep secrets. I'm going to try to tell Zack when I see him tomorrow. I'm not sure how Jan will respond. Even less certain about Zack."

"You have a crush on him."

"Yes. A little. I'm not in love with him. Don't be frightened. Don't worry."

"But you're not going to speak about us to him either, right?"

"No. I can't, Paul. Please understand."

"I do. Of course I do. What made you decide all of a sudden?"

"I don't know. Maybe you. I don't know. Mother. What's happening to her."

I gaze into the white globe of the lamp overhead, wondering what it would feel like to be blinded by light. I close my eyes and watch the colors swirl, rubbing my hand across my forehead and wondering if I want it to end. How little time changes anything. The world moves as slowly as a snail across a road with neither whip nor goad to quicken it. I understand nothing. I love my brother. He loves me.

Mother is having a very bad morning and refuses even to try to get out of bed. Gerald has left the house for part of the day, promising to be back by at least late afternoon. By one o'clock her coughing has driven me out of the house, too, leaving her alone, her two sons not pitiless but useless, or so she rightly tells us. I work in the backyard. Mother no longer tries to conceal her suffering and concentrates on her pain as if it might reveal something to her that might save her yet. Twice, trying to find words of comfort, I mouthed platitudes and started to sob. She stared at me resentfully.

It's hot, the air heavy and sweet. Clouds from the west hang motionless in the sky, like a dark wool blanket, Mother would say, over the earth. Working in the back with my bare hands, I rip the vines off the picket fence to which they've so long clung that they are now its only support. From time to time, I toss the pile of twigs I've gathered into the gully that separates our property from the woods in back, kicking the rotten pickets over one by one until the whole fence lies in pieces on the ground. My skin itches like bug bites under my clothes. I long for rain.

Two houses over, the golden retriever begins to bark randomly. It hushes and barks, barks and hushes over and over. Across the street, a bell on a bicycle jingles. I can hear even the hum of its tires on the sidewalk, then the crush of the driveway gravel beneath them. Over head, a squirrel leaps from one branch to another. Briefly rustling in the breezeless air, the shaken leaves release a dead limb that topples to earth, splitting as it falls.

The back screen door squeaks open. "Paul," Gerald yells. "Paul."

I crawl fast up the slope. "I was getting rid of the old fence and the vine at last. I was trying to pull out some of that overgrown honeysuckle."

"It's Mother. She's fallen in her bathroom. I can't open the door."

Zack steps out beside him. Clearly Gerald has told him nothing. Sometimes a failure to speak, to tell the truth, can survive as a kindness. I start to wail.

The afternoon that Mother learned her cancer had spread beyond any stopping of it, she went straight to her room, locked the door behind her, and cried for nearly two days. We couldn't hear her crying. She wasn't careless that way. But both of us listened for it and knew what she was suffering no matter where we were those forty or fifty hours. Wounds that heal are a mere annoyance, meaningless, not wounds at all. They are breakdowns in a machine that can be repaired. Cancer is the devil of a sensible hell who knows just when, where, and how to cut the flesh so that the spirit will always be open to bleed. After she was done, she opened her door around suppertime on the second day, found us in our separate rooms waiting, took us by the hand, directed us down the stairs, and had us sit on the living room couch to listen to her where she sat between us, one of our hands held in each of hers.

"There no use my beating around the bush." She didn't look at either of us. "I'm dying and there's no good my denying it to you or to anybody else. Least of all to myself. There's nothing anybody can do."

She'd turned her head toward Gerald, but I could tell her eyes were closed. "Don't, honey. Don't. Please. It'll be better for me if we're all real strong. I'm hardly worth a fig anyway. I'm just one of those that was forgotten a little, that's all. I merely want you to know I won't go back to that hospital." She squeezed both our hands. "I want you to have my body burned as quick as you can. Don't keep my ashes around here. Let me vanish. Disappear."

Gerald's right hand covered his eyes. Mucus had begun to flow out of his nose. "Yes'm."

"It's Dad," I said. "You don't want to be buried because...."

"I've got my own reasons." She let go of our hands and patted them like a distant elderly aunt. "I better go fix our dinner before all of us starve."

She started to stand up, but her legs buckled slightly under her. After she had sat back down, she cocked her head and closed her eyes. A smile creased her cheeks as if some sweet, long forgotten thought for which she had been searching had suddenly returned to her. She relished it for a while, tossing her head lightly back and forth.

"I was just thinking about a long time ago in Chowan. My own mother used to hunt with her father on a swamp ridge near their home. She was just a little girl at that time. She and my Grampa Eure were fascinated by the Chowan Indians since part of their land bordered on the Chatanooka Cut where the old Indians had once farmed.

Anyway, one day they discovered all these mysterious carvings on large trees. But all the carvings were so old and overgrown their messages couldn't be read. The single legible carving was the picture of a man upon a large beech tree. And you know what Grampa Eure said to Momma when he saw that old Indian carving? He said, 'That's your late husband, little missy. He's been imprisoned in that tree.' And Momma started to howl so bad Grampa Eure had to carry her in his arms all the way home.

"She never forgot that incident. She told me about it when my Frank died, when your father died. She thought Grampa Eure had prophesied the future, only he'd gotten it wrong by one generation. It's funny how you remember certain stories when you least expect to. I'd like so much to see Grampa Eure now and ask him things about life, about the odd shapes and patterns it takes."

I twisted uncomfortably on my cushion, enough to make Mother break her thought and rise to her feet. "Now I better get going on that meal I promised you and not tell you any more strange tales about your great grandpa. He used to make me smile so. And then I always felt so sad."

"I'm going to call Zack," Gerald tells me the day after Mother's death. "I can't wait any longer." He looks so changed since he saw so much of her blood on the bathroom floor, some of it the blood in which she drowned, that I can't read from his face anything of what he's feeling. He's gone blank, shut down, for the last many long hours.

The call could have lasted only ten minutes or so. "Do you want to talk about it?" He shakes his head no.

Jan's letter arrives the following day, the day of the cremation, and lies unopened for two days thereafter. We have said practically nothing to one another since the men from the hospital came for Mother's body. Gerald keeps to his room, occasionally coming downstairs to fix himself a sandwich or to pour himself a bowl of cereal. He won't let me cook for him. I try repeatedly to re-read my essay on Uncle Earl, to be critical of what I've written, to find some meaning in it. The intolerable truth is that no one can ever experience or feel another person's suffering or sorrow. No one. Not ever.

When Earl was running for re-election, his alleged madness a real issue, he asked a crowd whether they wouldn't rather have a tried and true man, admittedly as crazy as he was intelligent, rather than some bladderskite for governor. The people voted Jimmy Davis back into office, the man who wrote "You Are My Sunshine," about whom Earl had said that he loved money like a hog loved slop.

Too many photographers had snapped pictures of Earl while he was scratching his balls, I suppose. He died almost three years ago and I think he might have been the last natively good man in the South. Maybe I caught some of the quality of the man in my essay. I don't know. Re-reading it, I notice that I've failed to mention his brother Huey. I'll send it off someplace tomorrow or the next day, a distraction taken from me.

Pretty soon, I'll have to start thinking about death. About Mother's death. Maybe about my own. Certainly about Gerald's. Even more certainly about my father's. I've been considering chopping back some of Mother's shrubs to let some light into the house.

That night in his room, I ask Gerald once more if he wants me to cook him a hot supper. "You need to eat. You're losing weight faster than I think you know."

"I'm not hungry."

"Force yourself."

"What for?"

"For me." His throat makes an odd, cough-like noise that he quickly swallows to conceal the hurt of it. "Why won't you read that letter from Jan? It's lain on the mantel for three days now."

"I know what it says already. It doesn't matter anymore. Maybe it never did."

"All right. Don't then. I'm going to go for a drive. You want to come?"

"I thought I didn't have any more crying left in me," he says, "just as she said she didn't have any more crying left in her when she learned Dad had been killed."

"Yes," I say. "Me too." He turns over in bed and pushes his face deep into the pillows. "I'll switch off the light."

He flips over. "Paul."

"What?"

"Don't be gone too long, o.k.? I need you."

All either of us, Gerald and me, can feel any more on our skin is the shock of the world. What can we do? I drive downtown, talking to myself wildly, almost babbling all the way. One part of my mind is clear, another part shattered so absolutely by the pain of it that it stands in need of complete reconstruction. I can't imagine why it occurs to me. But out of the blue it seems important to me that, probably because Dad was away in the war when Gerald was born, he's circumcised and I'm not.

I park my car near the library and go in, waving to the familiar hunched back of the circulation librarian as I pass her. I wander through the too familiar stacks like someone eating popcorn at a movie, filling myself without paying attention to what I'm doing. I try to read book titles and watch them blur, no matter how hard I try to focus my mind. Walking down aisle after aisle, I confirm that there's not one book I want to read.

I start to panic. I don't begin to shake. My blood beats no faster. I sense no sudden urge to flee. The shell feels nothing. But the nerves of the beast have just been dropped into boiling water. There is a moment of perfect pain, perfect sorrow. Not even a second passes. Death immediately follows. And then, for no reason, it's over. I know what we must do.

I walk uncertainly toward the front entrance, bumping clumsily into a comically perfect picture book little old lady in a pill box hat whom I hadn't seen entering through the door. She squints at me in understandable irritation, points herself in the right direction, and makes for the front desk with all the dignity she can recoup from my blundering rudeness. As I stand on the well-lit steps, I wonder how I've managed to scratch my arm slightly near the wrist and lick the blood off with my dry tongue.

Back home, I notice that Gerald has left both the porch light and a light in the living room on. I run up the stairs two and three at a time. He's sitting on his bed, wearing only his briefs, staring down at the opened letter and its envelope which are spread across the sheets. The table lamp which at the moment is the room's only light is too dim to illuminate the pages. Gerald's biting his nails, a habit I thought he'd broken long ago.

"You can read it if you want to. You've read all the others. I should have minded, I guess. But I don't. Fair's fair. We'd said long ago there'd be no secrets between us."

I do a weak job of not looking surprised, flinching a little, feeling guilty as I should, a caught spy. But he's right. No secrets. I pick up the three pieces of stationery off his bed and carry them over to the lamp, rearranging them into the proper order.

> Dearest Gerry,
> I've been reading and re-reading your letter every five minutes since I got it. I don't think I understand. Why did you write me such a letter? Are you testing me? Being mean? I've got exams and essays to think about and out of nowhere your letter comes and stops me short.
> I believe love is sacred, the highest principle in the world. I love you so much sometimes I want to burst like a bud and break into a flower. Do you think I'd ever forget that night we talked till dawn in my car near the dorm. I told you I would help you and I meant it. Oh, Gerry, I love you and I know you could never be what you said you

were in your letter because I've held your hand so hard I thought my own would break into little pieces and kissed you and hugged you until I believed we were one body. So don't give up on us.

Why don't you re-enroll in the fall and we'll live together! We couldn't tell my family. We'll need to keep it a big secret. I promise I can keep it, too. We could be so close and so perfectly in love.

My darling, you must never write me such a letter again and say such things to me, such obvious, bewildering lies.

I have to stop for now. A big bio. exam in the morning. Come to me soon. Bill Craig says you can stay at his frat house. He says it's almost empty during the summer. They may even want to pledge you next year.

I long to see you again and hold you and kiss you. And we can forget you have ever said such bad things to me. After all, we've got all of eternity before us and the Good Lord looking down on us with all His beneficence and abundant grace.

Your true love,

Jan

"I didn't know anyone called you 'Gerry.'"

Gerald finds my eyes for the first time in days. "It's hopeless. It always was. I've been a fool, Paul. I'm sorry.

"So have I. What did Zack say?"

"That if I ever get near him again he'll beat the hell out of me."

"I prefer Zack's response."

"She doesn't understand at all, does she?"

"No. How could she?"

"No one can. No one ever will. It's hopeless, you and me. We've no one else now." Gerald jumps off the bed, finds his clothes, and dresses so quickly that I don't seem to be able to find the words to stop him. "You've got the car keys. Give them to me."

"Tell me where you're going first."

"Away. Away from all of you. From Jan. From Zack. From you.

From Mother.

Give me those keys, Paul. Now. I mean it."

I stand firm for less than a minute before he pushes me. As I stumble backwards, I hit my head against the wall. I reach into my pocket and hand him the keys. "Where are you going? Please tell me."

"I don't know. I'm scared, Paul. Not of you. Of everyone else. Somewhere impossible. Somewhere I'll feel free. I don't know. Out. Somewhere out."

Gerald gone, I lie on the floor of my study, the lights off, thinking once more about what I've tried not to think about all week. Father's death. Whether we attack or whether we stay where we are, there is only death. So General Saito on Saipan. A Japanese officer beheads his little band of enlisted men with his sword before he is shot down by his would-be captors. Japanese soldiers swim out to the reefs of Tanapag Harbor where most refuse to give up and are machine-gunned. Hundreds of civilians leap from the cliffs of Marpi Point to the knife-like rocks below. At times, the waters beneath are so clotted with the bobbing bodies of men, women, and children that naval small craft cannot steer a course without running over them. Almost the entire garrison of thirty thousand Japanese on Saipan is wiped out. Three thousand six hundred and seventy four Army and ten thousand four hundred and thirty seven Marine Corps personnel are killed, wounded, or, like my father, missing in action.

Seven lives to repay our country. The largest mass suicide yet in the Pacific. I advance to seek out the enemy. Follow me! The old general eating canned crabmeat, drinking saki. A ceremonial sword or is it a dagger? Blood flowing, a pistol shot. The lame, the halt, the blind. The sick and wounded from the hospitals come forth to die. Three hundred too weak to move killed in the hospital by their comrades, their brothers-in-arms. Marines lying down to sleep amid already rotting corpses because no spot is free of dead bodies. Mothers and fathers stabbing, strangling, shooting their screaming children, hurling them into the sea and leaping in after them. Wounded children still lingering on whose parents had failed to finish them off before taking their own lives.

I see my father charging toward the bayonet that will pierce his side or his guts or his heart, his face thrown back in terror. I feel dead myself, as if he had thrown me over a cliff into the sea the moment that he died.

God made us out of nothing and we each of us seem to strive only to bring ourselves back to nothing, dying in our own blood if need be. Like our poor Mother.

Earl Long's favorite poem was "Invictus," written by a man in a tuberculosis hospital. It tells us that it does not matter how strait the gate or how charged with punishment the scroll, that we are masters of our fate and captains of our soul. I wonder how Earl regarded his favorite poem when he was being peed on by a madman mistaking his room for a toilet in the asylum in Galveston. Earl had to be half crazy to come back and answer the charges of craziness made against him as he did. I think he was able to do sane things only because he was more than a little crazy. Sometimes I think he might even have been as insane as Miz Blanche seemed to want people to think he was. But he was a survivor, at least until some bad pork at a barbecue and a worse heart felled him. His eyes, I see it in every photograph, long ago had cracked like a mirror.

I try to imagine the sanity of my father at the moment of his death, the clarity of my mother at hers. It is real, the wound is real, as the man saying "I love you but I can't love you because the world won't let me" is suddenly real to his panicking lover, his body clearer and more necessary than ever before. I begin to cry for both of them, my mother and my father, and for my own lost past, my chest rising and falling as my lungs gasp for breath between sobs, though my mind nonetheless remains keenly alert to the slightest sound that might indicate that tires have turned up the driveway, that a car door has been slammed, that Gerald's home.

The grief subsides even as my fears for him increase. I get up off the floor and begin to pace, trying to find signs of light through the thicket of shrubs and bushes smothering the window. I turn on a lamp, try to read tonight's paper, try to summon interest in reading something, anything, give it up, and turn on the radio only to switch it off, having heard maybe the first five bars of a song until I realize that nothing can distract me from him, that I have wrung only darkness out of the darkness, only pain out of our common pain, mine, his, our dead parents'.

Sometime, it cannot be much before dawn, I wake up where I had fallen asleep perhaps only a few minutes earlier. Gerald stands over the sofa where I lie, looking down at me curiously, his left hand dripping blood onto the living room rug and the coffee table, his face badly scratched and bleeding.

He's a little drunk. "I crashed the car. I don't think it's too bad. I hit a tree making a turn." He lifts up his hand for me to notice. "I did this when I slammed the door."

"Let me look at it."

"Later. It's o.k. It doesn't even hurt."

"It will. Where have you been?"

"To a couple of beer joints. Some dives way out on 440. I didn't know where I was going. I couldn't know. I just took a ride, stopped wherever I saw a flashing neon sign." He digs a handkerchief out of his back pocket and wraps it around his hand to keep it from staining the carpet further. "I got out of the car every once in a while and ran some, but I always was still drunk when I stopped running. I guess that's why I hit that tree. But I'm o.k. now. I'm so sorry, Paul. You understand, don't you? Why I've been behaving as I have this last year or so? That what I was crazily hoping for was to live a normal life? Like everyone else does?"

"Yes. And now?"

"Now I don't anymore. I never really did because I know for sure now I never could. It was all a mistake. Jan. Even Zack. It's too bad about them, losing them, especially Zack. But it's true, isn't it? I haven't really a choice, do I? And even if I did I think this is what I would choose. You, I mean. Us."

I brush his lips with my fingers. "Maybe that's why human beings so often fail at life. Wanting it to be normal. Maybe that's where all the need to hurt comes from. From being normal. How's your head?"

"It's fine. Really clear. For once." He pushes my legs toward the back of the sofa to make room and sits down, grabbing my right hand in his, almost as if he means somehow to shake it. "I've been thinking. I've been thinking a lot. I've got to learn things. I don't know enough. I've never known enough. But I don't think I could stand going back to school. I don't want to see people anymore. I mean it. Not for a long time anyway. I've got to read things, Paul. I want to find out about stuff. I know sometimes I get it all wrong. I've got to start all over. I've got to be educated."

"What do you want to know?" I take his shoulder in my arms, push him gently aside, and get up, walking toward the fireplace. He follows me like an eager pupil.

"I hope this doesn't sound dumb. I was thinking we could begin with the Greeks. With Homer maybe or the tragic playwrights. They were the first ones, weren't they? We may as well start at the beginning, don't you think?"

"All right. We'll start with the tragedies. The stories of people who suffered because they couldn't change."

"Not like us." He kisses me. Passionately.

The wind gusts, scratching an oak tree limb across the top edge of the picture window. Startled, I glance over Gerald's shoulder and catch a glimpse of my face on the pane staring back at me out of the dark. It looks like the face of someone long buried that's been imprinted on his shroud, slightly smudged and boneless. Like our father's face in a faded photograph taken his last day in bootcamp. How much the dead must miss us to imprint their lives on ours.

"No," I say, not wishing to lie, holding him tightly. "Not like us at all."

"Free," he says. "You and me."

"Yes." I release him to close the curtains. "Free."

My Father

1.
The earth under my feet is trying
to sink me. My bathtub's a creek,
its water blackened from ash-like soot.
I wash what grime I can off.
My father pounds on the door, shouts,
"What're you doing in there? It's school time."

The streets of Memphis are burning. Tanks
crush a revolt in Budapest. Young boys
in Algeria are tortured, die tangled in wire,
burnooses, tied to posts.

                              Asleep,
I'm seized by a nightmare I dread,
a century old sunk ship near my home
rises out of the sand. Kidnapped by
a press gang, oh fatherless, I disappear.

2.
I sit on a curb. No streetlights are permitted
in my neighborhood. Like someone dying, I wander
from home. In his slippers, pajamas, robe, my father
searches for me in the dark, calling my name
down the long driveway. Nearly visible in the night,
I glide down the street, toward stone walls, an iron
gate and a lawn as meticulously shorn and tended
as a country club green. In my room, the wind's
whistling through loose panes, a ghostly intruder
in my brain, no stalker, no fantasy, the rain
again, the bracing winter rain, the hail and ice.
Listen. The key is in the lock, the latch clicks,
the door opens. All this I hear. Not a burglar,
my father's home. Why fear anything, anyone,
if I'm never alone, night my friend, the graveyard wall.

3.

Sprawled on a bench, a man in wine-soaked,
bedraggled clothes is feeding gulls, and crows
from a box of corn cereal while wailing.
His hands and forearms are black from mud.
Striped white and blue, a wind surfer's sail
flies over the dunes like a lost balloon.
A punk on a motorcycle guns his engine. A kid
on a bicycle races past. Dressed
in sweats, pony tails tied in ribbons,
two girls jog around him. The bum shoves
chips from the box into his mouth, chokes,
wheezes until he spits it out like vomit.
He stinks. What kindness was ever done him?
Mist refracts a blackening sun. Am I no one,
my father, a child of the wild and bitterly cold?

4.

It's solitude made the world and left undivided
dark from day. Last night, I watched fog swallow
a whitewashed moon and the streams of the milky way.
Mist fell like snow to cover the world, to blanket
and comfort the life below, the dead in the ground
still struggling to breathe. The sea near my cliffside
cell cracked like ice, roared louder than a surging river.

Father, my father. The heart begins and ends
in betrayal, the mute farewell of those who say
goodbye when it's long past time to say it.

White is my body, the earth still whiter, pallid
as the sky. I write this last note with my breath
for a pen to tell you I'm a thief of lies, a solitary
prisoner permitted to see nothing except
the white of your eyes, loveless in their clarity.

After Bronzino's Portrait of a Young Man

Looking out his window on the fourth floor of his stark, barely furnished two-room apartment on West 24th Street, Wes watches passersby slip and slide on the icy sidewalk below, the sand and cinders scattered on it earlier that morning no deterrent to the occasional pratfall. He wraps a scarf around his neck, dons a suede bomber coat, fleece lined gloves, shit kicker flier's boots—not remnants of the war he'd fought in, but clothes he'd bought used in an Army Navy store in the Bronx. Pretending to be an airman who flew in raids over Germany, he likes the look of fakery about them, the irony of his disguise. He was a buck private in the Pacific, a corporal twice, demoted twice for wising off. He was no hero. He survived. The costume lets him strut if he wants to.

Because it's a Saturday, Wes is free to roam where he likes, to wander impetuously through the city, to take a look, fast or slow, at whatever strikes his fancy. The sky's overcast, a dingy mud-gray. A north wind's blowing, stark, rheumy, threatening more snow by afternoon. Uptown, by the park, as they wait for a light to change so they can cross the street, people huddle near the curbs, massing closer together against the cold. Wes prefers to keep his distance, jaywalks whenever he can.

Block after block, his soles and heels click clomp, mocking his soldier's stiff strut, his marching stride. He walks further up Fifth Avenue all the way to the Met, enjoying the admiring glances he occasionally gets, and buys a hotdog smeared with mustard from a sidewalk vendor by an entrance to the park. He devours it in four quick bites, always hungry since he's been back, ravenous for three years now.

Inside, the museum's chilly as a marble vault, vast as an airplane hanger. He races through cavernous rooms filled with art, paintings, sculpture, tapestries, pottery, though he barely looks at any of it. It's not paintings or sculpture he means to see anyway, at least not today. He's after a hookup, the luck of a chance encounter. He's discovered museums are better for what he's after than bars, the johns at the Met better than the Modern's. Or a stray, yet meaningful glance in the room with all the Greek marble nudes. Despite how cold it sometimes feels, it's a sensuous place, the Met.

And fast. A boy, maybe five or so years younger than he is, is standing next to a half-length portrait by Bronzino, the wall label says. He's posing, aping the sneer, the arrogant stance of the boy in the picture, thinning his lips, mimicking the posture of aristocratic disdain. Wes thinks he sees in both an agony inside. Their pride makes them look less afraid, like soldiers sometimes. Wes keeps his distance, turning around for an instant to check for guards before he approaches him, not wanting to scare him, fearing he might call out.

When he glances back over his shoulder the boy's already gone. He imagines him walking off, seeking more images to try out, maybe lost in the holy blacks, vermilions, and Prussian blues of the Spanish Renaissance, though what painting in the museum could suit the boy better than the Bronzino, his face and the boy's in the painting nearly identical, eerily the same despite the passage of centuries and the living boy's mussed clothes?

He searches for him, taking his time, moving from room to room, country to country, century to century, but he's nowhere to be seen. An hour later, as Wes leaves the museum without him, he spies the boy again. He seems to be waiting for him, next to the Met's outdoor pool. A glove, undoubtedly his, is floating through icy water toward the fountain's center. His right hand's pink from the stinging cold. Dashing or brash or merely foolish, Wes can't tell which, he tugs off the other glove and hurls it in to join its mate, slyly grinning at Wes. He knows what it's all been about. He saw Wes checking him out. He wanted to be pursued.

He doesn't speak as they ride the subway further than they need to, to Sheridan Square in the Village. Without saying a word, both knowing what they want and why they've met, preferring quiet to too much talk, they walk to Washington Square where they sit, comfortable as old friends, for a while on a bench. The shadow of the arch is gray as old snow darkened by coal soot or city grime. Wes asks the boy his name. He says, "Jack." Wes doesn't believe him and doesn't need to say so. The boy can tell from the look he gives him and tries again. "Rick. Gus. Tony. It doesn't matter to me. Some guys have a fantasy name they like to call me by. You choose."

"O.K.," Wes says. "Jack it is, then."

"I'm not for rent, if that's what you're thinking. I do what I like."

"I'm not thinking at all," Wes says.

"Good," the boy says. "I should tell you, too."

"What?"

"This is a-one-time-only thing."

"All right," Wes says.

Jack abandons his apartment too soon. Wes is already missing him. After they'd screwed twice, with little time to rest between the sex, he'd dressed so fast that he left his slightly torn briefs and a comb with broken teeth behind. Wes lies on the mattress he'd shoved while Jack stripped into the brighter, warmer of his two rooms and snuggles beneath the covers, tugging a blanket under his chin. There's no sun. He's cold. And infuriatingly in love. Without reason. Without any sense to it. Passion.

When he wakes from his too long nap, feeling deeply anxious as he slept, snow has cloaked the roofs, the fire escapes, the ledges of the buildings across the alley where aerials, poles, slack wires forest the tenements with a fresh coat of white. Sharp, nearly carbolic cooking odors seep under his door. Garlic, onions, Indian spices. Black clouds drift over head.

It feels like night. He likes December again now that Manhattan's even more lit up that it used to be before the war. The sky's hushed, moonless, ignoring the holiday lights and bustle below it, the cabs, buses, cars, neon signs, store windows, distant, dissonant sounds of clashing Christmas musics.

At first, as he'd held Jack, their bodies had embraced, had fit together as easily as two sheets of paper he'd folded along the crease in the middle. Their bodies were made for each other, belonged together. The rhythm they'd found, their spontaneous movements, felt like a shared pulse, like an inevitable beat, what the heart must do to survive.

There were together a little over two hours. They'd made love twice, twice, Wes repeats to himself as he recalls each moment, wanting to keep each detail right. They'd switched roles, places, like exchanging bodies. No, it can't be a-one-time-only thing. This, what he has now, what's left, is as suddenly nothing as Jack was everything.

He's napped too long. He cannot sleep. There's no food in his refrigerator worth eating.

Next morning, bereft as he'd felt some dawns during the war when friends hadn't made it back from the night before, he watches the ferries dock, commuters disembark, pigeons swarming round their feet, not frightened, not in panicky flight, but slowly preparing to fly away if necessary. He follows people randomly north. Walks on and on. Workers are fitting girders on the top floor of a new building at Fiftieth and Park. Nearby, in a hole in the wall deli, he drinks coffee, munches strudel, and, angry at fate, contemplates work on Tuesday, his lousy job, his security guard's garbage salary. He strolls further uptown, meaning to check out the skaters in Rockefeller Plaza and its absurdly oversized Christmas tree.

On the fancy store windows, people's passing faces blur like a film frame melting on a movie screen. At Forty-Second, he reads new graffiti scrawled over the old. He tries to decipher the palimpsest on the subway's stairwells white tiles, cryptic, violent and crazily drawn. For fifty cents, he buys a triple bill for a show of bad reruns he mostly dozes through. It's dark when he leaves.

Near the park, the night's clear. A brash wind rattles tree limbs along stone walls. Five hansoms linger in line. The tang of horseflesh and piss hangs in the air. Limousines and taxis wait in front of bustling hotels. Buses zoom back and forth.

A bum stumbles and thrusts his bird claw hands under Wes's jaw. Weightless as a ragged robe, his body sags on crutches. His purple lips are swollen. Wes drops all his change into his encrusted palms. The beggar falls, crashing flat, hard on the sidewalk, cracking bones.

Wes calls for help. No one stops. He finds a cop and points him to him. What more can he do? Escaping, he runs down the stairs to the subway, crowded with shoppers.

In front of his building, he hesitates, its façade menacing and raw as the bum's scarred face. In his room, he strips and lies flat on the floor. In reverie, like the easy fantasies of guys he'd conjure as a boy, he touches Jack's sable hair, smells his skin, tastes his tongue licking his, their bodies floating weightlessly, like leaves in an autumn breeze.

But he can't keep the fantasy alive. The beggar he effectively left for dead, in the hands of a cop who could hardly care what would become of him, stretches out his skinny arms to hold him instead. He recalls strange words he'd learned from scary movies his parents had forbidden him to see. Kebold, gogmagog. A zombie who's snuck from his lair into the city is pleading with him. The bum's unwanted face before his eyes frightens him.

Two weeks ago, on a ride home on the A from the clothing store in which he works, which he's supposed to guard, he hesitated as a mad kid on the train, a tiger's face stitched on the back of his shiny, Jap-made jacket, slashed at a wounded soldier leaning on a cane, at lovers necking on a bench, at a woman wearing a smart gray cloth coat and a santa cap, jabbing at all five with a knife, long, broad, sharp as a bayonet until, from behind, Wes grabbed his wrist and hurt him enough to force him to drop it. A hero. Even the cops praised him later. But he hadn't been so scared since before he'd reached San Diego in late '45.

A knock on the door breaks what spell he's in, the spirits of darkness memories conjure against his will. He hesitates to answer it, dresses fast, calls out "I"m coming" even as he opens the door. Jack falls into his arms, his face battered and scratched, his clothes badly torn. He coughs, swears, licks blood off his lips, his body shaking, buzzing like a fly's as it dies, as his buddy Ray's did in Trinian that time. And Curt's, too, on Okinawa.

Those who beat up Jack did so like pros. It would have taken more than one to do this to him, surprisingly strong as he was despite his slim, still boyish body. He's passed out. As he sleeps, or seems to rest, he grins as if he's dreaming of something lovely and gentle, his smile as sly and elusive as a Buddha's. He sleeps until dawn when the city's harsh, sometimes piercing first light sneaks back through the alley and seeps through Wes's useless shades. Sleet's falling intermittently. Wes opens a cedar chest, his one decent piece of furniture, and throws Jack another blanket, sweet with the smell of pine and a hint of camphor.

Jack draws it up to his chin, stares at a bulbless socket, his face sad, like an actor's peering through the curtain at an empty house, his expression both real and an actor's flourish. Wes contemplates the same patch of plaster Jack's eyes are exploring, cracked and crumbling, trying to find what he's seeing there, what secret he's keeping.

"What's wrong?"

"Nothing. Everything."

"That's no answer. Who worked you over?"

"No one."

"Jack."

"You fought. You were a soldier, right? You did tell me that, didn't you? I get confused."

"For three years. I'm not one now. Or I try not to be."

"O.K. O.K. Listen," Jack whispers. "I'm a deserter. I jumped ship, I guess you could say, but it wasn't as easy as that sounds. I knew they'd look for me. I knew what could happen if they found me. I was supposed to be sailing for England. I couldn't go. I was afraid. I didn't want to fight. I didn't want to die. So I hooked up with some old creep who let me stay with him long enough to get away from it. From them. Those who were trying to find me. I knew I'd get shot if they did. No one knew where I was. I kept changing daddies. Addresses. I've been hiding for five years, here and there. Tricking mostly. But I'm not a kid anymore. It's not working so good for me. I'm twenty-three. Or will be early next year. I was afraid of the Germans. I didn't want to die. That's all. That's all. No convictions. No c.o. Just a coward. But now I'm nothing but ashamed. Ashamed and afraid. A shit, that's who I am, a lousy piece of shit. Earlier last night, I was in a bar, having a beer. A straight bar, not looking to get laid, not looking for another place to hide. Just some dive to have a beer in. This big, brawny, ugly hulk of a guy walks up to me saying he recognizes me. Saying he knows who I am. The fag who jumped ship. He starts cursing me. Then he calls over some of his buddies. He'd already slapped me around. There was no use me trying to fight back or denying it. If he meant to beat me up or break my arms, he would. 'Live with it, creep,' he says to me after he's done." Jack shakes his head. "As if I don't, you know?"

"How bad do you hurt this morning?"

"It looks worse than it feels, I guess."

"Why didn't you stay here with me? I mean, for more than a few hours? Damn you, Jack. Why didn't you ask me to hide you the other day? I would have."

"I don't know. It didn't seem right."

"I don't care about you jumping ship. I don't care what you did or didn't do," Wes says.

"But you just told me you went. You fought."

"Yes."

"Where?"

"It doesn't matter. Islands mostly. In the Pacific."

"You saw your buddies die."

"Lots of them."

"Were you scared?"

"All the time. Every second. I was a lousy soldier. I never wanted to be one. I hated every bit of it."

"You don't hate me?"

"Why should I? And your family? What about them?"

"What family? My older brother was wounded at Anzio. How could I write them? How could I ever face them again?"

"You could have told the army what you are. Who you are."

"Right. My folks'd rather have a coward than a pansy to despise."

"You could stay here," Wes repeats. "I'd like you to."

"No. Thanks. Not now, not after you know about me. That's always when I usually leave. When I have to tell them. I couldn't."

"It doesn't matter to me. Not a bit. I swear."

"It should. It will."

"Maybe. Or maybe I could be better than that. I'd like to try. Is Jack really your name?"

He shakes his head, wobbling slightly on his feet, wincing with pain as he stands up to leave. "It's Cal. Cal Ryan, from Worcester, Mass."

"All right, Cal. I believe you. Don't leave. Please."

"You shouldn't care for me so much," he says, kissing Wes on the cheek. "I'm nothing but a liar. Oh, it's true I deserted. I did do that. And I do use my body to keep from getting found. I thought that's all you were. Just another place to hide in. But I was wrong, you were different, and I had to do what I did to get over that feeling real fast. This," he points to his wounds, "this roughing up yesterday? Forget it. It was no vindictive bruiser. I just like rough sex. I let it get out of hand. Way out of hand. I like pain. Fucked up, right?"

"But you came back. You came here."

"I had nowhere else to go."

"And now?"

"I'll be all right. Don't worry. But I have to go now. There's someone else. I'm living with him. He'll be expecting me back, to return to him pretty soon, all black and blue."

Wes doesn't try to stop him as he walks out the door, closing it firmly, though carefully behind him, without making a sound, as if Wes were in a bed asleep and he, Jack, Cal, was being careful, as he left, not to wake him.

No more wars, Wes longs to say out loud, now it's too late. No more torturing ourselves, Jack. Let's us two pretend we could be free, in California maybe, tanning on a beach somewhere while seabirds clatter and a tide comes in lapping pebbles along the shore. I've dreamed since I was a kid of living in California. Not just shipping out or shipping in. I love the light there, the sun, the clear blue skies. You will too. Let me show it to you. Let's lie on a beach together, side by side.

Let's walk down stairs carved from rock, the cliff behind us starry from quartz or in a beachside shower let's watch steam mist the room as metal doors slam and shoes shuffle behind us while we shut off our two faucets at the same time and, reaching for the same towel, touch. Let me taste the wax in your ears again, Jack, let me kiss your fingernails' moons, kiss your lips, the zipper scar on your beautiful ass. Let the sun shine on us somewhere far away from here on a beach by a sea where no one's fighting, where all is peace. Mexico maybe. Or Hawaii. Or Key West.

Let all this mourning stop. Let memory, yours, mine, ours, everyone's, be freed from its pain. I want the war to be over. Everyone does.

Wes opens his window. "Jack," he shouts into the cold. "Cal."

Two men momentarily stop they're shuffling in the snow to look up, shake their heads, and walk on. A taxi skids on a patch of ice. The lights inside and the big red neon sign over the door go on in the hamburger joint across the way. Wes is hungry. He closes the window with a force too strong for it and cracks a pane.

Three months after he'd walked away from him and out of his life, Wes is sure of it. He needs to quit it. He needs to stop looking for Jack beside the Bronzino portrait of him, of his face and proud stance and hands, or by the fountain at the Met, on subway cars, in gay bars, in the alley behind his apartment. He needs to cease searching for him somewhere in the din of the machine shops, trucks, and piers by the Hudson. He mustn't explore for him anymore where men's faces leer out of the dark, guarding the way to an open yard fenced in by corrugated tin and sheet metal, requiring a card or a pass to enter.

He won't again cross in his head or in reality that ramp past a bebop blast and the stench of grease, sweat, beer, urine, leather, jizz to a steel-like ring of men hunched over, drunkenly cheering buzzing yelling swearing like betters huddled round a cock pit or crap game, whips stinging flesh while guards hold torches like monks ready to light the faggots they've piled. He refuses to see other men's shadows falling across his body as Jack or Cal or whatever his real name is smiles, his eyes too proud to admit his need to seek a pain only more suffering can save him from. In order to save himself now, Wes needs to keep himself from searching more. No more quest. No more hunting for him like a lost dog. No more fantasies. It's gone on so long, his seeking him, seeing him everywhere, he's no longer sure what either of them looked like naked in bed, lying side by side, making love.

One night was all it was. Less than a night. Two hours of mute happiness, of silent fucking, of wordless passion, a kind of abandonment, their two bodies entwined together alone, whether real or make-believe it was impossible to tell. It didn't matter. It doesn't matter. One night is enough. It has to be.

No more. He can't comfort his suffering. He can't love him anymore. It has to be as it is. The silence. The absence. Jack, Cal, Rick, Gus, Tony, whatever his name is.

Why must a war go on and on inside you long after it's over? It killed millions millions. Why doesn't that suffice whatever god there is? Why isn't it enough? Why must he also love Jack, Cal, and his pain, the agony, the wound he saw he was hiding inside that pose he assumed, imitating the Bronzino, that infatuated Wes and made him pursue him? He's lied to himself more than Jack ever has. It's suffering he's been in love with. No more.

Outside, the evening's clouds are darkening as if the sky were ink and they were tuffs of cotton absorbing it. The second time he left him, Jack forgot his jacket. It seems he intends always to be discarding, abandoning things. One by one. His clothes. His body. His soul. Himself. Until he's nothing but his absence. Wes draws its collar, sticky still from Jack's dried blood, higher and tighter around his neck.

But some Jack within him won't leave him. Wes's desire for him, for it, scares him. He can't seem to stop what he's feeling. He remembers holding in his hand a grenade from which he'd pulled the plug that turned out to be a dud. He's almost as afraid as he was then, as if once again he's waiting for only a second or two to pass before he will explode into a thousand picccs.

In a room across the alley from his, a great looking guy, a hunk, a babe, his shades up, strips as if he's deliberately taunting him while the moon slips behind a building much taller than Wes's or the man's. As the night slowly deepens, many of the more imposing buildings in lower Manhattan start to look almost like giant picket fences or massive plinths. Declining behind one of the tallest, the moon leaves a strange curving shadow in the sky linking building to building, a trace of where it's been, like an arc it's cut out of the black sky beyond it, a shape like a rainbow's drained of light and color, as if it were making Wes a promise, like a psychic's or a preacher's, too dark to know what it means with any certainty: he'll return.

Heavy Fog on an Early Morning in Late July

A pale gray day, the fog so thick
it could be smoke pouring from the earth,
though without fire, damp and cold.
A branch falls from a tree, a stick
I step on snaps. What is the world worth
when you cannot see it? Sounds. The old
rhythm of waves piercing the clouds
I wander in, eucalyptus
drizzling, a crow invisibly perched
close by cawing through billowing shrouds
of mist, on the highway an N-Judah bus
starting its engine, he whom I've searched
for, his voice undying despite the sea
dividing us, calling, calling to me.

Snow Cover

The second weekend of the new semester followed two blizzards that were separated by less than four days, covering the campus with snow piled three or four feet deep in many places. Northern winds had blown higher banks against our dorm, five feet or more, obscuring windows. Yet most of those who could leave campus that weekend, despite the risky traveling, did. It was the first road trip of the spring semester, part of a tradition at least forty years old. Or that's what we told ourselves.

Wells, Vassar, Smith, Bennington, Skidmore. You name any girls' school within four or five hours driving time from our college and some of our guys would be there making out with his date or eagerly looking for one. An all male school affected how you saw the world and what, in the back of your mind, many, most, found missing.

Those who didn't own a car or couldn't bum a ride weren't able to go, of course. Some, a few, for reasons of their own weren't interested in the promise of it or the pursuit. Whether recently pledged or not, freshmen were mostly confined to their monastery of a dorm or huddled together in one of the bars in the village, lamenting their fate, doomed to trek down and climb back up the steep, ill-plowed walkway on the hill in the dangerous cold. Otherwise, the campus appeared to have been abandoned, emptied of students for a few days

But our team had a fencing match against West Point our coaches had perversely scheduled at least a year ago for that Saturday night. I'd been given no choice. I was forced to stay. We attracted maybe ten spectators from the Point who'd ridden up with the team on their bus and maybe three times that many from the college, faculty and their wives and a few bored classmates.

I'd won my match. I was pleased with myself. The cadets were our toughest competitors. All our team had succumbed to their greater strength and finesse except for me and Kingsley Colvin. The locker room after our loss was glum. We always lost to West Point. But the Kingman and I had a great time of it stinging each other's butts with the flick of a towel, lunging at each other, greeting others coming out of the showers with an arm flourish worthy of a musketeer. We were crowing, insufferably smug, just as we'd intended to be.

After we'd dressed and sufficiently commiserated with one another, I said goodnight to the other guys at the field house door. The Kingman invited me to his quarters in the Deke House for a nightcap but I demurred. I was tired, and one of my roommates, Randall Smythe, was waiting for me and the news, he felt certain was to come, of my fifth straight victory that season. I didn't want to disappoint him. He seemed to enjoy my conceit even when I was at my most preposterous, as Will or Andy could readily attest.

Randall never left campus during school terms except occasionally for a drink or two or three or more at the Inn in the village, never went anywhere but home to Manhattan during breaks. He claimed he was being faithful to his girlfriend Anne. Perhaps he was. We had no reason to doubt him.

Every house party, there he was arm in arm with Anne or standing possessively beside her, a picture perfect Sarah Lawrence girl, meaning half of her like Bennington, the other half like Vassar, beautifully dressed and coiffed but happy to party. She danced every dance with him, drank almost as much as he did without its ever showing in the slightest, the two of them clearly having a great time together all weekend long and managing somehow to disappear, no one ever knew exactly where or how, as the late night riots began.

The Smythes lived on East 71st Street, three brownstones off 5th Avenue. I visited him there a couple of times. His quarters were on the top floor, his own almost private penthouse, with floor to ceiling windows, sloped on top like those in a hothouse, looking at an angle, slightly distorting, toward Central Park.

On his white, otherwise blank walls he displayed a Kline ink drawing, an enormous brown-gray Motherwell, a festive Grace Hartigan, and a small, cracked, moon-lit, romantic Ryder, maybe a fake Randall confessed, that looked like a work that had been stored in an attic for far too long, dusty and neglected. All these he'd bought himself. They weren't pictures purchased by his parents whose taste in art was far more conventional that their son's. Their favorite opera at the Met was Faust. I'd never been to the opera. Nor did I much like the pictures Randall had collected. I didn't get it. He needed to tell me what the artists' names were and why they were important. I didn't feel any interest in knowing either. But it made Randall happy when I said, lying, I enjoyed his mini-museum.

Whenever a professor, reading the roll on the first day of class, pronounced his name 'Smith,' he'd say, "It's 'Smythe.' It rhymes with 'life,' Sir." And it did, more or less. Call him Randy Smith and watch his face. We did it all the time.

During my walk back to the dorm, the campus looked even more calm and peaceful than it usually did. It was quiet in that way snow, falling lightly, can silence everything in the world, even the voices, the noises inside you, just flakes drifting down with the hushed whooshing sound of wind through woods. The lights from dorm and frat house windows and the lamps on the quad were as soft as if they had been shaded by thin layers of fine cloth, the trees leaving strangely glowing shadows on the snow packs. I had won and was happy and at ease with myself and the world. I knew my future and it was good. I belonged to it. I fit in.

"How did it go?" Randall asked me immediately after I'd walked into our suite on the second floor of Carnegie, the second oldest dorm on campus, late nineteenth century, with thick dolomite walls and lead windows in a Tudor pattern. We shared three rooms, a living room and two bedrooms, each with twin beds and two desks, and a full bath. I shared my room with Andrew Courtenay, Randall his with Will Mason. We'd furnished it ourselves, mostly with chairs, couches, lamps, and rugs we'd bought from last year's graduating seniors the previous May.

Randall had lit the logs he'd arranged on the andirons in the fireplace. Two of our frat's recent pledges had piled them and more kindling that morning in a receptacle beside the hearth. He was sipping a bit of scotch out of an Old Fashioned glass, as he was apt to do evenings when he was alone, sitting on the couch, gazing into the fire, his legs resting on a hassock.

As I was walking back from the field house, I'd been chilled more than I noticed until I'd entered our rooms. The heat felt comforting, like home. I plopped on the couch next to him. He took a glass from a tray, poured me a finger of scotch, and handed it to me. "Cheers," he said, clicking his glass against mine.

"We lost. I won," I informed him.

"So you're pleased with yourself."

"Of course. I couldn't be more so," I said.

"Cocky bastard," he said.

"Indeed," I said.

He nestled deeper into the couch. No less than forty or fifty years old, it had outlasted many generations of seniors, passed down from one year to the next, enticingly plush, wonderfully worn, befitting the needs of men's butts for soft, cozy cushions, redolent of well-aged leather on its arms. It belonged to everyone, we believed, us and those before us and those who would follow, like a benevolent tradition meant to be observed and bestowed on all. No one looked better or more noble sprawled on it than Randall. We three had at once ceded him the right to occupy it as his own whenever he chose to recline on it like a daybed, his body half-covered with an afghan.

He rested his head on a back cushion and sighed. Randall often sighed. It was his signature sound. "Less than four more months," he said and sighed again.

"Meaning what? Is time moving too quickly or too slowly for you?"

"Oh, I don't know. Both. Wharton for you. Some law school for me. The inevitability of it all."

"Yale, Randall. You know what your father's said. It has to be Yale."

"Maybe. Maybe not. I don't think I was made for the practice of law, do you?"

"Having second thoughts?"

"Of course. Or third or fourth thoughts. Don't you?" He poured us both a second round. Or at least a second round for me. He'd probably been drinking for a while already. It was what he did. But it hardly ever showed. On me, alcohol worked almost instantaneously, especially when I was already high from any victory. Just a couple of beers after any match I'd won would throw me off my feet. And I'd babble. Whenever I got tight, I'd babble. I was a nuisance to everyone. My dates hated it.

"Everything's been planned for us, hasn't it?" Randall said, "right from the start, from kindergarten through boarding school to here. Next law school or business school or grad school. Then we join our father's firm. Or the firm of someone who's our father's friend. Or a friend of a friend. It doesn't leave much space for anything else, anything strange, anything extraordinary does it?"

"I'm not complaining. In fact, I feel grateful. Why should anyone feel ashamed for what they've been given? And who wants to be strange? Not me. Not Andy or Will or most of the others. Not you, either, Randall. A few eccentricities are fine, of course. A bit of rebelliousness. But not forever. It would be too confusing."

"All right," Randall said. "Listen to this then. See how it sounds. This is my destiny, David. Anne and I will marry. We'll find an apartment close by my parents or anywhere somewhere relatively, I stress the relatively, modest in the Upper East Side. I'll just be starting out, of course, but I'll practice at my father's firm. It's in the cards, as sure as the stars, that I'll become a partner fast, in no less than ten years. Anne and I will produce three children, two boys, one girl. We'll vacation in the south of France, have a getaway in the Hamptons or rural Connecticut or maybe in northwestern Jersey. We'll grow old and more heartless and then, some day, probably by that time wishing it might come sooner than later since we all know how boring and unattractive old age is, we'll die. Does that scenario sound familiar to you, David? Happy, contented, unreflective, smug snobbery. Doesn't that bother you?"

"Not much. Here's mine. Quite similar to yours, in fact. I'll find myself a beautiful, talented girl, a sandy colored brunette with ample but unflamboyant breasts. We'll buy a home close to my parents in Brookside. I'll work at Merrill. Or maybe link up with some young ad agency on its way toward greatness. I don't know how many kids we'll have. Two or three. Something like that. Nothing ostentatious. And they'll all be brilliant just to shame their father." The fire, Randall by my side felt increasingly relaxing and good. So did the scotch. He poured me another. I was already a little high, tighter than I care to be. I am sometimes a reckless drunk.

He set his glass down on the tray, stood up, and jerked a window open. A harsh wind blew in through it. The room grew quickly cold. I shivered. Randall beat at his chest like a cartoon ape. "I'm going to take a dive," he said as he started to shed his clothes. "Come on, coward. This might be our last chance. We have a record to beat. Remember the challenge from Spence last year?"

"I'm freezing," I said. But he looked too serious for me to deny him. He'd already stripped down to his briefs. Snow dives were a rite at the college, like a winter's plunge into the Atlantic off Long Island or into an ice-free but frosty upstate lake, a proof we could take it like superior men, that minor things like subzero temperatures weren't going to deter us from demonstrating our right to rule in any way we chose to. The cold couldn't matter. We were aristocrats, by birth or aspiration, and therefore born to be stoics or well-taught ones at least.

The dive was folly, of course, but that was the point of it, a gesture toward the wildness of a youth that was too fast disappearing. You had to grasp it while you could, contest or no contest to win. It couldn't really matter who had dived the most in a single winter, of course. Yet it was the stuff of legend. Everyone knew about Doug Ashby and his hundred dive winter back in '55. He'd emerged from his record-setting year unscathed and heroic.

That's what Randall wanted me to do. To act wilder, to become legendary by achieving something obviously meaningless, like diving myriad times almost naked into snow. Fencing, soccer, hockey, lacrosse didn't count. They had history behind them. The point was to do something daring that had no point to it at all except to show off.

If he could bear the cold, I could too, the mad swan dive deep into the frigid snow. He'd performed it at least six times since the turn of the year. He was the master of the bold, imperious gesture. Besides, he was right. If you'd had enough to drink, it could be a lot of fun so long as you didn't crack your skull or break your arm on a rock or loose brick hidden in the pile or a chunk of ice. Emerging from the cold, you'd let the spirits inside you warm you back to life, the adrenalin and the booze.

Except for my briefs, I'd rid myself of my clothes in no time and joined him at the open window. The winds had picked up. Fresh snow was falling. "Who's first?"

"Me of course," Randall said and out he went, arms stretched out wide, legs held straight, two floors down into a pile of still soft snow taller than either of us.

Despite the snow that had at once covered him, I could easily see where he'd fallen in and aimed a couple of feet to his left, managing an almost full somersault before I'd hit it. No one saw my feat, of course, the extra bit of dexterity, of panache I'd displayed. There were no witnesses. But it made me happy I could do it. Or nearly accomplish it. I landed flat on my back. My spread eagle body made a deep hole in the snow that at once caved in over me as it had over Randall. I'd never been so cold. I fought my way out, shaking, nearly trembling, rubbing myself frantically, trying to get the snow that clung to me off me and my gelid blood pulsing again.

Randall had extricated himself before me, of course, and was idly standing in front of an ancient elm. It was the strangest sight. He wasn't leaning on it. He was just waiting there, for me, I supposed, as straight and still as the trunk of the tree behind him.

He wasn't moving. He was spookily quiet. And white. All white, as if he was still covered with snow, as if he were a remarkably life-like snow man. Only he wasn't, of course. He'd freed himself from the snow bank without a trace of snow on him, somehow had removed it by shaking or rubbing or wiping it off, though with what I couldn't see. Yet his whole body, face, neck, arms, torso, legs, feet, all of Randall was whiter than his always scrupulously white briefs. He appeared to be pale and blank and mute as an apparition. I couldn't explain it. I never could. He was scaring me. It occurred to me he intended to.

I raced to the door to the dorm, rushed up the stairs and into our rooms, and took a hot, steaming shower. In my and Andy's room, I dressed in fresh jeans, a shirt, socks, my inevitable Weejuns, and a natty wool crew neck sweater. No longer looking like a ghost, Randall had put on his flannel pajamas and a heavy robe, rested back on the couch, and poured himself another drink. The bedtime outfit made him look ten years older, especially the slippers he must have filched from his grandfather's closet. He should have been smoking a pipe and reading, late, The Wall Street Journal, checking up on his stocks and yesterday's market. He offered me more scotch, but I refused. I'd had enough.

I found Andy's new Beatles album in the rack under the record player we shared and put it on. Randall hated the Beatles, especially John Lennon. He thought him an ill-mannered brat. His favorite composer was Chopin and he let everyone know it. It drove the rest of us a little crazy at times, but we'd listen when he made us. Lying on his deathbed, Chopin, Randall had lectured us, might have heard his own music being played and sung, an arrangement for voice and piano of a mazurka or the third nocturne or maybe a movement from the cello sonata. Randall said he couldn't remember which. Chopin was probably too sick to hear it, his mind intent on immortal things. Or on his despair. Yet what a way to die, he'd said.

If Randall meant to tell us something about our lives with that story, I couldn't figure out what it was. I had no reason to think about death. When the Beatles started singing, I kept the volume low to appease him.

"That was fun," he said as I sat down next to him on the couch. "My best, cleverest dive yet." He'd closed the window shortly after he'd followed me in and laid another log on the fire, a not completely dry pine, it was obvious, from the resiny smell of its smoke and the way it would spit and pop.

"I guess," I said. It hadn't been fun for me really. I regretted it. My back stung. I'd bruised my elbow somehow. It felt much better to snow dive when a crowd is watching than when you're only two, me and Randall. It was the sort of stunt that begged for applause and a date's admiration. "I think you're getting seriously tight, Randall," I said as he emptied the rest of the scotch bottle into his glass. "Set that aside, undrunk. That's enough for tonight, o.k.?"

"It isn't and I'm not," he said. "Not at all. Not the least bit. I wish I were." Most of the color had returned to his face and the rest of his body. His eyes had always been the palest blue I'd ever seen, an icy blue you nearly could see through, like the pale blue in some otherwise clear glass when the light is right.

Randall had never allowed anyone to see inside him. Neither had I. Neither had any of us. We were ironists, compelled to stay that way by fate and the laws of discretion, more firmly engraved in stone than the ten commandments. The best expression to assume, in most instances, was a blank, empty one that might mean anything or nothing at all.

He lay his head back on the couch. Lately, he'd started wearing his hair much longer because, he'd said, his father hated it when it wasn't trimmed precisely every ten days or two weeks. He enjoyed rousing his father to quiet fits of fury over nothing at all from time to time. "My neck hurts a little," he said.

I was about to hand him the plump throw pillow to my right on the couch for his neck when he reached over me, I thought, to grab it. But instead of picking it up and placing it under his head, he ignored it and lay his outstretched hand on my thigh for a few seconds, then let it drift over my lap and across my crotch, resting it on my other thigh, next to his, pressing down on it, ever so slightly caressing my muscles.

I couldn't breathe. I didn't want his hand there. I didn't want him touching me like that. I didn't want his touching me at all. But I couldn't say it. I couldn't say, "Stop it." I shoved his hand off me and jumped up. "You stupid bastard! You've ruined it," I shouted and ran out the room, slamming the door behind me so he'd know, without having any doubts about it, exactly what I'd meant. What I had to do, how I'd have to behave toward him from then on.

The few guys remaining in our frat house over the weekend were surprised to see me walk in the front door without my having worn any kind of jacket or coat to hike through snow across campus. When they asked why I'd been so dumb or foolish, I ordered them to shove it. My room during my sophomore and junior years was on the third floor. I knew the sack room next to it would be deserted that weekend, at least until Sunday night when everyone returned with lingering hangovers and their not quite believable stories of beautiful women and love and conquest.

I snuggled into my old bed, the two blankets, Gary's I think, were pleasingly warm, and I slept under them surprisingly well, without thinking much about what had just happened or what Randall and I might have to say, or attempt to say, to each other the next day. I was praying it might be nothing. That he might understand that a certain chilliness and silence were to be the law between us for the days ahead and the weeks and months and years after that. I'd meant what I'd said. He'd ruined everything.

I should have worried a lot more than I did. After eating a breakfast I'd cooked for myself in the house's kitchen, I returned to our rooms in the dorm. Our suite was a shambles. That is, Randall's part and portion of it were. Everything, including Randall, had gone missing. His clothes, his suitcases. But also his books, his files of old essays and research materials for his senior thesis, his writing materials, pens, pencils, paper, his typewriter, his radio, his records, his small paintings, the ones he'd painted and the ones he'd bought, his collection of mugs and crystal glasses, his porcelain dogs and cats, everything was gone. Not anything that belonged to me, Andy, or Will had been touched or disturbed. Only everything he'd owned.

He'd been scrupulous. He'd entirely rid us of him, himself from us. By which I was sure he meant me. He must have feared I'd tell Andy and Will. Everyone. I had no intention of saying a word. But I thought he'd done the right thing, for both our sakes.

"What the hell" was the first thing Andy said upon entering the room, back from his road trip to Smith.

Will reacted in much the same way a few minutes later. "What the fuck happened here?"

"I wish I knew," I said. "I slept at the house last night. When I got back, he was gone. Vanished."

"Gone? You mean he's left school? To go where?" Andy said. "Why?"

"Apparently he's cracked," I said and shrugged. "Who knows why?

Guys do sometimes. Think of Ormsby."

"Where's all his stuff?" Will said.

"He must have taken some with him. His suitcases are gone. He must have packed his clothes."

"And everything else?" Will said.

I pointed to the window he'd thrown it out of. Into the snow bank. Everything, I'd bet. I could see some of his records on top when I went out stupidly looking for him early that afternoon. "Everything else must be buried in it," I said, though I hadn't looked or explored. It was too deep and cold. "It'll all be covered over if it keeps snowing like this much longer."

Andy groaned. "And it's only February."

"It'll probably be spring before we see that typewriter again," Will said.

"What a waste," Andy said. "He was a great guy. A tad eccentric. Unusual, you might say. But a really great guy."

"I'll call his sister Julia tomorrow," I said. "Let her know what's happened if she doesn't already, in case Randall hasn't told anyone yet."

"What about his parents?" Andy said. "They should know he's flown the coop. They'll be worried sick."

"You bet they will be. And mad as hell. I'll call his sister first," I said. "It'll be safer."

She hadn't heard a word from him when I spoke to her the next day. But she had by the time she called me back twelve days later. He'd taken the train down to Manhattan, stayed home for a while until, after he'd argued fiercely with his father, he escaped from the house and booked a room in the Lexington. By the end of week three of his disappearance from campus, shocking everyone with a two sentence telegram, he announced he'd signed up to join the Marines. Their parents, Julia said, were frantic. But he wouldn't be dissuaded. They blamed everyone but him and themselves, me, Andy, Will, the college which had apparently terribly misunderstood him, they blamed everyone except themselves and their son for his astonishing flight from success and the life to come. It was all nonsense. But the Smythes were geniuses at self-protection from uncertain reality. So were we all.

The telegram he sent me was identical to the others I read. Will might have kept his. But Andy and I tossed ours into the fire, too mad at him to want to save it. Or I pretended to be angry. I never said a word about what had happened. About how I probably was the one who ought to be blamed for what had led to him to flee. I knew I never could tell anyone, not ever. It was worse than keeping a secret. It was my life I had to keep hidden. I missed him, but I was relieved he'd gone.

Randall Miles Smythe was killed in action in the Que Son Valley on June 2nd of 1967. He was twenty five. His funeral was held three months later in The Church of the Heavenly Rest, the same church Randall'd referred to, smirking, as The Church of the Perpetual Snooze. He'd been cremated. The story was that there wasn't much of him left to put in a coffin as his family would have wished. Andy, Will, and I sat side by side in a pew. It was the last time we three were together.

I was sadder, more grief-stricken, than I allowed myself to show. We all were. But sometimes, I've found, mourning is true to who you are. You don't want to display it. You hope some day soon it will end. Yet you also fear it might stop inside you and leave you with nothing at all.

2.

From the landing upstairs, my wife gently calls to me where I'm standing in the den, watching the snow fall. Both our daughters are sound asleep in their rooms. It's the second weekend in February. We like to leave the city behind us from time to time. We've had a quiet night of it, just the four of us playing bridge in our Connecticut country retreat my wife has re-named Stoneridge, having removed the signs with the former owner's name on them and replaced them with her choice, a bit haughty, if not strictly pretentious, I suppose. But that's my Claudia. We've owned the cottage for over a decade.

It was in fact originally built of stone and does indeed sit on a sort of mound, though not quite a ridge of any kind. Over the years, we've added a room, like a pantry, in the back downstairs and two small bedrooms upstairs, all constructed from wood and other materials. It's difficult, nearly impossible, to find the right stones to match the house's, its once light gray stones having weathered as dark as storm clouds.

My daughters are nine and thirteen. I work for the Alexander Palmer Ad Agency, a small but thriving business. I met Alex through a Wharton connection I was happy to use. My wife is on the board of numerous charitable organizations. I hope, or rather I suspect, though I can't know, that she's content with me, with us, with our lives together. Happiness or contentment are not the sorts of topics either of us likes to discuss, our world being what it is.

When we met at a cocktail party given by friends we shared, she was studying at Juilliard for a concert career as a pianist. I didn't ask her not to continue. She decided on her own no career was likely to happen. She wasn't talented enough for a professional career, she'd said. So she chose me instead. It made me feel odd, after I'd proposed, when she told me that, as if I was a substitute, at most a second best option. The man she chose when she feared she'd fail at what she would have preferred. But all of life is a kind of substitute for failure, isn't it? I've tried not to mind. We get along well enough.

Her favorite composer is Chopin. I find her preference slightly eerie, of course. She enjoys playing some of his pieces before she goes to bed every night. The girls sleep through it. I pretend to listen. Occasionally, I actually enjoy it.

Tonight, when I don't respond to her call, she walks down the stairs to our living room to ask me what's wrong. "Nothing," I say.

The truth is that I'm concerned about the snow, how it's weighing down the limbs of so many trees, breaking branches. I'm worried about our roof if it doesn't quit snowing soon, the pressure on it, wondering if the new beams are strong enough to hold it.

David Gardiner. David Francis Gardiner. That is what she whispers sometimes at night after we have sex, more to herself than to me. I once asked her why. She said, "Because you surprise me. I never am quite certain who you are. Saying your name over and over reminds me when nothing else does."

Before I married her, her name was Claudia Joyce Revell, originally from Alexandria, Virginia, her father a sound Republican lobbyist for textile companies and the like. I've never liked her name, not any of it. I love her, I think, I hope. Or I try my best to love her when I can. But I have never cared for her name. I wish I could change it. I wish I could change many things. My girls are Susan and Abigail. Claudia chose their names.

At work, I live in a world of men. At home, I live in a world of women. I'm a stranger in both, a secret outsider. I'd like to think it adds a touch of mystery to my life, but it doesn't. There's nothing profound about me except what I've driven away and what I keep secret. Or so I like to think.

Claudia clicks on a table lamp near her baby grand to play some more Chopin. A late nocturne. I know that much at least now, after years of her tutoring. Randall might be proud of me, even though I can't recall which one it is or hear what key it's in.

She thinks it pleases me, that her playing comforts and relaxes me. She says I've been on edge lately. Perhaps she is right, though the music tonight sounds like a lament for a dream that has come true too late. I am forty-two years old and the city we live in is plague infested. She plays me music late at night to calm my spirits, but my spirits wander where they will nonetheless, out into the dark of night, much of the time, or the greater dark of the past.

In my world, the small, seemingly tidy one people who don't belong to it refer to disdainfully as privileged, your life is supposed to be what you've chosen it to be. By which I mean the life you've chosen which happens to be identical to the one that was chosen for you before you were born. In that sense, I've chosen my life, or most of it, but it turns out not to have been the life I'd wanted after all. I obeyed the rules but the rules were wrong. I was wrong.

The problem is that I think I see him from time to time I mention it to no one, of course. They'd think I was losing my grip or going mad. People look at you curiously if you even intimate that you might believe in ghosts. I guess, no matter what I tell myself, I must know in my soul, no matter how much I distrust the word, that I killed him, that Randall died because of me. It's foolish, I'm sure, to confess such nonsense even if only silently to myself, but some sorts of folly can be more real than the plainer, simpler, more rational sorts of truth most of us can admit to, whether altogether willingly or not. And I admit it now, at last. I did kill Randall and that's the end of my story. It's the only part of it that makes any sense.

The plate glass window I am standing by is nearly frosted over, yet there's a patch of almost clear glass near its center where I keep watch over the woods near our cottage. That's where I've seen him most often recently. In the woods, in winter, when it's snowing. He's all white, not shaking or trembling, not seeming to mind being dead and ghostly pale, but all white nonetheless, white as a fresh snow bank or as his scrupulously laundered underwear I used to stare at in amazement, wondering how through the day he managed to keep it so clean, as if nothing about him ever could be dirty. He's everywhere, I seem to feel, whenever it snows.

My wife plays Chopin's music lovingly. She loathes Beethoven and Brahms. She's a peculiar woman. We live alone together and don't seem to mind or care. The snow pile by the cedar grove must be four feet high by now. It will remain there until late March or early April or maybe later since the tall thickly needled trees will keep it shaded, away from the sun's warmth, allowing it to melt more slowly than most of the rest of what winter's left behind that's layering the ground, blank and clear. I can wait. I admire snow's spirit of defiance, its insistence on staying cold and inhuman.

Andrew, Will, and I recovered a few of Randall's possessions once the snow had melted completely, though little worth keeping and nothing that we saved past the end of the semester. That year it was early April before we could retrieve it. His typewriter had already rusted and was hopelessly broken and clogged with mud. Andy discovered what looked to be a diary, but wet snow and spring rains had rendered it impossible to read, the ink smeared, most of the pages stuck soppily together.

I tried to read it anyway, wondering if he'd written my name on any of them. But it was hopeless. I'd never know what he'd been feeling about me before the rupture that seems to have destroyed both our lives, what signs I'd given him he'd misread or understood too well. I guess he must have suspected how much I cared about him. For him, I should say if I were being candid.

We three threw everything away into a trash barrel. If we'd known what was going to happen to him, we might have preserved something. Some of the mugs, a few of his objet survived the fall and the long hard winter of our final year of college quite well. But what could we do with them? We were leaving the hill soon, destined for much greater things, ambitious, greedy as only the already well-off can be, wanting more from life than it can give to anyone, immoralists of a sort, the carefree sort, ending their trivial spree. Romantics of a young Byron's temper and stance. Seriously superficial. Ambitious, magnificent jesters.

Randall was the one who had acted unwisely, precipitously, mysteriously, wildly, not us, Randall the one who had made the grand refusal for no reason anyone but me could make sense of. For that very reason they, his friends, considered it to be all the more marvelous. To risk everything and to lose. His was the rash, gratuitous act everyone envied and never could admit to envying because it would mean everything else they believed in was wrong.

They'd all grieved, of course, when they heard, three years later, the news of his death, grieved and were quietly relieved that the path they were bound to travel on was the right and only one to follow if they wanted to survive. No courtship with death for them, for us. No risking a great love. No daring an overwhelming passion from which you'd probably never return.

You stupid bastard. You've ruined it.

Claudia lifts her hands off the keys and calls to me again. She's whispering my name into the moonless dark. What does she want? Is she wondering once more what has gone so wrong between us? How could I confess to her what I'm really thinking? How tell her I must hurt us both for either of us to discover some way to live as more free, happier than we've been? She would denounce me for all my faults, impossible to enumerate because they were so many, and I'd nod and silently acknowledge she was right. And wound and wound her again and again.

Let her stand next to me, us two truly close for a moment. Let her imagine with me the snowbanks outside melting in a few more months. It's what I do these lonely nights: fantasize about what I might discover when the sun warms the earth again, about what the coming of spring might expose to eyes looking to find what's been hidden in the snow, what if anything has survived the long winter covered by it and ice, that I've left too long unspoken of, that I've abandoned to endure, if it can, on its own in the cold.

Fresh Fallen Snow

it's low tide. The sand's been washed to the color
of reaped hay. Shallow pools lie scattered along
the shoreline where gulls calmly float in the water.
The fog mutes the cawing of ravens, a wren's song.
Wearing waders, elderly Chinese cast in the surf.
When the fish's too small to keep, they toss it back in.
In his wetsuit, a guy wonders if the ride's worth
trying on a sea slick as snow. The ghost-white sun's moon's twin.

In a house near a meadow, a man watches as a blizzard
obscures night. The snow's covering the world in white.
When the moon appears later, it's pale as his face
in a window. The world outside is clear, unmarred.
He hears a late nocturne playing silently in the light
of a snow that shines with the moon and the stars' slow grace.

When Summers Were Younger

Seven ripe oranges sit in a row on Eric's kitchen window sill, aromatic, acidic and sweet. Gnats swarm over them, darting in and out of a swatch of amber sunlight that falls across a polished hardwood floor. The morning's bleaching the already white walls even whiter. The sky's a pure cerulean, the ocean bands of green and blue turquoise, the waves's crests white and sandy and almost translucent like the skin of an onion being peeled. There's no wind, no sign of fog, no haze. Beneath so dazzling a sun, Eric thinks, the light feels nearly as heavy as rain.

Fifty feet down the hill of the canyon, wearing only gym shorts and flip flops, a neighbor poses for a snapshot, squinting against the light. As he and his friend shuffle back into his house, their sandals flap against the bottoms of their feet. Eric darts inside to grab an orange, brings it to the deck, peels some of the rind, squeezes it between his palms, and sucks its juices. They dribble down his chin. Removing a handkerchief from the back pocket of his jeans, he wipes his face clean.

There's a fluorescent glow to the scirocco-like air, an intensity to it, the way it heightens the appearance of everything around him, inside him, all his senses, his nerves keener, febrile and attentive. Yesterday, the Santa Ana winds unceasingly blew over the mountains, filling the basin with a desert's heat and electric charge.

On these radiantly clear Pacific summer mornings, Eric likes to stand on his deck, content, the past blank to him, empty of meaning, no longer calling him back to the pine woods and soft hills and long, quiet rainy days of his childhood in Carolina.

On his last visit, not liking the way he'd changed, not wanting to have to listen to his talking so freely about his boyfriends, his sister had argued that Californians worshiped youth because youth was the only age they ever experienced throughout their lives. In the South, everyone understood how quickly it faded, fast as spit on a sidewalk, she'd said, or jasmine after a frost. "But L.A. has no seasons. It's always summer there. How can you bear it, Eric?"

Because he's happy there, he replied. And he is, more peaceful in the transient, impermanent, earthquake prone place where he lives now than he'd ever been in what his family insists on calling his home. He's freer. He can live his life, day by day, without regret, without his heart's tugging him backward, homeward. He can't think of a moment since his move west when he's truly mourned the loss of where he grew up. It was never his home. Not really.

He slides the tinted glass door closed behind him. In the kitchen, he assembles what he'll need for their breakfast, his and Todd's. Bowl, spoons, butter, jam, bread for toast, cereal, cold milk, fresh ground coffee. Wearing only his baggy, droopy boxers, Todd strolls in. When he smiles, his boyish face changes slightly, forming tiny creases, signs of the wrinkles that'll appear some day far away from now in the corners of his striking, beautifully pale green eyes. Stretching, he holds his back straight as a dancer's. His hair's uncombed, dark and curly. He scratches an itch by a nipple on his hairless chest.

No, Eric wouldn't go back, not to a world that expects its young men to find themselves a good war to fight in before they spoil fast, like fruit under too much sun or cotton under excessive rain. The worst times for a country, his father had argued, were the quiet years, like the useless era between Korea, his second war, and Vietnam, which ought to have been his son's first. A nation needs a war, righteous or not, to keep its senses and its spirits alive, he'd said. Battle hardens a man, gives him what it takes to survive in peacetime. Camaraderie and the risk of death, he'd said, there's nothing to equal it for the rest of your life. That irreplaceable, unforgettable bond.

Thankfully, he's been spared the bellicose gene that seems to have run in his family, in his town, his state, that whole benighted part of the country, maybe everywhere, Eric couldn't be sure. His brother and his two best buddies fought in 'Nam. Only his brother and Gene came back. What good had it done, was it doing anyone now? The many years the fighting continued, unrelentingly, the killing, the being killed. Six, seven years, or more. Who knew, could truly tell, when it'd started? Or how? He'd torn up his draft card at a protest rally at his college but didn't mention it to his family or the board. If he were to be drafted, he wouldn't go because he knows the solution. Tell them the truth.

He should write the board a letter today, Eric thinks, as he finishes preparing breakfast. I'm gay. I'm gay, thank the Lord. You can't get your

clutches in me. But of course it would be too late. He was too old for
that sort of bravery. He no longer needed to confess anything. Not to
anyone. Time and luck had spared him. The war had begun to be called
over for more than a year.

Todd puts on his sunglasses that were lying on the coffee table where
he'd tossed them last evening right before he and Eric had begun strip-
ping each other naked. They'd met at a bar in Manhattan Beach just an
hour before. Wearing just his sunglasses and his ragged shorts, he almost
glides onto the deck where he sits on a chaise longue while dexterously
holding the bowl and spoon Eric's brought him in one hand and the L.A.
Times' sport section in the other. He lays the paper on his lap, grips the
spoon in one hand, grasps the bowl in the other and eats and reads.

Remember this, Eric tells himself as he sits directly across from Todd,
placing his own bowl and cup of coffee on the glass top table. Don't forget this scene. Or him. How beautiful it is, he is. How beautiful both
will always be in memory. Home? This is home. This is where I belong.
He stares at him and admires how easily Todd accepts his staring. He
will leave me. Or I will leave him. Maybe today. Or tomorrow. Or
sometime soon. Pay attention. Look as hard as you can. And never forget him. Any of them. Remember all of their names. "Todd," he says,
as if to himself, "Todd Eader," and smiles when Todd winks at him. No
happiness, no peace that one finds in such sunlight, could be finer than
this early morning's.

Flushed from the heat, sweating some, Eric sits near the front of the
bar, sipping his beer, swiveling back and forth on his stool. He's loosened his tie, unbuttoned the neck of his shirt, removed his sport coat,
and draped it over the back of the empty barstool next to him. He takes
another sip of his beer, wipes the foam off his upper lip with the back of
his hand, and checks his watch. It's early, only five after five. Todd's not
really late yet. Not quite.

The bar's nearly empty. A few men talk around a low table next to
the dance floor. A man in his late forties or so, wearing chinos and a too
tight Lacoste, drinks an occasional scotch at the far end of the bar where
it's darker. He's pretending to read a local gay rag. He catches Eric's eye,
smiles a smile with no meaning to it, no intention behind it except to be
pleasant. The bartender is experimenting with two fans, pointing them

first in one direction, then in another, to discover which way might cool the room more quickly.

"Waiting for someone?" he asks Eric. The bartender opens a beer for himself, drinks it from the bottle, and, having set it down, crushes ice inside a towel with a hammer. "He'll show," he says. "You're not the kind of man a guy'd deliberately forget a bar date with if you get my drift." He winks and shoves the crushed ice into a bucket. Eric is glad for the compliment but isn't so sure.

The room is filling up fast. By five-thirty, it's crowded, most of the men standing in small groups talking, only a few of them sitting alone on a barstool or on one of the benches along the walls. Eric's working on his second draft when Todd, picking Eric's coat off it and setting it aside on the counter, slips onto the stool next to him.

"Hey. I'm sorry I'm late. The surf was fantastic. I lost all sense of time."

"No worries. It's fine. California easy time. You're not late, not really," Eric says. "Want a beer?"

"No, thanks. I don't drink, remember?"

"Right. No alcohol. A Coke?"

"A ginger ale would be great." Eric signals to the bartender.

"Fantastic day, huh?" Todd says.

"I left L.A. at three," Eric says. "Got off work early. It was a beautiful drive back down. Sometimes I think I should live up there, Westlake or Echo Park maybe, and avoid the commute back and forth to Laguna. But, especially on days like this one, the ride each way is too fine to miss."

"What is it you do anyway? In L.A., I mean."

"I thought I told you the other night. When we met."

"You probably did. I forget. Probably wasn't paying attention. Too busy noticing other things."

Eric reddens with pleasure and stares at an ashtray on top of the bar. "I'm a lawyer. Just starting. I passed the bar out here only six months ago. I work for the city."

"It sounds like a swell job."

"I'm getting used to it," Eric says. "And you?"

"A part-time gardener, full-time surfer."

"Right. Lucky you."

"Yeah, lucky me. Mowing lawns, pruning roses, killing bugs with pesticides that are probably poisoning me, too. It pays well enough to keep me from having to really work. It helps keep me out of trouble. I've been surfing since I was ten. I grew up in Gardena, moved out when I was seventeen, lived in Manhattan Beach ever since. That's my story. Nothing much more to add. Nothing important anyways. I'm a beach bum, I guess, simple as that." He pauses, takes a deep breath. "I could use a little weed." He grabs Eric by the arm. "You're funny, you know that? You're the only guy I've hooked up with who told me to wait a week until we met up again. And here I am again, I actually showed, and you're not even surprised."

"Why should I be? Aren't I a catch?" Eric says slyly. "You got the day right. So did I. You remembered. So did I. I never thought you wouldn't show. I never expected to be stood up. I rarely am."

"Good for me, then. I don't always, you know. Show up, I mean. Do the right thing. I'm a bit of a stoner. But you're correct, if immodest. You're worth remembering. You said five-thirty, Friday, right?"

"Five," Eric says. "It was supposed to be five. Not five-thirty."

"Do you care?"

"Nope. Not in the least. Sorry. That was just me still back at my job."

"Split the difference." Todd leans back in his stool, stretches his arms out wide, stands up, drains his ginger ale in three swallows. "Let's go. I have to stop by my apartment and pick up some fresh shirts. I haven't been there since yesterday morning." Todd waves and yells "Later" to the bartender.

"You two friends?" Eric asks outside.

"You might say that. I hang out around here a lot," Todd says, smiling so cockily Eric understands immediately what he means. Why doesn't it bother him? The two of them more than friends, maybe former lovers? Who cares whom or how many other men he's slept with? Todd's with him now, this second, minute, hour, day, at least one more night. Every beginning demands an end. He'll take what he can from what's between them. The brief spell—a couple of days, a few weeks, a month—after love, or whatever he should call what he feels at the moment for Todd, has started and before it finishes. He'll relish it, cherish it for however long or briefly it might last. That's the part that Todd can't comprehend about himself. For some, maybe most, it's sex, just sex as they like to say. But not for him. For him, what he feels must be love. Passion, of course, but love as well. It always will be, time after time. Why doesn't it matter to him if it doesn't last?

"How did you get here?" Eric asks.

"Walked."

"You don't drive?"

"Not a car. A bike. A motorbike. It's getting repaired. Brakes. My place isn't that far away. Just a couple of miles. Right by the beach. I like to walk." He punches Eric gently on the shoulder. "Exercise, man. It's great."

Todd tells Eric how to get there, when to turn, where to park. He lives in a three-story stucco building on a crowded street one block away from the ocean. Except that it's been painted licorice for some peculiar reason, maybe because the paint was cheap, it's nearly indistinguishable from the ochre colored motels on either side of it. All three could use some serious repair. Todd's apartment house faces only thirty feet or so of the sidewalk, but extends a hundred feet back to abut the rear of a similar building's row of garbage cans.

Near the stairwell, Todd opens the car's door and says, with a sweep of his arm, "Come on up. Two flights."

An ice machine rumbles outside his studio apartment near the front of the building. The sofa bed's still open, pillows and yellowed sheets are strewn over the floor, dirty dishes and aluminum trays lie scattered in odd corners. An air conditioner clacks and churns and wheezes in a window over a cracked black leather couch. Except for two posters, one of Mick Jagger, the other of Jim Morrison, that hang over the refrigerator, the walls are bare plaster, painted a thin, skim milk white.

Todd has pinned torn bits of paper on a cork board he's nailed to the back of an old wardrobe he uses as a second closet and a room divider. He's noted on them chores he has to do, dates for his gardening jobs, some friends' addresses, a few phone numbers, two of them scratched through, a couple of passes to a club near Silver Lake, another in West L.A.. Two wetsuits dangle, drying, over the bathroom door. Todd grabs a grocery bag from under the kitchen sink, opens the closet, and tosses some fresh shorts, a pair of socks, and a couple of t-shirts into the sack.

"Polish luggage," he says, walking out of his bathroom, adding a toothbrush to it. The phone rings. "Let's go," Todd says, ignoring it. "It'll just be somebody wanting something I don't want to give them right now."

Eric surveys the room. Todd reminds him of a guy he knew in high school. All the girls adored him, flirted with him, wanted him to be their boyfriend. And he was their boyfriend, in a way, one by one. It was easy for Eric to understand why they'd made such a fuss. If he could have, he would have made a fuss, too, tried to entice him to kiss him, embrace him, sit next to him at the movies, holding hands.

It was Carroll's casual carelessness, the way he carried his handsomeness as the rich do with the assurance that wealth gives them, as if it had been owed them from birth, a superiority they deserved to be granted, that attracted most people to him, Eric included. Not one of the girls seemed to mind at first that he wouldn't stay her boyfriend for long. They'd share him if they had to. It was like being blessed.

It felt good at the time, it wouldn't last, none of his conquests lasted, yet they'd be able to remember it for the rest of their lives, those moments with Carroll like no other. Eric had envied all of them, all of Carroll's girls, each in turn, and imagined, as if their pain had been his own, how they'd sigh and moan and even cry after he had switched his attentions to someone else. Who would dare to be ungrateful to Carroll? At the end of their days, they'd still be one of Carroll Cooper's girlfriends for a while once upon a time.

Eric listens to Todd's phone as it rings on and on. "You hustle, don't you?"

"Sure," Todd says, "a little. When I need the extra dough. I try to keep it out of the rest of my life." The phone quits for a second, then begins to ring again. "Fuck it," Todd says, lifting the receiver up and placing it back in the cradle. He locks the door behind him and drops the chain of keys in his jeans' slightly torn front pocket.

The freeway's jammed with rush hour traffic, the Laguna Canyon Road backed up, most of the way to Eric's. It's almost eight when Todd, his bag in his hand, follows him for the second time in a little over a week up the stairs that lead to Eric's cottage perched high on the bridge of a nose-shaped hill overlooking the Pacific.

Eric clicks on a light. "There must be a dozen varieties of fuchsias around here," Todd says.

"Fortunately, they seem to survive on their own. I'm always forgetting to water them."

"They could use some pruning. Some TLC. These over here don't look too happy."

"You're welcome to do to them whatever you'd like to," Eric says.

He opens the door, inviting Todd in. The living room's western wall is mostly window, part of which slides back to open onto the narrow deck. Bookcases cover the other walls from floor to ceiling. Prints and photographs hang in the few remaining spaces. Todd sets his bag down on the coffee table.

"Welcome home," Eric says, kissing him on the cheek.

"Thanks. It feels real familiar. I like it."

"The bedroom and john are back there," Eric says, pointing to them.

"Yeah, I remember. It's only been a week. I'm not an idiot."

"I was joking," Eric says.

On the deck, they eat a cold supper Eric had prepared ahead and enjoy the end of sunset together, not talking much, drinking strong coffee.

"This is my favorite time of day," Todd says.

"Mine, too. Just after twilight, before it's night. It's almost the solstice. We arrived back just at the right time. Check out the horizon, that golden red. Amazing," Eric says.

"Night's good, too. When it gets spooky and dark. You know what I mean? Maybe better."

"It can be. Depending on who you're with. How old are you, Todd?"

"Twenty three. Or I have been for a couple of weeks."

"Happy birthday," Eric says. "You sure?"

"Sure I'm sure. I wouldn't lie to you. I don't lie, Eric. You need to know that. I don't lie. Not to anyone. I may not always behave like some people say I should. So what? I never fucking lie. Why do you want to know how old I am anyways?"

"Just curious. I'm thirty. Seven years difference." Eric sets his cup down on the deck and stands up, yawning theatrically, not sleepy at all. "Is it too early to go to bed?"

"It's never too early for me. Or too late either. Look. The sun just slipped out of sight. Only the horizon's still glowing red. It'll be dark soon. Stars. Moon."

"We get great night skies here," Eric says, "when it's not fogged in. You'll spend the night again? I'd like it if you would."

"Sure," Todd says grinning, pursuing him in, grabbing Eric's butt. "Why not? You brew up a swell cup of coffee, night or day. Wakes a guy up, you know? So do you."

In his bedroom, the light of the moon sneaks through a window. It fills the room like mist, as the ocean fog fills the depths of the canyon most mornings with its ghost-like radiance, a light impossible to touch or hold, like a wave in the ocean a boy is playing in up to his waist and tries to catch as it breaks, delighting in it as it flows through his fingers.

As best as he can, Eric watches Todd strip in the nearly dark room, touching him to see him better, more clearly, as they fall into bed, their bodies wrestling, striving, as Eric searches for, reaches, kisses, tastes his flesh, his hardness, him within him, each in the other, seeks everything he can find in their pleasure together that he'll need to remember him by.

A heavy fog had settled overnight on the gray northern strip of the coastal crescent that appeared to be suspended between the gauze of the sky and the oyster shell colors of the ocean. It's late in the morning before the thick mist retreats, the sun slowly burning it off. Eric and Todd meander up and down the beach much of the afternoon, stopping a couple of times to watch a volleyball game at the cove.

Sandpipers skitter along the sea's edge. Todd and Eric play frisbee near the public beach, stopping for a soda at the snack bar. At the end of a pier, they sit on a bench, their thighs and upper arms touching. Two old Chinese men are meticulously hooking their bait. When they cast their lines, the gulls and pelicans scatter.

In the dim evening, just before dark, two hummingbirds hover over the deck. Todd calls to Eric to come look but they fly off before he can see them. Before dinner, he lights a joint.

Lit from within, windows flicker over the hills and down into the base of the canyon. Inside, while Eric is cooking dinner, Todd listens to a solo jazz piano on the record player while flipping through the pages of some of Eric's books, ones he's removed from the bottom shelf below a stack of art magazines. Since they've come back to Eric's place from their day on the beach, Todd has wanted more people around him. He thought getting stoned might help. It's the Fourth of July. Fireworks start to explode. None of Eric's books interest him. He tries to find another that might bore him less.

"It's started, the celebrating," Eric says as he places two glasses of wine on the table. He sits next to Todd on the couch. "Just tonight," he says. "Drink some. Just taste it if you want to. It's a holiday. And our third date."

"You think we're dating?" Todd says. "What is a date, anyways? I've never understood how a date's different from just two guys being together."

"Our third hook up? O.K.? Better?"

"Not really."

"Forget it, Todd. It's just that it's been weeks since I saw you last. I'm glad you phoned me."

"Why call it anything? You and I? Me and anyone?"

"All right. I won't. From now on, I won't. Christ."

Todd continues to flip idly through pages, stopping only to pick an old newspaper clipping out of the middle of a picture book on the history of Ancient Greece. He'd hoped it might be full of statues of humpy guys, but it's only architecture, mostly temples and theaters.

"Who's this?" he says, taking a second look, holding the clipping closer to a lamp, then passing it to Eric for him to see it better. "He's really handsome. A hunk twice over. A real babe."

Eric takes it from him. "Shit. I'd forgotten I'd saved that. I must have stuck it in there when I was in college. For a class I took when I was a freshman. Good lord, that was eleven, twelve years ago. I must not have opened it since. Or maybe I did skim through it once or twice since and managed somehow not to see it. Maybe it clung to a page as I skipped it. Who knows?"

Though the paper has turned straw-colored and is torn in two places, the print, though faded, is still legible. "I had a crush on him when I was in high school. Of course." A tall boy's displaying a silver, punch-bowl size trophy he's just won. The column below the picture describes the boy's accomplishments and the many successes of the football team during the four years he's played on it. "'A state championship,'" Eric reads aloud, "'eluded him only in his final year, but it's near a certainty that new victories await him at N.C. State where though only a freshman he'll be a starter in the fall.'"

Eric lays the clipping on the coffee table, away from the wine glasses, careful not to tear it more. He picks his glass up and walks out onto the deck. The night's been warm, uncomfortably muggy, but a slight, cooling breeze, carrying a hint of incoming fog with it, is blowing from the ocean.

Todd follows him out, leaving his unwanted glass of wine on the table, and embraces Eric from behind. Startled by how strong Todd's grip is, Eric nearly drops his glass over the rail, spilling some. He takes a last sip out of it, sets it aside, and with his palm wipes a wet red spot off the wood.

"He's a gas station attendant now at a little four corners garage where he's lived with his wife since he flunked out of college. He messed up somehow. Got kicked off the State team. They have two sons. That's all I know. I could find out more, if I wanted to, I suppose. My sister or older brother would know. He was a year younger than me. I never knew him. But I went to all his games. That's the whole story. His name was David. David McCrae. My big crush long ago. Or one of them. The best one, the most imposing, I'd say, as crushes go."

Todd releases Eric from his embrace. "You dream about him still, I bet. Jerk off to him, too."

"Sometimes. At first, you might have reminded me of him in some ways. Maybe that was why, without my knowing why, I was so turned on by you that first night when we met at the bar. I didn't say to myself, 'He looks like David McCrae,' unless I did so deep inside me, in some place where the past works without anyone's knowing about it. I didn't give it a conscious thought. None. Not for a second. Not till now."

"How? How do I remind you of him?"

Is Todd teasing him? "Your curly dark hair. Your chiseled chin. The dimple," Eric says, touching it. "Your perfect nose."

"I've broken it twice," Todd says. "Hit by my board once, once on a rock I couldn't see as a wave tossed me over and over."

"That's what I mean. Broken. Perfect." Now it's Eric's turn to hug Todd from behind. "It's strange. I don't understand it. I mean the way some fantasies stay in you, with you forever, never letting you go. Maybe it's just being young, just a teenager, feeling things for the first time, not knowing what to do with them, especially when you're not supposed to be feeling them, that makes them so strong, so enduring even after you've mostly forgotten all about them. About him. Them. All of it. The misery, too, all that impossibility."

"So he's the one, huh? That guy in the clipping?"

Todd breaks free and moves to the darker side of the deck. The firecrackers and rockets and flares have stopped for a while. "We all have someone like that inside us, Eric. The president of the class. The baseball player. The star swimmer. The hunk and a half we sat behind in homeroom and stared and stared at the back of his head, hoping he might turn around just once and look at you as you wanted him to look at you, to notice you. Mine was the leader of a rock band. I went to every dance he played. He works for an electronics firm in the Valley now, no kids, unmarried. I wonder once in a while if I should give him a call. His number's listed. But that would be crazy. Those dreams, those stories we told ourselves late at night, lying in bed, getting hard. Those faces, those bodies. They're in us for good, right? What can you do?"

"Nothing, I guess," Eric says, "except try not to forget them. Honor them whenever you remember them, when they come back to you as if out of nowhere. Thank them for giving you something to hope for, to cling to at night when there was no one else, nothing else, but them to comfort that fear in you you tried to make sense of by telling yourself it would be disappear some day, life would be all right, if they just would love you a little."

"It's better now, isn't it?" Todd says. "Not falling in love with straight guys anymore. No longer making yourself miserable over what you can't have. Being out. Finding others you like as well or better than them who find you sexy too."

"I know. It's just…"

"It's just what?"

"I don't want to lose them, Todd. The old fantasies. I'm thirty years old, a pretty good lawyer, I make decent money, I live in a great place, and I still want them to fill me with that desire you feel when you know the quest is hopeless, that it will never come true. I don't want my life to become too real. That's how parents, all my family have lived, or thought they did. By the rule of reality. Good sense, they'd call it, being reasonable. I don't believe in God, but I want the promise of paradise to be true nonetheless. I don't want to lose it, that promise, that sense of joy when you're about to enter it. I want to have that gate to heaven up there waiting for me to walk in even if I won't ever enter it. I don't want to lose that crazy dream. I don't want to lose you either, but I will, won't I?"

Todd shrugs. "I'm a good lay. I'd make you a lousy boyfriend, Eric. I said I wouldn't lie to you. I won't."

"You're right. You'd be a lousy boyfriend," Eric says and laughs. "And an even worse lover, Todd. I know. You are what you are. I'm glad you're here, however brief it might be." He points to the houses below them. "Do you think anyone in any of them, man or woman over twenty, has ever forgotten he's gone to high school? Not one of them, I'd say.

Not any of them. They're all dreamers, too, or else they couldn't stand it, the boredom of it, how ordinary it is, the dull repetitiveness of it. Of life, I mean. Jesus, I'm talking too much. I need some more wine."

"And I could use another toke."

"That's fine with me. I like it when you get high."

"I'm always high, man."

"That you are," Eric says. "In every way. So what? Why come down if you don't have to? I mean, as I have to, or do, every day, every hour almost. Crashing when I don't want to."

After eating a quiet supper, Eric clicks on a movie on TV, a western Todd sleeps through the end of. They wait for midnight before going to bed, watching what they can see of the last of the fireworks exploding through the thickening fog, so heavy it's begun to drizzle on the windows, reminding Eric he needs to slide the doors to the deck closed.

As he reenters the bedroom, the sight of Todd, resting his head on a pillow, naked except for his boxers, waiting for him, so obviously anticipating the next minutes, the next hour or more of their being together rushes through him, makes him flush, redden, the pulse of longing in him too great to last, to be anything but what it is, joy, this moment of it, the wave of it pouring over him, drawing him into the elation he feels at seeing, at being embraced by Todd's outstretched, welcoming, encompassing arms.

Last night's dream has lingered too long, haunting Eric most of the morning and early afternoon until Todd arrives, very late, around three. He says nothing about where he's been, assuming Eric knows. They eat a delayed lunch on the deck, the air tense between them. On his way up, Todd tore some twigs of scotch broom off a shrub that shades the steps near the road. He's stuck them in a drinking glass on the porch table. Hanging from protruding beams, several potted fuchsias sway in the breeze, dropping an occasional petal on the floor.

"You're watering them too much," Todd says.

"Too little or too much," Eric says. "That's me."

Fifty feet below them, a young girl wearing a shift throws crumbs into the air for the circling gulls to catch on the wing. Glittering like silver sequins beneath a hazy sun, the Pacific's glassy and calm.

Todd pitches bits of his uneaten crust toward the birds who swoop up to catch them. Eric sips a second cup of coffee. They clean up the cottage and hose off the deck. Taking out the trash and garbage, coming back up, Todd stubs his big toe on the last step, curses, hobbles into the cottage, and washes it off in the bath tub.

Eric leans against the bathroom door. "I used to do that all the time as a kid. I was a barefoot boy in the wilds of the woods, the calluses on my feet thick as mocassins."

Todd says nothing, applies some iodine to the wound, pulls the string of a band aid, decides not to use it, and limps down the hall, through the living room, and onto the deck, touching the floors with only the heel of his injured foot.

Eric follows him out. The sun has begun to set. The canyon and the surrounding hills glow as if they'd been lightly brushed with a rust colored stain. "Your toe's not bleeding anymore. It should heal well."

"I hope so. No beach. No surfing for a couple of days at least, damn it." He leans on the railing. "Listen, Eric. It's time. I've got to go."

"Now?"

"No. I really want to spend the night with you. One more night. But tomorrow, after I leave, it's over, you and I. More or less. O.K.?"

"'More or less'? What does that mean?"

"It means more or less," Todd says.

Eric leans over to inspect Todd's toe again. "Just be careful where you walk for the next few days. You don't want to hurt it further or have it get infected."

"You're not listening. I can tell."

"Yes, I am. I'm not going to make a fuss, Todd. I'm not going to protest. I understand. I'm all right. This isn't really news, you know. We haven't been with each other that often during these last four weeks since we met, have we?"

"Maybe not, but when we have it's been great," Todd says. He's shivering. "I've got to put a shirt on."

In the bedroom, he's looking for one of the extra t-shirts he brought with him the second night he stayed at Eric's and left behind, not knowing when or if he might need it later. "They're in here," Eric says, opening a closet door. "Your clothes. What did you mean, 'more or less'? Explain it to me, Todd."

"It means I'll call you."

"When?"

"I don't know. In a few weeks. Sometime next month maybe."

"We could have dinner together. Take in a movie," Eric says.

"Sure," Todd says. They lapse into an awkward silence.

"How are you getting home?"

"I said I want to spend the night. I still do. I like you, Eric. I genuinely do. We haven't just been tricking."

"Tomorrow then. How are you going to get home tomorrow?"

"I have a car. I left it on the street so you wouldn't see it until I was ready to tell you that I needed to split. Now I have."

"Whose is it?"

"Some guy I met two days ago. Rex something."

"You're not crying, are you, Todd?"

"No." He blinks his eyes. "I'm not. Screw that."

"It's all right. It's summer."

"You'll let me stay. You still want us to fuck tonight?"

"Of course. I wouldn't miss it. It's what I want more than anything, one more night with you in my bed," Eric says and kisses him. Over and over. Passionately, ardently kissing his lips, his face, his body. Believing in, trusting in that ecstasy he knows only when emotions like love or whatever it was he'd felt for Todd are nearly over, past having, even though his desire, his need for him has never been keener.

Maybe only whenever the best of life's coming to an end, the uncanny, sad intensity of last times, moments of parting, of saying a final goodbye, maybe only then does the fantasy of what it might have been begin and the joy of it, of him, whoever he was, become shockingly real. Perhaps the rarest joy, Eric thinks, though he's trying hard not to think at all as he holds Todd as tightly as he can in his arms, is the life we make up from the life we've lived. Though careful of his hurt toe, he leads Todd swiftly toward his bed.

After they'd made love, Todd falls easily asleep, but rest eludes Eric. There's a party going on somewhere down in the depths of the canyon. He carefully slips out from between the sheets and steps as quietly as he can onto the deck. The noise from below grows louder, even though it is very late, but he yields to it, to the rock music and the shouting and the loud laughter until he is certain Todd is about to disappear from his life for good as surely as if he had never been in it. Neither will ever call the other again. It's summer, he forces himself to remember. "It's summer," he whispers to no one. He will remember him in the summers to come.

He must. A light clicks on in his bedroom. Having woken up, finding Eric's side of the bed empty, Todd is perhaps wondering where he's gone. What, if anything, his absence means.

In L.A., like God, the sun is love. Or so Christopher says, smiling, admiring himself in the mirror over the bar at The Breakers. Eric's immediately smitten. Christopher tells the friend he rode down with he'll find some other way back home.

Late in the night, just before dawn of the next day, on the drive up the coast highway toward his place in the city, lights from a police van and ambulance swirl red and blue around a wreck, the car's hood crumpled, side smashed, windshield shattered. One body's shrouded. "Night's scary," Christopher says. "Like death."

"Or the rainy season," Eric says. They laugh.

Once in L.A., Eric deliberately takes a circuitous route to Christopher's apartment. At a diner, they eat omelets and watch the sun come up, tinting poster palms, wide glass façades, cars on La Cienega an apple jelly gold.

"This is wrong. I shouldn't have let you talk me into it. We just met. I'm not taking you home yet. I refuse to," Eric says as they walk back to his car. "I don't want to let go of you this quickly. Come back with me to Laguna. It's Sunday. We've got another day, another night before us, if you want. That's all I'm asking for. Twenty four more hours. We can spend part of it at the beach, if you like."

"We just got here," Chris says. "It won't take that much longer to get to my place, Eric. It's nice there, too, in Echo Park. You could spend the night with me in my bed."

"I'd need a change of clothes for work in the morning."

"Borrow some of mine. They might fit you well enough."

"All right, I tell you what," Eric says. "Let's flip for it. Let's let chance decide."

"Agreed," Christopher, says, reaching for a quarter from his pocket. "Call it."

"Heads," Eric says.

Christopher tosses it. It lands heads up on the sidewalk. "You win, Eric. Back to Laguna it is."

"Don't look so disappointed."

"I'm not. I'm not disappointed at all. It's just…."

"Just what?"

"Nothing. I need to change. I need a bath."

"If I could fit in your clothes, you can fit in mine."

"I wanted you to see my place. I wanted to show it off."

"Next weekend. I'll drive up next weekend. How's that?"

"Sure," Christopher says. "It sounds like a plan. I'll let you know for certain later. I'll have to check my calendar first."

They hold hands walking up the steps to Eric's. The kitchen's bright, a bleached sun blazing in through open shutter slats where gnats swarm over oranges on a sill. A furry creature, like something new to nature, crawls across a wooly rug. Far off, the sea's banded pewter, polished silver, pearl. Tattered clouds scatter in a powder blue sky. From the canyon, a strong scent of scotch broom blows through the cottage's rooms.

The radio's reporting fires are still burning in eastern Riverside County. A jet's cattail trails above pelicans flying in a line parallel to the horizon. More light spills from a bulging sun. Pulp from a lime Eric squeezes oozes out the rind and spots the floor. A squirrel scampers up a pepper tree. Christopher's undresses in the bathroom, takes a quick shower, and, towel wrapped around his waist, walks into his bedroom. So that's how it is, how it will be this time. In sunlight. In full clarity. A day's enough for a lifetime, Eric's thinks, excited, rapidly removing all his clothes. A day's enough. And always will be.

Throwing the towel off his body, lying back upon a sheet still crumpled from last night, despite the shower he's just taken, Christopher smells hot, sweaty, like Laguna, like L.A., like a summer wild for embraces, for love, for the bliss of this white morning.

A Last Dance

Ill fortune. Bad luck. My beach town haunts are gone.
The Breakers is long torn down. Where the Pacific
Coast Highway intersects with the Laguna Canyon
Road is now reserved for families. No disco music,
no gay boys dancing in their speedos on the deck
or the beach on Sunday afternoons, no July Fourth
orgies when all the hunky guys from L.A. would trek
down from Hollywood, Westwood, Silver Lake, or north
from Dana Point or Del Mar. No more noon revels.
Laguna is a straight town now, in a hurry
to crisscross the hills. What's sounded in its ocean's swells?
A gull whirls by me, as if in a twister's fury,
and breaks free. You are my past, my love, never done
dancing, we two, to the great blazing round of the sun.

A Story of Love and the Sea

Dessert over, with Ty's help, Howard finishes clearing the dining room table of everything except what he believes best enhances the after spell, the glow inside each diner, of a good meal. Like the five flickering, slightly smoky candles, the heirloom white linen tablecloth and embroidered napkins, thin stem wine glasses, and two half full bottles of wine, one red, one white. They are done with eating. These few good things, precious in a way, left to contemplate ought to suffice, he hopes, to keep the night cheerful. He and Ty sit back down, each at their place at opposite ends of the large table.

They are the only survivors of thirty or more close friends that once, forty years ago, saw each other nearly every day and most nights at the bars or on the dance floors, these the six among their group who are left, who have come to enjoy sitting around a table after a meal for the simple comfort, the ease of being where they've gathered many times before for old friendship's old familiarities and the always nostalgic, moving view of the sea and the beach that Howard and Ty's cottage offers them from high on a promontory at the end of Blue Bird Canyon Road. On fog free nights like this one, under a bright moon and starry sky, the Pacific seems to curve and shine like a scimitar out of its sheath, meant only for display.

Without being asked, Ty pours them all another round of wine. In the silence among them that follows another brief toast and the clinking of glasses, they listen. Howard's put on a different CD.

"What's that playing so softly in the background?" Will asks. "No wait. It's the Kinks, isn't it? That's naughty of you, Howard, this late into the night. Nineteen seventy-two, wasn't it?"

"You're two years off," Ty says. "Nineteen Seventy. Before you'd arrived among us, I believe, still in the closet back home in a wind-blown North Dakota."

"Yes," Will says. He studies the stem of the glass he's holding and sips.

"'Lola,'" Howard says, pleased with himself, not quite smirking. "Lo Lo Lola." He waves a finger in the air as if dancing.

"Please, Howard," Jules says. "What are you trying to do to us? This music. It breaks my heart. So long ago."

"I used to love this song. I still do, I guess," Sam says. "Remember our hearing it for the first time at The Shrimp, Mitch?"

"I do, as if it were yesterday," Mitch says. "Thanks, Howie."

"More Sauvignon for you, Jules?" Ty says.

"Yes. Please. Red gives me terrible headaches. Just one little taste and I'm down for the night, craving aspirins."

"It always has," Will says. "A shame, I'd say." He swirls his glass gently. "How lovely wine looks by candlelight, the amber or ruby glow of it on the tablecloth."

"Yes, I suppose it is a shame. 'Always' seems too long, though perhaps you're right. Has my constitution always been this weak? Perhaps," Jules says. "That was a wonderful lemon soufflé, Howard. Just scrumptious."

"Do you remember Norman's soufflés?" Ty says to them all at once, to his four best friends in the world and his lover Howard, spreading his arms out wide as if to embrace each one simultaneously in the memory of one of Norman's many miracles in the kitchen, of his preparing for their Sunday morning brunches pleasures rare and delicious. "The work, the sweat it took him to cook them. And the result? Heavenly."

"The taste and texture of them," Mitch says. "Inimitable."

"The way he was always proudly handing out his recipes," Ty says, "as if they were precious secrets only he knew. And maybe they were."

"The book of them he made one Christmas," Howard says, "and wrapped as presents for us all."

"Did you ever try one?" Will says.

"I wouldn't have dared," Ty says. "My reputation was at stake."

"Me neither," Howard says. "A certain disaster if created by anyone but Norman. My, he was a lovely man. Lovely, simply lovely."

"Oh, the sweetest man on earth," Jules says. "And generous. Those little dolls he used to carve from driftwood and gift us with on our birthdays. The toy dogs he'd assemble from old coat hangers."

Sam takes a careful sip from his glass. Like the others, he's a little tight from the cocktails before and all the wine poured during dinner. It's nearly midnight, yet none of them is eager to leave, though two of them still have jobs to go to in the morning. "I wonder why in the world Norman let Craig go," Sam says. "It seemed so perverse at the time. So wrong. Do you suppose he already knew?"

"I always thought so," Will says.

"Yes," Jules agrees. "It would be like him. To let him go before the worst of it started for him, when it would begin to show and no one could doubt it was happening to him now, too. Clark Humboldt did the same with his partner. What was his name, Will? You'd remember."

"Tony. Antonio actually," Will says. "Tony Sabatino."

"Yes. Yes. Of course," Jules says.

Howard fumbles with his napkin. It's a habit of his Ty's never managed to break him of, twisting and knotting his napkins, even in restaurants, after a meal. "Yes. That was like Norman. Sad. Certainly sad." He rips a corner of it. "Craig didn't want to go, of course, didn't want to leave their home. But Norman left him little choice, did he? And then Craig...."

"Howard," Ty admonishes. Howard's face reddens. He tosses the napkin, a touch defiantly, not quite at Ty, more toward the center of the table.

"He was alone forever after that. Completely alone," Sam says. "Till the day he died."

"He had us," Ty says. "So did Craig."

"That's not what I meant," Sam says.

"I know," Ty says. "Of course I know. We all do."

"Craig was such a beauty," Will says.

"Oh, we all thought so," Jules says. "Didn't we? I envied Norman. Didn't everyone?"

"He wasn't faithful," Howard says. "That's what Norman said."

"I don't think that's fair, Howard," Sam says. "'Not faithful' is too strong."

"What phrase would you prefer?" Howard says.

"If he'd been mine," Jules says, "I wouldn't have cared. It's all I wanted. All I've ever wanted. Craig could have done anything he liked so long as he came home to me eventually."

"No? Maybe you wouldn't have been bothered by it, Jules. How would you know? Norman did care, though. Very much."

"That's unkind of you, Howard," Jules says.

"Sorry." Howard twists his head to gaze out his window. "It's utterly clear all the way to Dana Point. A perfect night. Just fine. No signs of fog forming yet."

"Who was faithful really in those days?" Sam says.

"Howard and I were," Ty objects.

"You two were different," Mitch says.

"Craig loved Norman. I know that. He told me so often," Sam says. "Norman knew it too."

"I'm sure he did," Howard says.

"Think of Tomàs and David. Think of Adam and Brendan. Scott and Ray," Sam says.

"I do," Jules says. "Don't we all? Every hour of the day."

"The fog will be on its way back in eventually tonight, no doubt about it," Will says. "I left my windows open."

"Such a pessimist, William," Howard says.

"And you're the optimist among us, Howie?" Will says, smiling.

"Not the only one, I hope," Howard says, "and not without reason."

"You live too close to the ocean, Will," Jules says. "Your place is always damp and cold. I need two sweaters on me whenever I visit these days."

"So I've observed, Jules," Will says, smiling even more broadly. "Should I move just for you? Maybe so."

"Certainly not. Don't mind me, Will," Jules says. "I'm just getting old and cranky."

"Getting old?" Will says. "We're old already, aren't we, every mother's son of us?"

"We're lucky to be here, Howard and I," Ty says. "Up in the hills. It's good we bought early. Before all the rich bitches and their oh so grand corporate husbands moved in and took over our town. They own it now and rule it, damn them."

"Our town," Jules says wistfully. "Ours. Once upon a time."

"I've been trying to think. What year did Craig die?" Sam asks.

"Oh, quite early. Late in eighty-two, early in eighty-three. Less than a year after Norman."

"Casey Evans had quite the crush on him," Ty says. "You remember how he mooned over Craig?"

"Casey was a boy who certainly could swoon with the best, couldn't he? Like a romantic girl in movies. Like Natalie Wood in that William Inge film with Beatty," Jules says. "What was it called? Don't tell me. Oh, yes. Splendor in the Grass. Ah, well. Craig and Norman certainly gave some special parties. Do you remember their Halloween bash in, what was it?, seventy-eight, I think, at that place they rented for a while on Catalina with all the carryings on in the bushes behind the garage? Goodness me."

"That was the same night David Brandt met Tomàs Garcia," Howard says. "They'd both come dressed as Luke Skywalker. They were meant for each other."

"They were always so dear together. All the way until the end," Mitch says.

"I don't know. Tomàs could be quite the little bitch sometimes," Jules says. "A real spitfire."

"Oh, Jules," Ty says. "Please."

"Well, he could," Jules says.

"Don't get upset, Jules. We all know why you didn't like him," Howard says. "It was just a misunderstanding between you and him."

"A misunderstanding? It was more than that, Howie. He'd slept with my Cody."

"Cody had already left you, Jules."

"I know. But he came back when he was sick, didn't he? To me. Love at first sight and so much more, I'd foolishly thought. He knew who would take care of him. And I did. I did. I took care him. I let bygones be bygones. There was no reason in the world not to. I cared for him to the end, didn't I? I know he didn't love me anymore. That he probably never had. But I did what I had to do, no matter what, didn't I?"

Howard pats his hand. He is often patting Jules' hand. Jules pulls it back. "You sure did," Howard says. "You're a good man, Jules."

"Those last months were awful. Blood. Shit. Thirty-five years ago and I still have nightmares. Poor, poor Cody. I've never felt like that again for anyone."

"I think we all have our nightmares," Ty says.

"And always will," Jules says.

"Tomàs and David. So committed. Inseparable. Having to die apart like that," Will says and shudders.

"What good times we had before though," Mitch says. "What fun."

"Do you remember those muscles numbers, every one of them somehow or other a stunning blond, who used to drive down from L.A., or Hollywood as they'd insist, on weekends to dance at Dante's or The BoomBoom Room?" Sam says.

"Who can forget them?" Ty says. "Who could forget one second of it? The pure joy of it. The beaches around the bars crowded with nearly naked men, every one of them gay. My lord, it was paradise."

"Do you remember how Tracy chased one end beauty all the way back to Westlake one night? What a story," Sam says. "He was so proud of himself. Just beaming whenever he told the tale in all its glorious, intimate details."

"I've never understood why Tracy returned to Mississippi at the end," Jules says. "It made no sense."

"Family," Howard says. "Or that's what he told me just before he left."

"But they'd expelled him. Told him never to come back. I don't get it. I never did, and I never will," Jules says. "Families at their best are still perverse. And Tracy's was one of the worst."

"He was tired," Mitch says. "Too tired to resist them."

"He was a brilliant man," Sam says. "Harvard. Irvine."

"Wild, too," Mitch says. "Remember that resolutely straight kid he met in San Diego and pursued until he'd caught him and held on to him for almost six months, even living together for part of that time. How did he manage that? And, later, he was best man at his wedding a year after they'd broken up. Amazing. The boy was some kid from deep in the heart of Texas he'd seen in uniform from afar and decided he had to have and wouldn't quit until he did. He chased him and chased him and finally caught him. What a wonder Tracy was."

"If I had been in love like Tracy was with him, I couldn't have been best man at his wedding. I'd be too upset and jealous," Jules says.

"Was he really that much of a hunk? I never met him, did I, Howard? Tracy never brought him here to visit us, did he?" Ty says.

"Never," Mitch says. "Tracy was frightened we might scare him off. He said he didn't want all his faggot friends flirting with him or trying to grope him or grab his ass."

"Oh, the pity of it is that if he really was all that Tracy said he was I think I might very well have," Sam says.

"I'm sure you would have, Babe," Mitch says.

"Oh, dear, dear Tracy," Ty says. "How I miss him. So smart and so funny."

"And Cam," Howard says.

"Of course. And Cam, too. They made an exceptional couple once Trace decided to finally settle down. More wine anyone? Please help yourself," Ty says.

"The Sauvignon is almost gone," Jules says.

"You've only yourself to blame," Howard says. "I fear my friends have all become drunkards."

"Howard," Ty protests.

"Sorry. It's true. I am a little tight," Jules says. "Maybe it's best if I didn't drink any more. Please don't open another bottle on my account."

"Did any of you ever read Dwight Carter's last novel?" Mitch asks. "Try as I could I couldn't get a publisher interested in it after he'd died. I thought it was good. Very good. His best."

"It was about us, all of us," Howard says. "He let me read a few chapters. I told him I thought he was being needlessly cruel to his friends at times. You all might guess to whom I might be referring. I particularly didn't want to read any more after I'd finished his chapters on Robert Schofferman. Maybe Dwight felt he had to let all of Bob's nastier cats out of the bag because he'd been quite ugly to him after their breakup. Bob was a wicked gossip, of course. But I liked him. Quite a lot in fact. It was such a transparent description of him, didn't you find, Mitch, of everyone really? All Dwight really did was disguise us all under different names. I don't think a good, decent, honest, truly kind person can write a roman à clef, do you? Or should. He must have been keeping some sort of diary which he decided to use at the end when the light of inspiration was failing him. Failing us all, perhaps."

"You didn't much like how you got depicted in it either, I'd bet," Mitch says.

"Of course I didn't," Howard says. "Why should I?"

"Howard carried a torch for Dwight for quite a while," Ty says. "Quite a fiery one."

"I didn't," Howard insists.

"Oh, Howie. You think I didn't know at the time? And for Luke Beaumont later, poor man. I didn't mind. Why should I? You never had a chance with either of them, sweetie. Sooner or later I knew you'd come to see that. And you did, each and every time you found a new crush to dote on for a while."

"I never truly loved anyone but you," Howard says.

"I know," Ty says.

"And those mind-blowing July Fourths, remember those?" Sam says, "year after year."

"The bands. The dancing. Barbecues on the beach. The partying. The fireworks," Mitch says.

"The sex," Will says.

"The joy of it," Mitch says, shaking his head.

"We were all so young," Jules says.

"Yes. And free," Ty says.

"And horny," Sam says. They laugh for a few seconds, then uncomfortably stare at one another, at what they'd rather avoid, rather not see, each other's faces and necks and hands. They're old men now who know it's getting late, who feel a keen need for bed and sleep.

The room becomes suddenly silent. The six men look away from each other, glancing instead at a picture on the wall, at a still burning though sputtering candle or out the window, at some bric-a-brac or a magazine cover on the nearby coffee table. Sam takes Mitch's hand in his. "It's time for us to go home, sweetie."

"Ghosts are passing through us," Howard says.

"Yes. I can feel them. We all can," Will says.

"We should change the conversation or call it a night," Howard says.

"I've heard it said, some famous writer has claimed, that only the homely ones survived. That all the beauties died," Jules says. "What does that say about us?"

"Jules," Howard says, frowning. "No more."

"You know that's not true," Sam says.

"Yes, Jules," Ty says. "Look at us. Still manly hunks, still gorgeous babes after all these years."

"Yes. Look at us," Howard says, "old, beginning to fall apart, and becoming too often maudlin whenever we few gather. Perhaps we ought to consider some new rules. Like no more reminiscing."

"Not so old. Not so wrecked. We're living our lives," Mitch protests, "as well as we can."

"Are we?" Howard says, pushing back his chair. "What's left of them, I suppose. It's really is late, gentlemen. Ty and I need to clean up and get to bed. I'm very tired. You must be exhausted, too. Tomorrow's Monday. Ty and Jules are still working men."

"We six. All that's left," Jules says. "Out of how many?"

"Hush," Ty says. "Howard's right. We've been looking back too much tonight. We mustn't live in the past. Mustn't live only in regret for what might have been if that terrible disease hadn't happened. Perhaps nostalgia is ruinous to old folks like us."

"But it really was a glorious time, though," Sam says, "wasn't it?"

"It's the wine," Jules says. "It goes to your head. It affects the heart."

"I have an announcement to make before it's too late this evening. It's my birthday," Howard says, turning so to face each one in turn. "I didn't tell you because at my age, I am the oldest as you all have so often delighted in establishing, at my time of life birthdays make me very unhappy. So I asked Ty to promise not to tell you either. None of you could have known it. For years, I've tried to keep the date a secret. Birthdays didn't always used to affect me like this. Only since, well, you know as well as I do since when. Since it began. But here we are now, we six together. So I tell you. I confess it, I suppose. I'm now seventy-three. Seventy-three since this morning." He checks his watch. "Seventy-three years and almost a day in a few more hours."

"A true survivor," Ty says. "Worth celebrating."

Howard drains the last wine from his glass, pours himself what remains in the bottle into it, and drinks it down fast. "Yes, a survivor," he says. "Alas for that. Goodnight all." Carrying the empty bottle, he swiftly disappears into the kitchen.

Mitch and Sam let themselves out. By a vote its neighbors held, it seems, at least every four years, the canyon road remains unlit and often dangerously dark, though tonight the way down is clear since the moon is nearing full. As they head toward town, not one car passes them in either direction. They park on the main drag near the street that leads to their house. Sam holds Mitch's hand tighter as they stroll slowly north on the sidewalk. "Sleepy?"

"Not really."

When they reach Rose Street, they cross the Coast Highway, walk down the steps toward the sand, and sit by the promontory, tall as the cliff from which it juts out into the Pacific. Its southern side was a favorite cruising spot in the old days, safely hidden from the eyes of those on the other side of it, whether unsuspecting, curious, or bluntly censorious. Sam wraps an arm around his husband's shoulder. "Feeling sad?"

"Every time we go to Howard's these days, most of what we talk about is the past."

"It's all he has left, he and Ty and Jules and Will. We've got each other. Ty and Howard are different from us, less in love still. And Jules and Will live alone. They're not like us, Mitch."

"But I miss it, too. I miss the fun. I miss our friends."

"Yes. Me, too."

"I sometimes think the past is all any of us has left." Mitch nods toward his left. "You know every time we come back to this spot lately I think I can see Luke Beaumont's bathing suit still lying where he left it all those years ago for someone to find in the sand. I guess that suit was his way of leaving a note. No one else would have dared to wear it, I mean absolutely no one, except Luke. He's the only one who was bold enough. Or perfect enough."

"You. It was you who found it. It was you who knew right away it was Luke's suit. I think it was you he'd wanted to have found it, Mitch. He wanted you to know first. He knew you liked to swim at night, too, no matter how cold the water was, just as he did. Who else? Only you could have known what it meant. That he was gone. That he'd made up his mind that it was over. No more suffering."

"Maybe. I did love him a little."

"No. You loved him a lot."

"We all did, didn't we? Of all our friends, his was the star that shined most."

"There were a lot of stars back then, Mitch. It was a crowded sky."

"Luke was the brightest, the handsomest man I ever saw."

"The best dancer, too."

Mitch gazes at the setting orange moon. "We've become two old half drunk Chinese monks, you and I, sitting outside our cave, watching the water in the river below flow past us, enraptured by the moon."

"Writing poems about pretty boys and falling petals," Sam says. "You remember when some surfer Nazi had carved into the rock face 'God Burns Faggots in Hell' and Luke raced home after he'd read it and brought back a pickax to chop it out while a few of the kids and men in wet suits watched him do it, mad as hell at him for invading their turf. But Luke was the one with the ax and no one to mess with even without it."

"I sometimes feel he's in the sea, here with us," Mitch says, "having changed his mind. Trying to swim back in against the currents. Wanting what little life he had left after all. Yearning for it."

"That's where they all are. Where all our friends have gone. Into the sea. That's what brought us all here, out of love for it and the sun. And for the fog and the rainy days, too. We were all in our way beach bums. Maybe some of us still are. It lured us all away from wherever we'd come from and welcomed us into our new lives. The sea is who we are, the secret of what it means to be gay. It's what I want too," Sam says. "My ashes thrown into the Pacific right at the spot where we scattered Darrell's and Craig's and David's and Tomàs'. You promise me? You'll do it?"

"Why should you be the one to die first?"

Sam shrugs. "Just an intuition."

"Something wrong I don't know about?"

"No." He kisses Mitch on the cheek. "We should go home now. Get some sleep."

They help each other up, both stumbling in the sand and laughing at their clumsiness. "I used to race you the length of this damned strand four times over," Mitch says. "I'd beat you, too."

"I know," Sam says. "You won because I'd let you."

Mitch picks up a fistful of sand and tosses it into the air. "Liar."

"I love you," Sam says. "I let you win because I love you."

Mitch stoops to pick up more sand to throw, but thinks better of it. It's a stupid game they sometimes play. Neither ever beat the other. It was never a real race. "Promise me," he says.

"What?"

"Promise me you won't die before me?"

2.

Monday morning, Mitch wakes earlier than Sam, showers, dresses in shorts and a t- shirt, just as he used to decades before, both too tight and much too young for him now, and saunters back down the road from their Catalina Street home to the beach. Laguna has changed. It's not the town they knew in their twenties anymore. Their old haunts are all gone. By whichever name one recalls it best, Dante's or the Breakers, their favorite bar is long torn down. Its site, where the Pacific Coast Highway intersects with Laguna Canyon Road, is now reserved for families and their picnics. No disco music, no gay boys dancing in their speedos on the deck or on the beach on a Sunday afternoon, no making out shame-free under the sun. No more tea dances at the BoomBoom Room. No Memorial Day or July Fourth or Labor Day summertime parties which all the cutest guys from L.A. would drive down from Hollywood, Westlake, Silver Lake, or Echo Park for or the even humpier ones who'd take Route One up from Dana Point or Del Mar. No more noon revels. No more screwing by the shore under the moon. Laguna is a straight town now, everyone in it in a hurry to crisscross the hills to get to and from their jobs and to vote as far right as they can at every election. It's money not beauty that matters most now.

But it's not Laguna, his hometown for forty years and more, that

Mitch is mourning for. It's Luke Beaumont whom he's grieved for since he died. He cups his hands around his mouth and pretends to call to him. To Luke. To Heat. Surf. Beach. Sun.

Whenever he had the chance to see him in action, how he loved watching him move, glide, walk, run, ride, dance. Luke's boyfriends would come and go, sometimes two in a day. Foggy days he'd dance at The Breakers for hours. Gym-toned, tanned by the sun. Blond. He was the light that gave Mitch life before he'd fallen in love with Sam, his eyes like the Mediterranean sky, like the sea Luke loved more than anyone, the Pacific he swam in every day, whatever the weather, no matter how cold the water was.

Starting early in 'Eighty-Four, each day, each night Mitch watched, still longingly, still at a distance he could never bridge, as Luke's beauty slowly, deliberately, perversely faded away. Everyone noticed its going, and no one said a word. Luke couldn't die. Everyone else, but not Luke. He danced on, shoved death away as he would a stranger who'd tried to kiss him without first asking his permission to touch him, denying it his favors, dancing to the sun, it seemed, that had loved him most of all, dispensing upon him its abundance of favors. Our sun, Mitch thinks, that belonged, belongs only to us. And yet betrayed us.

The early morning fog that returned overnight obscures the horizon. Waves cascade in, roaring like a waterfall. Mitch stands at the Pacific's edge. No surfers are out yet today, no fishing boats, few birds. He hears Luke call to him from thirty-two years away. The sea is warning him it's too rough, too cold, too wild to swim in today, the rip tides vicious. Come back later, this evening or tomorrow. I'll be here, waiting, patiently waiting. For Luke. For everyone.

Luke's weird ways of having fun, his laughter, the crazy views he argued for, the games he played, the light he left behind him in each room as he left it, his speech too rapid sometimes to understand, his slow gait, the pleasures he took and gave in bed, at a party, on his job, the same look on his face whether he'd just heard a sweet enticement or an envious curse, his dying's absurd trials, his pain, his inimitable strut, whatever belonged to him alone, to no one else, no less clear to Mitch because Luke is decades gone, yet nonetheless a foreigner, a stranger now, someone whom he suspected he couldn't really recognize anymore: Luke is there, right in front of him, waiting for him at the ocean's edge. It was only at the end he let Mitch in like no one else. Neither knew why. He'd come back. He's here, near the beach.

Fog. Clouds. Mist. Wherever light and shadows meet. The sea echoing within the caves in the cliffs. Sun gleaming through the fog, off the white sand. Waves that seem to rise and fall at once. Watch me, he hears Luke say to him. He lives to body surf, to go a hundred yards or more out, sometimes tumbling over and over as he approaches the shore where the waves have gained more force than he'd expected. Undaunted, never afraid, always swimming out again for the rush of the trip back in. The rush of living just for the fuck of it, he'd say. The risk. As if some deity were daring him to do it, to be better than anyone, than a god.

Lie by my side, Luke. Take off your shoes, your jeans, t-shirt, shorts. Let me muss your hair, kiss your skin. Just tonight. Just this one time more and I'll let you go, Mitch says to no one, to the phantom in his head. All right, Luke replies with a cool guy's grin. I will.

Long ago, after so many others he'd loved, so many friends had fallen sick, Mitch had waited for him here at twilight as evening shaded the sea and the first stars showed, waited for Luke to come back to shore from his last swim of the day. And he had, and they'd made love, just that once. But he never does anymore, Luke never returns dripping wet and splendid, stepping out of the surf.

That he himself had grown old came as a surprise to Mitch, perhaps because, having seen so many others die young or almost still young before him, he never thought he might last. His dead don't leave him. He's like an old man wandering up and down the coast searching for something he's missing or lost, a key or a watch—he can barely recall which, maybe both—that he might have dropped in the sand or that fell out of his pocket, he has no way of knowing or remembering exactly when. Suddenly it's gone. It's all gone.

It's not only the many friends. It's not only lovers. It's not only them. It's so much more he cannot name or describe that he's mourning for. It's a whole world he's lost. A whole time. An era of the earth that's gone missing, irrecoverable.

Maybe he and Luke will meet again some day. Reality can't be as bad, as painful, the second time it's experienced as it is the first time you live through it, can it? Wondering if Sam has followed him down the steps, concerned about where Mitch's gone and rightly guessing where, Mitch looks back, sees he hasn't, and wades into the water at the Pacific's edge. What he wants more than anything, is waiting for every day, is the return of the joy they've lost.

The tide's coming in or retreating. Mitch forgot to check before he left the house and can't decide which, preferring to believe it's neither. Standing in the water a few yards away from the rocky face of the promontory that struts out from the cliffs–cliffs that aeons ago rose out of and are now slowly, ponderously returning to the sea–Mitch feels it lapping invitingly at his body as high as his chest. Luke is smiling, beckoning him to join him for one more swim.

The arc of the sky, just visible through the fog, is Luke's breath, the wind his pulse, the day as it clears his sea-blue eyes. Mitch's need for him, his enduring love for Luke, is cresting as waves do rising and falling, breaking hard on the sand, receding back into the sea. This is his life's sole solace, save for Sam his only comfort. Rapture, if it exists at all, must lie waiting in the stillness between one tide and another, in the silence between waves, in that love men at their best feel for each other where ends and beginnings are ever the same.

Laguna Beach

His knotted straw blond hair is covered with sand,
his bathing suit cut-off jeans. His lesions are raw,
livid on both thighs, one zigzagging his left hand.
He's coral pink from sunburn, red as a crab's claw.

He knifes his name in rock face, cutting deep,
not satisfied until he knows it can be read,
then dives in, swims out past where the shelf is steep-
est, beyond the surfers, invisible except for his head.

Wait for evening to shade the beach, the first stars
to show, though you really must let him go.
He'll not return. It's like in the time of the wars.
People vanish, are listed as missing. But you know.

Wander like a spirit up and down the coast.
Perhaps you'll meet again. Perhaps it's wrong
to write as he did after he learned he was lost:
This is the last story I'll ever tell you. So long.

Morning Light at Sunset

The city where I live is lost to me and I to it. Most of my friends, the heart of my life, died during the plague, those awful fifteen years and more when it was its worst. Though it's no longer news the way it was, it's killing still, just more quietly and not so many at once.

The few friends I had who survived moved away or retreated into their rooms like recluses, unable to bear the sight of the outside world, all the familiar faces they no longer saw that they nevertheless kept passing on the streets or seeing in the bars.

I am continuously surprised about how often dead friends return to me in dreams or in daytime illusions. Apparitions, ghosts they were once called. It's not magic but solitude that conjures them up.

My straight friends stayed by my side for a while, though slowly they, too, left or disappeared from my life, though obviously for different reasons. I don't know why they never call or write me anymore. Maybe I bore them or take the wrong views about the world. Content people usually retreat from the company of those who are not happy.

There is no reason for me to think, after all, that I am the slightest bit likable, not anymore. Most people avoid those whom they see to be in a state, near obsession, of perpetual mourning. I try not to complain. I try not to drone on about this or that, whatever inside me depresses me. I make an effort to take the stoic attitude. But it's no good. They see it on my face. The sadness. The self-pitying loneliness.

Perhaps self-pity is a survivor's right. Or maybe it's merely his plight, another kind of failure. The day comes when you finally are no longer tolerable to yourself. It is when you discover how much you dislike life that you have two choices. The one I took was to depart as well, to leave San Francisco, to return home, to the town I came from. To end where I began. Doesn't everyone do that, whether they mean to or not, sooner or later? I mean, go back home.

Stonefield the town is called, founded in the eighteen forties. I was born there a hundred years later. It began as a general store and tavern

where two plank roads crossed. In those days hundreds of large stones
and dozens of boulders lay scattered over a grand meadow nearby. It gave
the place a primeval appearance, some of the earliest recorders reported, a
sense of a time when giants dwelled on the earth or else, like a moonscape,
no one at all. Not that it was barren. The soil was fertile and yielded
fine crops. The trees that were cut and chopped to construct the earliest
cottages and barns were almost as monumental before they were felled.

Not many of the original boulders are left. On one the town's name
was carved during the first year of the new century. The rest were slowly
chiseled into stones to be used for the new, modern homes' façades, as
decor, to give them a fashionable antique look.

It remained a somewhat unprosperous village until the decade before
World War Two changed it into a bustling suburban, commuter town
happily aligned with a train that ran six times a day from north central
Jersey to New York City and back. Stonefield is near the southern end
of its route. My father rode that train to and from Manhattan five days
a week for forty-two years. He carried two newspapers with him in his
briefcase, one for each way, the local paper and The New York Times. He
liked to think of himself as well-informed.

We, my parents, my two sisters, and I, lived on a poplar and elm-
lined street in a remodeled, partially restored Victorian. I say 'Victorian'
because of when it was built, not how it looked. It was a big white
clapboard house. It had a full basement with a coal furnace in it, an attic you could walk upright in despite the pitched roof, two floors with
old-fashioned high ceilings and views of the neighborhood ("charming-
ly nostalgic," it was called), a porch on the northern side, a sunroom
on the southern one, with a yard in back that was shaped like an upside
down L surrounded by trees so dark and green they appeared to be
mementos of an ancient age, too, like the oaks in a Gothic forest or the
pines along the Appian Way.

Paradisal, my mother called it, and she was almost right. It felt like
a private, secluded park. My father was an adept, orderly, yet passionate gardener. It was his only hobby. His flowers flourished as if hot
house blooms.

Why was I so eager to leave it? Why did I need to go anywhere else?
I was a happy child, wasn't I? My sisters have often said I was. Then what
would explain my carefully hidden discontent? Perhaps it started when I

was six or seven, the age when to my horror I discovered, as if it were an unassailable conviction, that some day, inevitably, everything I was would be annihilated.

I'd started my life satisfied by my comparative solitude, the quiet late child in the family. As I grew older, however, in early puberty, I grew less confident in my little piece of the earth. In turn, my parents increasingly were impatient with me.

They insisted I make friends with the outside world or at least strongly encouraged me to seek companionship with the neighborhood's boys my age, Leslie, Bruce, Teddy, Cam, Eddie. To me it was as if I was being forced awake in the morning from a dream I'd wanted to keep dreaming. I had no desire to be part of reality. Quite the contrary. It was reality that would do its worst to me.

My older sisters had their own friends, of course, and by that time had started dating and staying out late and playing their records too loud. I counted the days until I was free of them and they happily on their own in some remote college. The curious fact of my life is that it begins and ends in solitude. What I clung to when young, however, now I would be freed from. It makes no sense.

I yielded to my parents' wishes. On rainy days, I encouraged my friends to play make believe with the clothes, sheets, curtains, draperies, furniture my parents had stored in the attic since they disliked throwing anything away. Swashbuckling pirates, feudal knights, cowboys on the range. The fantasies of small boys seem made much of the same old stories. Had we all read them somewhere, in the books we were given thought fit for small boys? Had all of our parents read to us from Sidney Lanier, Walter Scott, Robert Louis Stevenson, and Zane Grey? Or was it some manifestation of shared memories beyond our own experiences that we were performing, enacting to each other?

It worked for a while. We were buddies, friends, companions. All of early childhood is a kind of pretense, isn't it?, though one perhaps less strenuous and compulsive than that of adults. It was my father who first complained that I was too imaginative. My four friends got bored with me before I did with them. They'd already begun to think more practically, more realistically than I dared to. Experimenting with chemistry sets, looking through telescopes, tending to aquariums, constructing small buildings out of blocks, making birdhouses, fixing bikes or rollar skates or radios. Rules, laws, a sense of order. Whenever I did what they did, I felt left out. Not so much by them as by myself.

The day I left San Francisco for Stonefield I took only what I could pack in a small suitcase that would fit in a plane's overhead compartment. I didn't mean to stay. I barely knew what I was doing. No, that's wrong. I didn't know what I was doing at all or why I was doing it. Perhaps I was merely old and lonely enough to want to go home, whatever that strangely haunting phrase might mean. I felt I was watching a movie I was so involved in that the only way for me to understand it, the only way it could satisfactorily end, was for me to enter the screen, to be in the film, to step into it, to make it my reality as some movies have had their characters do.

I chose to fly into La Guardia since that, not Idlewild, was the airport we'd always flown out of and into when I was a boy with my family on a trip. After I'd walked out of the plane down the stairs that men in coveralls had rolled up to its door, I strolled through the corridors. They looked exactly like old times. The whole airport did. It was in fact the LaGuardia of my childhood. So be it, I thought. This old commonplace of the dying. The world of your youth restored and returned to you. The final comfort. The last dream you dream.

I hailed a taxi for Pennsylvania Station. It was still there, in its glory. It hadn't been torn down yet. I had often seen photographs, of course, of how it had been ruined, nearly reduced to rubble, no more than tracks and efficient, ugly ways in and out of the building. It had happened more than fifty years ago, a famous disaster of city planning at its worst.

But no. It was just the same, just as I'd remembered it at its best, the vast vaulting arches of the entranceway and the waiting rooms with the light pouring through the cathedral-like windows, the long lines and crowds at the busy ticket counters, the massive stairways, the marble and steel solidity of it, the temple-like enormity of it all, the mythic god-like power it seemed to embody in its imposing, classic beauty. It had been the most beautiful building I had ever seen and so it remained. It didn't seem strange to me. Why should the world have changed when it didn't have to? Somehow, somewhere, it had survived its ruination and let me in. Another tall tale I was familiar with and simply accepted with a shrug.

I was pleased of course, even happy about it, but I didn't believe it for a moment. It was as if, having been given his vision in the olive grove at Colonus, Oedipus turned away, dismissing it, thinking no better of the gods than he had before. Yet nonetheless he'd enjoyed it while it lasted. At least it was better than being completely blind.

The trip on the train was as slow a grind as it had always been. Yet once I was through the crowded, overbuilt northeast Jersey that amounted to greater New York, it was lovely, every town's name taking me back, nearer, closer to wherever it was I was really bound for since 'Stonefield' was only a temporary substitute name for it.

It stopped in Cranford, Garwood, Westfield, Plainfield, Middlesex, Bridgewater, Raritan. When the train approached Stonefield, I flattened my face against the window as I would as a kid, always delighted by the sights I could see as it rolled into the station. I liked to pretend the town was endlessly new to me, as if I had never seen it before. I liked to believe it had been transformed by my having been away even if was only for a day trip to Manhattan with my mother and sisters or a lunch with my father freed for an hour from his law firm.

I read out loud, though under my breath, the town's stores' old families' names painted on their windows or awnings, the sign over the deli my parents liked to go to on Sunday evenings to buy food for our supper that night and watched as the train crept past the large expanse of the always meticulously cut and trimmed grass and the four story high flagpole outside Evergreen Elementary School. The station was only three blocks away from it. My favorite childhood excursion from school work was a trip we took in the third grade to Westfield and back on the train. A train is the best way for children to travel. Who among the young today understands that? The lure of trains?

Our house, the house of my childhood, sat close to the main entrance to the town's park, with its two creeks and hundreds of weeping willows and acres of well-mowed grass and the old groves of Dutch elms, poplars, and sycamore where I liked to play hour after hour, alone and safe from time, I'd hoped, as if I could live there forever, a child spared other people, dwelling solely among the squirrels and chipmunks and thousands of songbirds.

In the winter, I would sometimes sit in our sunroom, the light in it white from the reflection on the snow outside, and long for spring despite the fact that the cold brought sleigh rides and ice thick and smooth enough to skate on over the town's narrow streets and snowboard runs down Cranston Hill. Who wouldn't want to stay a child in such a place? In school, at home, I was being taught to think.

I didn't want to be forced to think. All I was, all I felt myself to be, was what the weather made me. The season didn't really matter to me. I wanted to be, in myself, by myself whatever the day's climate determined I was, the morning's light, the sunset, a moonless dark, snow or rain, the air pleasant or cold or hot. You must trust me. It didn't matter. I didn't want to have to choose. I don't mean this was happiness. But it was a kind of joy.

When I told the cab driver the address to our old house, I had the odd, if only momentary sensation that I was asking him to take me to a destination that no longer existed. Was I losing my conviction? As we arrived there ten minutes later, however, I was surprised how it looked to be exactly the same, the gray shingles, the gables, the dormer windows, the shutters painted green against the white wood siding, the stone walls, the two large pin oaks in the front yard, the boxwood lined sidewalk that led to the front door with its lead panes intact, the glass slightly distorting, and the brass knob, freshly polished.

I rang the bell. The sound of it hadn't changed either, more like chimes than a bell or buzzer. A small boy answered, carefully opening the door, half hiding behind it as he took a cautious look at me.

"Grandpa," he squealed. "Mother," he shouted into the house. "It's Grandpa."

The boy startled me, so closely did he resemble me at his age as I know from the photographs I still have and occasionally look at with the strange sensation of their being pictures of some other boy entirely, a stranger I might have wanted to have as a friend when I was his age.

Mother didn't come. Perhaps she was out back, watering some flowers in the planters. The boy called her again.

"May I come in?" I said. "I used to live here. Long ago. Sixty years ago. I'm not your grandfather, you know. You don't know me. I promise I'm harmless. I just want a quick look around and then I'll be on my way." On my way where?

"Grandpa. Grandpa," the boy insisted. He opened the door wider to let me in. I didn't feel like disagreeing any further. Perhaps he was right.

"What's your name?" I said, following him into the living room.

"David," he said, then asked with well-trained politeness, "Would you like a glass of water?"

Of course it was David. What is more unfamiliar to you than your own past? It takes a while to become accustomed to it, like a distant land whose people act and think very differently from what you are used to. The trip had made me thirsty. "Yes, I would," I said. "Very much, thank you. My name's David, too."

The boy frowned. "You think I don't know that? Grandpa David. My grandpa David. That's why I am David Elliston the Second, after you, right, Grandpa? I could offer you a ginger ale instead of water. Would you prefer a ginger ale? Or a beer? You always like your beer in a small glass, with the foam on it just so, Father says."

"Water's fine," I said. It is perhaps not so strange how unsurprised some children are at the return of the dead. Grandpa Elliston died when I was five. The David I was looking at was at least twelve. My youth was haunted by my family's dying. Both grandfathers. Both grandmothers. An aunt. All before I was ten.

David re-entered the living room from the kitchen with a glass sweating from the cold drink inside. He'd added some ice. I took a sip. It was pleasantly cooling and refreshing. "Are you here alone this morning, David?"

He shook his head. "I don't think so." He took a deep breath. "It's hard to know sometimes."

"Yes. It is. Your sisters must be out. It's quiet."

"They were at a slumber party last night at Sally Keating's. They won't be home till this afternoon. I was just going to the park. Would you like to go to the park with me? It's not very far. But you know that. You used to walk me there in a perambulator. That's what Mother calls it when she shows me the photo of you in your overcoat that touches the tops of your shoes and me in my knit cap and sweater coat sitting in it with a big grin on my face. A perambulator is a baby buggy." It was clearly a word that it pleased him to say. "Do you remember that day the picture was taken, Grandpa?"

"Of course I do, David," I lied. "I'd very much like to go to the park with you," I said quickly to cover it. "But shouldn't you ask your mother first?"

"She already knows. I told her earlier I was going to the park for a while."

"I mean about me. That you'll be with me. I don't want her to worry."

"She wouldn't worry more than she always worries," David said. He stood up and grabbed my hand. "Let's go. It's best in the morning before it gets too warm, though I like it then, too. It's good you came early."

The park was in full bloom. The park is in full bloom. I'm not sure which it is. I suppose I've (or I'd?) lost control of tenses and must settle on this one or that one at times just for convention's sake.

The smell of pink and white wild roses tickled his nose. My nose, too. There was a woody smell in the air, like wet logs set out to dry in the sun. The hedges' leaves shone dark green on top, pale jade underneath. Heavy with dew, the oak and willows dripped into the creek as if after a hard rain. The boy knelt to play there, to dig in its sandy bottom. Black beetles, ants, a few white grubs and milky caterpillars, red worms crawled or squirmed over rocks or slithered through the grass. A spider had knit its web among ferns that, shimmering, glinted in a shaft of sun. Wild ivy threaded in and out of brush whose gnarly stems meshed together like woven lace.

All, all was how I had remembered it. Imagined it. Thought it up. Written it.

With his small shovel, the boy dug out jagged pebbles and round slick stones that he carefully laid into his bucket. Treasures to prize. He removed his shoes and socks and waded into the creek that trickled around his ankles. It was a windless morning. It is a windless morning. And so it goes.

A few skaters zigzagged on the surface of the water or silently glided on the stream, leaving no ripples behind it in its steady movement. Threads of cloud broke apart, fragmenting into white wisps of nothing, like specks of ash, and blew away. I tugged on a patch of Queen Anne's lace and sniffed my palms. David. Davids. Me and him. A few dogs were running in the meadow, their owners throwing balls or sticks for them to chase. They might have been mine. Once upon a time. One stayed. The other my mother made me give away.

What you love first is never done with you. "I found a quarter in here once and later a fifty cents piece," the boy bragged. "I also found a stone that looked like it had flecks of gold in it. And four or five marbles. And a pair of rusted scissors."

I nodded. I knew. "Do you come here with your friends? To play tag or hide and seek. To toss a ball around. I used to, I think. I wish I could be sure."

"That's kid's stuff." He frowned his brow, looking thoughtful and five years older. "Not much. Sometimes with Leslie. Sometimes Bruce or Teddy. Mostly, we do other things now." He shrugged as if he didn't care. "Go to the movies. Watch TV. Play board games. Monopoly. Clue. Going to the theater with mother is more fun, though. I guess I'm friends with those guys still. I did a bad thing last year. I hit Eddie on the head with a hunk of slate I'd picked up off the path. He'd made me mad and I picked up a piece of slate and threw it at him. I hit his head hard. It gave him a concussion. I didn't mean to. I have a temper, my father says. I was born mad, he says. He says if I don't repair my anger I will end up bitter or in jail. I visited Eddie when he was home in bed. His father's a preacher. I got forgiven. But it's not been the same between him and me. I don't expect it ever will be. Between me and any of them really. It changed stuff." He looked away from me, glancing up the trunk of a willow. "I guess I know why."

"How did he make you mad? What did Eddie do? Or say, David?"

"I don't know. I can't remember."

He remembers. But doesn't want to.

He stomped out of the creek, dried his feet off as best he could in a patch of dry grass, put his socks and shoes back on, and grabbed his jacket. "Let's walk on the path for a while. There's a nice bench to sit on near the duck pond. You might want to rest. There's a pair of swans that swim in it, too."

Yes. I do want to rest. And, yes, there's a nice bench to sit on near the duck pond. And two swans. The scandal was that both were male. I recall when it broke. I lead the way. I led the way. No more of that. David's mood changed as we walked. "I don't like to go there on this path," he says. "Let's go back around the other one by the rose garden."

"What's wrong with this way?"

"Nothing. I just don't like it."

But it was too late for us to change directions. Four older boys and a girl, all in their middle or late teens, at least four or five years older than he was, were walking out of the door to the public pool, a stolid white washed brick building with a pitched, half glass roof in the summer, windows in it that could be opened to let in air. I could whiff the smell of chlorine. The tallest saw David first.

"Hey, Davey, little boy Davey," he said, giving a lilt to his voice that meant to mock him. "Such a sweetie pie, don't you agree, guys?"

"Don't," David says. "Please. Don't you see? I'm with my grandfather. Don't embarrass me. Not in front of him. Please, guys."

"You are, are you?" the tall one said. He checked around him, pretending to look. "I don't see him. Do you see anyone, Kenny? Alice? See any old man dragging his shoes around here?"

"Nope," the others say, shaking their heads.

"But I see you, Davey" the tall one said. "I see you staring at me in the shower. Spying on me. I see you sneaking in there for a peek at my cock, you little perv. Every morning since school's been out. At Kenny's and Dirk's too. Davey's a perv, isn't he, Alice?"

"Leave him alone," she said. "He's still just a kid, tall for his age. Curious, you know?"

"Yeah, a very curious kid," the tall one said. "You like me, don't you, kid?" he said, tickling his face with the tips of his fingers.

"Stop it, Curt," Alice said.

"Davey, Davey," the skinniest one said, looking for approval from the biggest of them, their leader, the big shot among them, the head of the pack.

Animals, I want to say. Criminals. Trash. But I'm afraid of what they might do to me if I actually say what I'm thinking.

"Hand me your lipstick," the tall one orders his girlfriend.

"What for?"

"You'll see." She dug in her purse and gave it to him.

Opening it, he twisted the stick higher. "Grab his head by his ears, Dirk," he says. "All of a sudden it's going to be Halloween five months early, Davey boy."

Dirk held David from behind while Curt painted David's lips a smeared scarlet red. When he'd done, David shook free from Dirk's grip and spat at him. Curt swatted his cheek, threw him on the ground, and with the lipstick printed FAG across David's forehead. "Serves him right, the little perv," he said as the five of them turned around as one to leave by the steps that led up to the street. They ran off, laughing.

Fear. Fatality. It begins on a June day, late in the morning, its light like sunset's fading, darkening, as if we were living in some land far north where in winter the sun barely rises before it sets.

I am helpless. I try to wipe all the lipstick off with my handkerchief, but none of it rubs away. David is crying. He starts to run, too. So young, he is much faster than I am. I lose him by the entrance to the park. I've lost him by the entrance to the park. I can't remember the right way out.

When I reached the house, I was nearly breathless. I am too old for this. I've always been too old, the years too late, for this. The door was ajar. I walked uninvited into the living room and up the stairs to his room. Sitting beside him where he lay in bed, his mother was washing his face with a cloth she dipped into a bowl of warm, soapy water she's resting in her lap. After she'd squeezed the cloth several times, the water turned bloody. His face was nearly clean, almost free of a lipstick called Viva Glam, but ruddy from so much scrubbing.

"Who did this to you, David?"

He shakes his head. "I don't know."

"You must. You must know."

"But I don't. Older boys."

"You've seen them before? They've done mean things to you before?"

"No."

"You're lying to me, David. I've heard you crying sometimes when you come home. You think I don't know what it means to feel hurt? But never mind. It's over, I hope. And it isn't true. What they wrote on your forehead. It isn't true. You must know that. You must forget that word. Promise me you'll forget all about it, David. It's just boys being cruel. It doesn't mean anything. People act ugly sometimes. Often are ugly even. But we can't let it damage us, can we? We mustn't. You just need to keep your distance from them. If you see them again, come straight home. Tell me. You understand? All right, David?"

She stood up, her back rigid, her face composed and firm, and held the bowl and washcloth against her hip. "All right," he says.

"Try to sleep awhile if you can. It's still not much past noon. Your father won't be home for another six hours. We'll have forgotten all about this by then, won't we, David? Not another word about it, especially not to him. You mustn't disappoint him, David. Not ever. Mum's the word."

"Yes, Mother. I promise."

I am sitting in my old favorite chair, the swivel chair at my desk, but she didn't see me. She turned her back toward him and with her free hand picked up Jerry Mahoney from where he sat propped next to an inkwell and pens. "And David. I think it would be better if you didn't play with this doll anymore. Let's put it in the attic."

"It's not a doll, Mother," David protests. "It's a ventriloquist's dummy. I'm practicing a show with him."

"You're still sleeping with it by your side, David. You're too old for that now. And all those pandas and bears in your bed. You mustn't anymore. You're practically a teenager. Up in the attic with them. In the chest with your other childhood toys. They're annoying your father. It's time to grow up, David. Watch what you do. Watch how you behave. You'll be thirteen soon, Son. It's time to start acting like it."

"Don't worry, Mother," he said as she began to leave his room. "I will. I promise you I will. I'll be good."

"I know you will be, Sweetie," she said, blowing him a kiss before gently closing the door behind her.

He slept until nearly one. I should feel hungry. I have eaten too little. It's been a long trip, but I have never felt hungry once during it. Now I am home. What he's supposed to be forgetting I'm remembering too well. I don't want to. Not this vividly. Not this clearly.

When he woke up, he said, as if startled to see me, "Grandpa."

Grandpa's dead. Grandpa's been dead for five years. For sixty-five years. No, longer. How I yearned to see him again. I loved him, love him the most of all my family. A man who would tear up, really cry whenever he passed a beggar on the streets of New York and give him a dollar bill. Who worshipped Stokowski, especially his Bach. Whose businesses failed twice. Who gave up. Who was kind. Who saw the world so far as I could tell not for what it was but as he wanted it to be. A fantasist, like me, like David. All Davids.

"Have you been dreaming, David?"

"I don't think so. I don't remember them if I did. I usually do. I need to dress now. Please turn your back to me." I did as he asked. I always still do as he asks. "All right," he said. "I've got my pants on." He buckled his belt and buttoned his shirt.

I offered him my hand, but he rejected it. "Where to next?" I said.

"Not outside. The sunroom, I think," he said.

The boxwood has grown no higher than it was when I was a boy. Father kept it neatly trimmed so that the light into the sunroom wouldn't be impeded, no shadows allowed in it during the day. A cheery room, especially in winter when the sun was shining off the snow and a fire burned in the fireplace. It is was almost always as bright there as it was outside, and, in storms, when rain or snow pounded the windows, it felt like the safest place in the house, in the world, because you could see how clearly, how completely it protected you, kept every torrent at bay.

"Look," David said, standing up on the couch and pointing out the window. "There he is, practicing on his crutches on their sidewalk again. He looks so, what's the word, graceful doing it, don't you think? It looks difficult to me. I'd be afraid of falling."

"Who?" I said, trying to see through the trees that lined the street in a well planned, too strict order, four to a house along the sidewalk, more on the lawns. The Hemmings' was down Crestview Road, the house on the southeast corner.

He stared at me as if I were stupid. "Tim Hemmings, of course, Bruce's older brother. He was in the war. A hero, too. Wounded by the Japanese. Bruce told me the doctors found more shrapnel they'd had to cut out a couple of weeks ago. He's had six surgeries. Isn't he beautiful, Grandpa? I wait for him here when it's sunny. I can wait for hours sometimes. Just a few days ago, Father came running in to scold me.   He'd heard a loud noise. He thought I'd been jumping off the couch. But it was that explosion we heard all the way from Perth Amboy. We learned about it on the radio. Isn't that strange? Don't you remember? It was in all the papers. Father thought it was me, being unruly and disobedient. At least he didn't catch me spying. On Tim, I mean. That would have been awful."

I do remember. The bang. The crash of it. The photos of the Perth Amboy blast site in the papers the next day. "Best not use the word 'beautiful' like that, David," I said. "Not for men. Not yet."

When then?

"But he is. He is."

I can see him again, racing up and down the sidewalk to the Hemmings' front door as if he weren't supported by anything, as if he wasn't using two crutches that, in his speed, were like wings. He was flying on them. My first crush. The most beautiful boy, lanky and tall, dark hair, blue eyes, a boyish, sly smile like a Caravaggio cherub's. Who knows what became of him, of any of them, Bruce his brother, Leslie, Eddie, Teddy, Mike, the others. If I had stayed, would any of them have loved me? Saved me from my solitude, the secrets I hid, that imprisoned me?

"You like Bruce, don't you? He's your friend, isn't he?"

"Sure."

"Then don't tell him you think his brother is beautiful, David. Just don't."

But I had used it, had said the word in the way I was warned not to by something inside me that cautioned me it was wrong. Dangerous. Fatal. It was too late now. It is eternally too late. I'd told Bruce. I told Tim, too. You're beautiful, I said to him, guilelessly. And so that ended too, how it had done so I'd almost forgotten, hidden as most endings have been for me in a shame too vague for me to understand or perceive where it had come from. I'd shudder at the thought of it and put it out of my mind. There is no tragedy without shame I learned in college.

You are shameless, a boyfriend said to me once. And I responded, I hope so.

Such nonsense.

I was watching, I am watching Tim on his crutches, moving back and forth on the sidewalk. And he is beautiful. His pain and his grace are beautiful. The wounded soul in him is beautiful.

It was then, that moment, that day, after I'd been painted and smeared and ostracized with lipstick, as I sat in the sun room gazing out the window at Timothy Hemmings practicing on his crutches, it was that exact moment, it is of course always that precise moment, still as it is, silent as it is, that I first knew who I was. Who I am. Who I will be, thank God, to my dying day. Who I want to be forever.

I long to go home, I tell myself, back to my final solitude, back to San Francisco.

"I have a train to catch soon, David," I said. "It leaves at three. Would you like to go with me? I'll leave a note for your mother. What do you say? One more excursion we might share today before the trip back on your own will bring you home, safe and sound to your parents' loving arms. Wouldn't that be exciting?" I meant no irony.

My family's buried in Bayview Cemetery. David's agreed to go with me. I don't mind dying, I hear my aunt say, it's the pain I despise. For me it's been fifty-five years since I was last here. For David it is new. Children his age didn't go to funerals then. His first, for his aunt, will occur when he's fifteen. Call this the future, then, despite the fact that a graveyard, no matter how large or small it is, is a place dedicated and sacred to the past.

Memory, that violent word, that can't suffice for the days, the promise of plenty, of relief, of peace that it denies. The calm he'll see in his aunt's eyes, her unsurprise at the end. Ghosts of people they loved invading everyone's nights. Mutti stirring her stew, daring the men in her kitchen to punch her stomach, who never wore a girdle or lost a strand of her amber hair to gray. Grandmother Louise, bosomy, zaftig, fast wasting away, telling stories of her years nursing the sick and dying, smiling, assured of heaven ahead, giving to her grandson a thin gold ring. The Danish grandfather he never knew, doctor, Hoboken dock worker, union organizer, who as a boy read about Lincoln's assassination in a Copenhagen newspaper.

Our dead, his and mine, rest together on a hill low enough to shudder from Atlantic blows. Soon I'll be mingled with their ashes, their bones. Though my dead talk, they never tell me what I need to know. If resurrection were true, it's Bayview where they'd leap from their crypts. I'm left only guesses, looking toward the harbor where ferries crisscross the river.

One is carrying my mother from her home in Hoboken to audit classes her soon-to-be-husband is taking at NYU. Her fiancé doesn't care that she's smarter or inches taller. Gripping the rail, she stares at the white water behind the boat.

The waves travel in a bobbing V, like the geese she'd seen beat their wings against gray clouds the previous spring to disappear like a dot, a period, fading into the sky. Stirred into life by the ferry, dissolved into the river's gray, the waves flow on and on. They both lie here too, husband and wife, father and mother. Mine.

David's getting restless, eager to go back home. Below us, across the harbor, an ocean liner is departing its dock. Tug boats and barges make way. I try to see them with David's eyes as I take his arm. He has memories too. He's crossing the Hudson again for the first time with his grandfather, the wind so briny it makes him cry. On the other side, a revival of Snow White awaits, a meal at Luchow's, a day on the town, his first without his parents by his side.

David, here I am beside you, wearing a black bowler hat and a great coat that droops to my ankles. My gloved fingers are tight, yet won't release your hand, gripping it harder. As a choppy high surf pounds the side of the ferry, as the whole boat pivots and rocks, though I slip and nearly fall, through all these absent years, no matter what role I play in my dreams, not once do I let you go, David, the grandchild of my old age, my only son, myself.

It was late when he arrived back home. His mother was understandably worried, his father angry. David explained he'd been at Teddy Fulton's. He'd been invited for dinner. Then they watched Milton Berle on TV. "Then why didn't you call?" his father boomed.

"I'm sorry," David said. "I should have."

"Apologies, apologies," his father said and sighed. "They're too easy, David. It's much too easy to say I'm sorry. No lawyer can, you know," he said as he paced on a Persian rug he'd inherited from a beloved cousin.

"Bedtime," his mother said. "For us all."

"Yes," David agreed.

"All right, all right," his father said. "But next time, remember."

For the first and last time, I suppose, I share his bed beside him. I promise him I do not snore and, though old, can sleep through a night without needing the bathroom more than once. He knows I'll be leaving in the morning. I'm returning to my city, I tell him, not Manhattan but the other one, the San Francisco he's yet to imagine or dream about. He knows, in fact, I've already gone.

Do we dream the same dream?

After a snake has slithered away from the rocks and stones we are tossing at it, chasing it back into the creek, shouting at it, Snake, snake, we both wander deeper into the woods on the western flanks of the Watchung Mountains, an easy drive from Stonefield. Resin has bled from the bark of a tree, forming phlegm colored clots we pick at, sniff and chew. High over our heads, its needles and the leaves of oak, sycamore, poplar, and elm allow only a soft light to seep through onto the bank of a stream where we kneel to drink.

Whacking a stick at the caterpillar tents, at the webs tangled in the vines, we trip over a knotted, gnarled root. We've cut our hand again and use a handkerchief we carry in a back pocket for a bandage. No one will ask why we have stayed away so long from home. We're free to roam.

In the densest part of the forest, we're alone except for the trees and wild flowers growing freely where the grass grows tall as weeds. A late spring mist is rolling in, heavy and low, the trees dripping as if it's just rained. Decaying leaves carpet the ground of what trail there is left, slick and easy to slip on. We grab onto an old oak's trunk, thicker than our two bodies bound together, and embrace it. Its sweet, dank, sharp sap, pungent as myrrh, sticks, clings to our skin. Dear earth. Dear life. How can we bear to leave it?

He's getting older and older and I younger and younger until we become one person, as we always were, as we always are, lost together in woods, wanting to go home, not sure of the way, anxiously following tracks and traces back until reaching a trailhead and the long way down toward home.

As the sun starts to warm my body through a dormer window, I wake up and begin to prepare to leave. The boy I was, the boy I am, takes my hand, squeezing it tighter, and pleads as he shakes it, "Don't lose me. Please don't forget me."

"I have to get back. I don't belong here. I'm sorry if I've intruded. Spoiled anything."

"David," he says.

Is it despair or hope I hear in his voice, my voice?

There's some lipstick left on his forehead his mother missed. I lick my fingers and tenderly rub it off as best I can. Only one small smear remains. Not Viva Glam, but Sunset Red.

The Not Done

You saw these things. I could not
watch how each ended. Reeling
like a drunk. Bleeding from his asshole.
Purple spotted. Emaciated. Blind.
Thirty years gone. The whole lot
of them gone. Our friends. Everything
we were. Would be. Stol-
en. We two left behind.
You good. Who brought food.
Who nursed. Who cared for
all. Not I. Oh, solitude,
now absolute. You stand
outside, waiting by the door
for me, offering your kind hand.

The Schlieffen Plan

An early May night in Manhattan, breezes gently flowing off the river, the park sweetly fragrant as if spring were still in its freshest first flourishing. They walk slowly back to Derek's apartment on the Upper West Side from the Met where they'd heard a stirringly old-fashioned performance of Lohengrin. Afterward, Derek complained that it was interminable and its story ridiculous. Did he really find it so absurd or, as James believed was more likely, had he hoped to incite a strongly worded reply from him? Any reaction might do so long as it was heartfelt enough, wasn't that true? A moment of passion. Of intense feeling, the kind couples need to survive on.

So James had waved his arms like a drunken conductor, praising tenor, soprano, mezzo, baritone, chorus, conductor, opera, all. "It's not a silly plot," he'd said. "It's deep. It's about faith, Derek. About how necessary and impossible it is. Absolute faith. No questions asked. The prelude to the first act alone tells you more about what spirituality means than the whole stupid bible." It was a good answer, Derek said, but not the one he'd wanted to hear. Which was what? James couldn't or at least didn't say any more.

The streets are filled with their usual late Saturday racket, the cacophony of New York that Derek enjoys for the randomness of it, the seeming freedom of the noisy bustle, though it sometimes drives James wild with rage, mock or not, truly felt or a show. He misses their boyhood, what they shared then, the quiet, the particular hush of Sunday mornings, the silence of woods, of cypress swamps, and the drained rice fields where they'd hike together.

They'd grown up in a small South Carolina low country town, not neighbors, they'd lived in opposite worlds, but classmates. Together they'd escaped to colleges and law schools in the North, one on scholarships, the other not, and never looked back, both finding jobs in the city at nearly the same time, employed by midtown firms. They returned to their childhood homes only on holidays. "Just friends," they'd answer to any questions which were fortunately rare and never from family. In fact they were lovers sometimes and sometimes not, depending on the weather, atmospheric conditions, and where their moods led them from day to day.

"Fuck buddies," a few friends called them. But it was more than that. It always had been more and still is. Thunderstorms back home had provided a good instigation or long rainy days or hot ones when they'd sit side by side, legs dangling in the water, at the edge of the public pool. It isn't quite like that in Manhattan. Yet a night like this one, after the opera, is reason enough to have sex. Or make love.

Their love-making had started in adolescence, lapsed when they were in college, James at Williams, Derek at Bowdoin, revived off and on during law school, was resurrected when they were able to find work in the city in offices only three blocks apart. It had survived their various and many infidelities, but to both never felt permanent, never like something they could count on forever, neither knew why. Or at least neither would say. They resisted labels, distrusted words, their own most of all. Deep or shallow, profound or merely pleasurable, passionate or merely an easy release of tension, how could they tell the difference between one and the other twenty years into whatever it was that had brought them together more often than it had driven them apart. They were used to each other, above all to each other's bodies. That was a large part of the joy and much of the trouble.

Despite the city's nocturnal brilliance, the bustle on the sidewalks, the raucous noises on the streets—tires screeching, horns honking, cabbies hollering at them as they recklessly jaywalk across Eighty-Sixth on their way to Derek's apartment—despite the random sounds, shrieks, cries, boisterous laughter that appear to stream straight for heaven like the city's intensest lights, despite the constant urban dissonance around them, high over their heads the sky looks almost silent, still, the few stars they could see seemingly fixed, unmoving, as if they'd been painted on a matte backdrop.

Gazing up, Derek senses, he says to James, a vast peace waiting for him, maybe for them, somewhere behind the night sky. Like the enormous stage of the Met, he explains, after the show was over and nearly all the audience had left the theater. He'd stared back at the curtain, thinking of the darkness and emptiness now behind it apart from the workmen breaking down the set to cart it to storage and fetch in the next day's show, Lohengrin to be replaced by Don Pasquale. He could hear nothing, not even shoes moving on the floor or the shifting of flats, but he knew what was happening, and it both scared and elated him, the invisible activity he knew was occurring though he couldn't see it, one world replacing another, utterly different.

A hope not altogether unlike fear that he'd long felt for the future was similar to what he swears he's just seen, or sensed, as he'd gazed up at the sky a moment before. As if it had been divided into two parts like the sea, the surface you swam on and the fathomless deep where if you'd stayed just a moment too long you'd die, drawn down by the currents or a riptide. He couldn't know to which he belonged, could he?, even if he'd had a choice. Below the surface danger lurked as it did behind the sky. So be it. God might be like that. The darkness of impossibility. The peace of meaninglessness. The awe of uncertainty before which one bows without hoping or even wanting to know what, if anything, it might mean.

He wants desperately to explain what he's just seen to James better than he can. He wishes he could tell James many things he's unable to say clearly because sometimes it, being alive, seems so simple to him, what they are to each other, all the important ways they'd been a couple without definitions over the years. Why need it mean anything? It simply was what it was, and is, like all beautiful things. Let it thrive as it was, as it is, as perhaps, in the goodness of time, it will be until the end of their lives.

But James always insists on depth. On something deeper he wants, longs for between them he couldn't explain either, couldn't say precisely what it was. Some hugeness he misses. Their love making, he'd said a few times, was like that between two people from different countries who'd never been able to learn the other's language. Bodies making love, aroused by desire, using a kind of sign language as they struggle to speak, to communicate, to say out of their need what they believe in. Derek didn't feel that way at all. It was love making. It was fun. It was often enough joyous. What more should one expect? Or want?

These differences they have long known about each other. Occasionally they talk about them, sometimes even discuss them. Or they rest content that they speak about them indirectly, silently or aloud, in the unsaid as much as the said, in disagreements they often express only bodily, perhaps sitting side by side as tonight while they listened to Lohengrin.

As they nearly always do, they walk up the narrow three flights of stairs to Derek's flat not side by side, but with Derek's following James one step at a time. The metaphor was too obvious to him to bother exploring. Or for him to challenge, for that matter. He'd always let James lead him, acknowledging James was ahead of him in almost every way. He always had been and always would be. Smarter, better looking, if not rich, then certainly comfortable as James' parents would say, stating a fact, not bragging. It was just his way, who James was, bold and smart always and slightly unhappy much of the time. While Derek was reticent and just smart enough to do the job, whatever it was, and largely content, day after day.

They were different. Everyone saw that. But their differences were pointless, nothing worth thinking about or pursuing or letting get in the way. Top, bottom, why should it mean anything more than the pleasure it gave? And gives, as it will tonight. Each enjoyed playing the other's part. They liked to switch, might even trade faces, their dicks, their entire bodies if they could.

After all, hadn't they shared the savage innocence of their boyhood's grappling with and groping for each other, their seemingly insatiable desires, their inescapable need for keeping their secret safe from others as if it were an unbreakable, eternal bond between them, the unspeakable fact that had kept them together throughout their younger, rougher years? As it did so still in a way, though they no longer had any desire or need for secrecy. Their present was inextricably tied to their past, all they'd experienced together, just them and no one else. It had made them in unnameable ways almost the same, the same and yet different, the incomplete knot that tied them together.

If they were together. If they were truly lovers despite their occasional wanderings. Neither could be sure from the start. They hadn't been certain for twenty years.   Neither is sure now. The word 'love' rarely arose between them. Yet 'lovers' is also a word they sometimes use about themselves when they're asked what they relationship is, maybe because some of their friends assume lovers is what they are, even their not so occasional tricks. It doesn't seem to count to those that think so that they have always lived in a place of their own. They were together a lot but also made lives alone.

Lovers. Boyfriends. Fuck buddies. It's James who needs to know what these words mean.   Derek doesn't care what language they use to describe themselves. He has James, James has him. They'd recently celebrated their two decades with an expensive dinner and a show it was hard to get tickets for, just the two of them, through the night holding hands as they had done, off and on, during tonight's Lohengrin. Of course they must know who, together, they are.

Derek had left a light on in the living room. He always keeps a light on whenever he goes out because he likes to return at night to a bright home, a lamp or two shining though a window. James is the opposite. Many times, using his key, Derek has discovered him sitting pensively, meditatively in a pitch black room. Such darkness, in a sense such deliberate obscurity, troubles Derek. It's like James' occasional fits of unhappiness, his bouts with depression. Whenever it happens, it feels to Derek like a waste of precious time.

When they were boys, looking for safe places to go, to hide in, Derek would seldom let James lead him. James was too fond of the woods behind his house at night, woods familiar to him but scary to Derek, afraid of getting lost, of what the dark might make him do or say or be. No wonder James loved Wagner more than any other composer, Tristan most of all. Or was it Parsifal? What did it matter which? Derek disliked both. Sex isn't death. Sex isn't a wound. It couldn't be and be so much fun, so exhilarating. And James was good at it. They both are good at it even when it hurts.

James uses his own keys, the ones Derek gave him when he first moved in, to unlock the two lock door. Derek doesn't yet know if James intends to spend the night or, if he does, when he should, in respect for James's preference for sex in the dark, turn the lights in the living room off and suggest they move into the bedroom, the room with the best view when the curtains were opened and the shades pulled up. James always draws them closed. Derek would rather see out. A useless struggle neither's resolved.

He pours them both a brandy. They'd learned to drink in college, but had been taught differently by different masters and developed different tastes. Derek loves the ritual of drinking more than the stuff itself, whatever the wine or liquor, while James occasionally drinks to get blind drunk. In bars, Derek would sip his scotch on the rocks and could make it last half the evening as he speculated happily, detachedly on the frenzy around him as if it were, after all, little more than a bit of inept improvisatory theater he was watching while James would strip off his shirt, exposing more skin, roll down his briefs to reveal the start of his thick black pubes, and, dancing with whoever would ask him, immerse himself in the madness and riot. He liked the mindlessness, he'd said, the freedom. Derek would smile and remain seated, watching and waiting for him to become exhausted enough so they both could go home and sleep in the same bed. Sex would often have to wait until morning, just before dawn the best time of all, half light, the night not yet over, the day just beginning. A compromise, in a way.

A snifter in each right hand, they sit next to each other on Derek's office-size leather couch, their legs stretching out, almost touching, their feet resting on the theater and art magazines laid out for display on Derek's marble top coffee table. "Should I put on some music?" Derek asks. "Or are you satiated by all that loud, endless Wagner?"

"You joke," James says.

"Not quite."

James finishes his brandy, drinking it too fast, not observing as Derek does the rules of its enjoyment, the etiquette for just about everything he'd had to learn almost too late by watching his classmates in college. Thereafter he strictly attended to the rules they'd taught him. Life proved to be easier to live that way. Orderly. Formal.

"No more music, please," James pleads. "Not after the wonders we've just listened to."

Derek ignores him and explores his CD case for the exact one he's looking for, removes it from its jewel case, and slips it into his player. "An antidote," he says turning the volume up a little. "Sorry, but I need one."

"Do you? For what toxin?" James slaps the cushion next to him. "Sit down. Stop fidgeting. I have some news I heard about just this afternoon."

Not exactly surprised by James' tone of authority, Derek does as he is told. "Good news or bad?"

"It depends."

"On what?"

"On you, I suppose." James reaches for a fancy, faux crystal bottle, pours his snifter half full, and tosses most of it down in one gulp.

"Do you know how much that stuff costs?" Derek says and laughs.

"Does it matter?"

"You make a lot more money than I do, James."

"I know. I'm sorry. I don't mean to, you know."

"You came from a better family. Had more much money back then, too. Servants. Mine barely made do. I got through college on grants and scholarships. Your father paid your way. I've never been sure how we became friends. We were so different. Are so different still. The color of our hair, our eyes, our features, our heights. The writers, the composers we most admire. How we see the world."

"Algebra."

"What?"

"You know what I mean. Don't look surprised, Derek. You weren't good at math. I was. You asked for my help. I gave it. Remember?" He rubs Derek's head with the back of his hand, runs his fingers through Derek's yellow hair. "I'm glad you asked for it. I'm glad you came to me for a little assistance. Here we are, more than twenty years later. Master, pupil. A tutorial, I called it."

"Pompously. Patronizingly."

James smiles back. "No doubt."

"You were my tutor in lots of things, James," Derek says. "Sex, too. What you don't know is that I was just using algebra as a ploy to get closer to you. I was actually a little wiz at math. If I hadn't come up with that trick I would have found another reason for you to spend time with me." Derek reaches for James' hand. "What about me turned you on, James? What about me attracted you? Why did you suggest that first movie date? I've asked you a hundred times or more and you never will say. Why not?"

"I don't think I used the word 'date,' Derek."

"Nevertheless, that's what it was, wasn't it?"

"Did you know any other gay boys back home?"

"Nope. Not a one. There must have been some more, don't you think?"

"I guess. Of course. The town wasn't that small. But all I knew were you and me. Reason enough, I'd think, for us two to hook up."

"That's almost cruel, James. Was I that obviously an available, easy catch? Get your rocks off with Derek? Why tell me that now?"

"Sorry. I was kidding, trying to rile you by playing casual as you do with me some times, Derek. I shouldn't have. I think maybe what I saw in you was a wound I was vain or young enough to think I could heal. A pain in you you still won't admit to. And, no, you weren't that obvious. You would never have been as popular as you were if you had been. Neither of us would have. I liked your grin, the way your eyes would light up sometimes, your nearly perfect nose and chin, the way you'd sometimes get a semi-hard on in the showers after gym and try to hide it with your hands or by turning your back to all the other boys even while or maybe because you knew I was looking at you."

"As I'm hiding a full woody now. Are you going to spend the night, James?"

He squeezes Derek's hand back. "Probably."

"Good."

"What is this we've been listening to? I don't like it."

"The Saint-Saens Fourth Piano Concerto. Second movement," Derek says even as his expression reveals that he doubts James is really listening to it. "Do you remember out first trip to Savannah?"

"Certainly. How could I not recall almost every second of it as wonderful and strange as it was, Derek, unforgettable. The seamy motel room where we spent our first full night together. Our first encounters with other gay boys. And men. Our first gay bar. That ante-bellum home Niles Schuyler lived in like a spider in her fully spun, sticky web. Everything he owned was meant to proclaim how marvelous he and his possessions were, the tapestries, the crystal, the old family portraits, the gilt frames, the silverware, the lace curtains. I don't know why you didn't turn out to be a decorator, Derek. It seemed to me you had the taste of one early on. Or maybe, I thought at the time, your admiration for all that crap was mostly just wrong side of the tracks envy."

"I don't deserve that, Jimmy."

"No, you don't. I could be a shit back then. I agree. All I wanted to do was get out of there, out of that crazy queen's mansion. I was certain old Niles had some kind of dungeon he'd built in his basement for naive, pretty boys like us."

"Maybe he did. You knew that world better than I did in those days. Still do, don't you, despite all your animosity toward it. You've informed yourself, Jimmy, along the way."

"I suppose. You're too trusting of rich people, Derek."

"Not anymore. But you're right. It was merely envy I was feeling, I reckon. I wanted to be rich more than anything when I was a teenager. Thank god I'm rid of that obsession now. We made our escape. We knew not to stay. We got away."

"Maybe. But, later, after we'd gotten home, you were itching to go back and take another look at Niles' world. Or so you told me. And so you went back to Savannah, that time on your own."

"He liked fine things. He seemed to like me. I felt sorry for him."

"Yes. He put on splendid orgies," James says, "with boys like you. Blond. Blue eyes. Like the too many others hanging around his mansion. He was a man surfeited by surfaces. Appearances. You fit the bill. A dazzling youth who was completely innocent. Completely. You'd have been ruined if you'd succumbed to him. I saved you. Often it's wise not to think the best of people. Or of life, for that matter. Or me either, Derek."

"So you've warned me."

"Did you ever sleep with him, Sir Niles of the Thousand Beds?"

"No. Of course not."

"Why the frown?" James wraps an arm around Derek's shoulder and pulls him toward him. "I was teasing. I like teasing you. It's so easy. Like a child, sometimes."

"Maybe so. But I'm not who I was, James. I'm no more innocent than you are. Perhaps I never was. I can be hurt too, you know, especially by you." He takes a deep breath and sighs. "So what's your big news?"

Slowly, James sets his snifter on the table, rearranges some magazines, and crosses his legs, delays he knows Derek will notice impatiently, as he does. "I've been offered a new job. A promotion. A big one. Huge, in fact. All I could wish for."

"Why am I hearing a 'but' in there someplace? More teasing?"

"It's in Cologne."

"Germany? Thousands of miles away? From me, our life together? And you're going to take it?"

"Probably. Yes. I think so."

Derek lays his head against James left arm and sighs again. "What about us? I know. We've never made promises. I guess I've just assumed...."

"I don't know." He holds Derek tighter in both his arms. "This is unusually sappy salon music you've been making me listen to. Turn it off, will you? It's awful."

"No. I don't think I will. I sat through four very long hours of Wagner for you. Let this play through to the end, James. It's nearly over. It's one of my favorite pieces. I used to play it on my record player all the time as a boy. I loved it. I love it still. But I've never dared to play it when you were around, not until tonight. Why is that? Brahms and Mahler. Those were your guys back then, gray and dreary like the smell of your father's library."

"You didn't seem to mind them when I played them for you long ago in my bedroom, did you? Loud as I could so Mother wouldn't hear us making out. Come on, Derek. This Saint-Saens is getting on my nerves. It's catchy but shallow, this piece. It's distracting me in all the wrong ways. Listen to that melody. It's banal. It's just a chorale-like tune, charming, but insincere. And listen to the neat little cadence just there. You hear it? Wait. There it is again, of course, just like that tune that keeps being repeated over and over with so little real variation. Precious. Seductive. Lovely even. Boom boom, boom boom, da dum da da dum dum. But predictable even when it takes sly little turns that Saint-Saëns probably thought were quite ingenious. There's nothing beneath it. Nothing to listen to or for except what it is, a fancy meal, maybe haute cuisine, but with too many sweets. It's more than a bit sickening, don't you think? Or have I just crossed a line?"

"All right, all right. Shut up. Enough. You have." Derek releases himself from James' hold, grabs the remote from the cabinet, clicks the CD off, walks to the window, throws the curtains open, and shoves a window up so hard that, as he forces it harder still, it creaks protestingly in its old warped frame.

"You're angry, Rick."

"Yes. Very."

Derek turns to confront James whose face's as dimly lit as a figure illuminated by a candle in a de la Tour. He appears to be almost as meditative, as rueful, as seraphic as Mary Magdalen, his head turned away, refusing to look at him. Derek checks his anger, not quite suppressing it, and says, "You've often maintained that I was France and you were Germany, even though we've neither been to either place. Yet it's true. I've become the subject nation, haven't I?, all these years, the place you've repeatedly invaded and left and invaded again."

"Not in the bedroom. You're more often than not the German there."

"That's not funny. And that's not what you meant by calling me 'France' either, is it? It isn't a joke. You mean that I'm frivolous somehow and you're the truly serious, deep one."

"It was a metaphor, that's all. Yes, I was talking about taste. I was talking about style. We both seem a bit lost in the nineteenth century but on different sides of the argument. That's all."

"It's not all. Your Wagner was a monster."

"The greatest, Auden said. By the way, Saint-Saëns was a Wagnerite and shared his antisemitism, too, you know. So don't look so superior, Derek."

"But it's not in his music. That's nothing monstrous about it. Not ever."

"And it is in Wagner's?"

"Yes. You could go to war to it. You could kill people to it, James, and feel justified. His music does that. It's been done. It's history. I heard it over and over tonight as I listened to that seductive, dangerous work. Abandon the world and follow me if you have faith enough. Otherwise, die. It's the music of a demagogue, all the more threatening because it is great, I agree. Give me Saint-Saëns any day. Maybe he wasn't all that good as a man either, I don't know, though I suspect he had to be a better human being than Wagner was. Most people are, thank goodness. Or try to be. But Camille's music never hectors, never exhorts, never turns into a mindless rant. It charms. That's all it means to do. I hate greatness. I despise profundity. They frighten me. It's like the dark beyond the stars."

Challenged, in effect dared to defend himself by his lover, boyfriend, long term fuck buddy, though he's not yet sure which he is or why he needs finally to figure it out, James stands up and walks closer to Derek. Through the open windows, the city's late night noises roar into Derek's apartment as loudly as if it were rush hour. A breeze rattles some panes and blows the lace curtains that rise and fall like waves, like people's arms do when they're saying goodbye.

"It's strange how we've always talked about each other, about what we mean to each other indirectly," James says. "As if we were metaphors, too, you and I, just metaphors to one another and nothing more. As now. As so often before. I, Germany. You, France. Yet, as you said, we've never been to either place. I want to go, Derek. Badly. I want to see it for myself. I'm not happy here. Maybe I will be there, at least for a while. You're not angry at me because of the differences in our tastes, are you? Because that would be crazy. You're mad at me because I'm leaving, going away without you."

Derek points to his chest, to his heart. "And me? Where am I supposed to go? What am I supposed to do now?"

"Why go anywhere when here's where you're happiest? You've said so yourself. Do what you've always done. You don't need me."

"Yes, I do. I'm happiest with you. Because of you."

"I don't think so. You've got a gift for happiness that for some mysterious reason I was denied at birth, Derek. You see the shine in things, in life, where I mostly see only what's fading. Besides, it'll only be for a year or two. Think of it as a separation. Not so long as our four years in college."

"I see more than you think I do, James. I know about pain. I'm not shallow."

"I'm sure of it."

"We could visit each other during college because we weren't living so far away. A day's drive."

"And now? A simple flight. You could visit me in Germany. We could take a vacation together there. See France, too. Paris, Toulouse, the Riviera. It could be like California two years ago."

"I don't think so, James. I don't think you really want me to. There's a river between us. There's the Rhine between us now, James. I think it is possible there always has been, this uncrossable border that I am only now seeing, some wide river without a bridge."

"Another metaphor."

"Yes. Another metaphor. A deep water uncrossable border. Each is better off on the other side of it. No more invasions. No more wars. No crossing over it. No von Schlieffen plans."

"Have we fought so often? Have we disagreed that much? Have we really been so separate, Derek?"

"I don't know. How could I? Sometimes it's felt like it. The other boyfriends. The other alliances, allegiances, yours, mine. It's like we've grown too used to it all, too accustomed to each other, even our separateness, our differences."

"So. A peaceful co-existence instead? Each confined to his own land? You in your old one, me in my new?"

"Something like that." Derek strolls across the room and clicks off the light. With his back to him, he says, "It's not what I want. I don't want you to go. Spend the night with me, James. Let's fuck. Let's scream as we come. Let's hold each other afterward. No more stupid talking. No more images. Just us, in bed, screwing, enjoying ourselves, one another's bodies, pleasing our pricks."

"I'm flying to Cologne in two weeks, Derek."

"Spend every night before you go with me then. Let that be my good-bye present, o.k.?"

"All right." James unties his tie, kicks off his shoes, unbuckles his belt. Wearing only his boxer shorts, he strides hesitantly, uncertainly as if it were his first time walking into Derek's bedroom and flops onto his bed.

Derek clicks his CD player back on. The same Saint-Saëns begins to play, starting where it had left off, in the return of the big chorale-like tune in the final movement. "Music to make love to," he says, joining James in his bedroom.

"Background music," James says. "Mood music. Like colored lights in a bar."

"No, a fine pinot noir."

"No, a whole dinner consisting of nothing but chocolate ganache."

"No, the shudder that comes from fingers sensuously touching a thigh. The delight of it that makes you want to sing a hymn to the pagan gods."

"It's merely mock passion, Derek. Formal, too polite, trying too hard. The pretense of feeling. A faked orgasm."

"Bullshit, James. That's not what I hear at all. I hear the happiness of passion after passion is over and memory's rejoicing in it, reliving all of it, wanting everyone in the world to know about it."

"There's something decadent about it, Derek. I detect in it the root-like odor of wild roses decaying in woods." James sniffs a little, playing his part.

"How can you say that? It's a fresh breeze blowing in from the Mediterranean."

"I beg to differ. It's the lovesick fantasy of a loveless man."

"Oh, is it? I see the opposite of what you're saying revealed in how your body's stretched out on my bed. This music's relaxing you, my friend, and maybe turning you on a bit."

"Derek, stop it. It isn't the music that's turning me on. You are. So lets stop this. It's silly. We're not kids trying to pretend he's the cleverest in my bedroom anymore."

"Of course, it's stupid. But it's fun, like any game if you don't take it too seriously." Derek strips off the rest of his clothes, kicks his white briefs onto the pile, and lies on the top of his comforter next to James. "It's all silly, James. Foolish. That's what I'm saying. I like things the way they are. Us. The world. It's just that to keep life bearable pretty much everything needs to be left alone. People only ruin things when they meddle too much and to try to transform them. Or think too hard. It's all meaningless. Accept that. Cherish what beauty you see or feel or hear and just let it be. Or embrace it if you can. But don't try to make sense of it. And don't try to change it."

"How can you say that, Derek? You're a lawyer, for god's sake."

"And no good at it. Or not half so good as you are. You're better at arguing. At winning."

"Am I? I'm leaving. In two weeks. Really."

"I believe you. Really."

"Touch me, Derek. Make love to me as if we could make us last."

Derek tickles his thigh. "Say you admire this music first. Say it."

"No."

"Like you mean it. Say it." Derek kisses him, licks his chest, cups his balls in one hand, tongues his stiff shaft. "I'm teasing you, but I mean it, too. I want to win this time. Say it."

"Oh, Jesus. All right. I love you Saint-Saëns."

"Louder. As if you've been truly inspired by it to new heights of passion."

"I love you Saint-Saëns!"

"Ah. La belle France." Derek laughs, too loudly, holding James tighter.

"I feel like a fool. No more of this game, Derek."

"Yes. A fool. Me too. I'll stop. But don't leave me, James. Please."

"I have to."

"You can't."

"I must."

"You won't. I know you won't."

"I will. In my mind, I'm already gone." He takes a deep breath. He hurts. And Derek hurts. The hurt, the wound is good, isn't it? Like the pain, though momentary, that Derek'll be feeling soon, the pain that's the beginning of their intensest pleasures, the reason for living, if it comes to that. It's the proof he needs that life and love matter, that Derek matters, isn't it, just as Derek has always said? Isn't the pain after always the best proof of love?

With two fingers, James probes Derek where his darkness deepens into night, preparing to enter him, his turn this time to cross the border between them, the sea, the forests, the river, to seek refuge in a country where he doesn't belong anymore. As the Saint-Saëns ends, as the concerto's last notes vanish into silence, another silence between them begins slowly to expand, one that sounds scarily like abandonment even to James.

Perhaps silence is profounder than any music, James thinks to himself at that moment, profounder, deeper even than love: this unbreachable distance, this separation that has no voice, no words, this ecstasy without a name. Or perhaps silence, the entwining of flesh, is beautiful because pleasure needn't make any sense. Which was it? Who is right, he or Derek?

He feels their bodies swimming on the surface of some great ocean. He doesn't know what to call it, its lapping waves, the sudden storm, its widening waters. Theirs is a shared cry out of nowhere, out of nothing at all. The namelessness of no place. Of absence heard. Of rapture. Derek not Derek, James not James. The afterwards of no more words, of being beyond language, where there's nothing like it in this world. Of a solitude that can never end.

"You could come with me. I could convince my firm it's all right. They'd find you a job," James whispers afterward, their sweat-drenched bodies still joined, the sheets wet as they are, the room as warm as if it were August. "We could live together."

"Maybe," Derek says, rolling off him, not knowing what to think of the sudden proposal. Which world was his? What in himself, in James, ought he to believe? He couldn't tell if the mystery of not being he'd felt before in their moments of ecstasy was the same strange sensation that he now fears. Had he confused the bliss of it with dying? That tired old Wagnerian cliché? Had James all along in his way been right? His asshole hurt but he liked the itch James' cock had left behind as he withdrew. Was that what it meant?

"I'll need to know soon," James says.

"Yes," Derek agrees. "Soon. Of course."

At daybreak, as James showers, Derek watches the coffee brewing while the morning light slowly seeps through the curtains into the kitchen, warming his unclothed body. He's recalling a summer rain when they were fifteen that fell gently on jonquils, ivy, dogwood near a creek, a late April paradise far from town, the sun in a vast sky, warm and good, a late August patch of sweet corn taller than either of them as they trespassed through the fields, watching chipmunks, fat squirrels being taunted by crows and a circling hawk. Lying in grass so many times with James, what had he felt as a boy, a mere teenager? An unsurpassed peace. What he feels now.

In the bathroom, he offers James a sip of his coffee as he dries himself off while standing on the rug outside the stall. James. His gait, his way of talking, of arguing, what pleasures he seeks in bed, on the job, at a party, at the theater or a concert, his lovely dark moods, his troubled joys, his turmoil, for good and for ill. How could he lose them, him, the deft way he moves through air, his poise, what he hears in music, how years and the ages work to deepen and change them both whenever they're together, however long or short the time?

His nakedness is making James appear impatient. He drops his towel onto the floor, accepts the cup from Derek's hand, takes a hearty sip, and licks his lips from the taste of it. "Well?"

"No," Derek says.

Two men, ordinary, unexceptional in the usual ways, little different from how most people are. Losing each other. Their love failing them. Yet to themselves, to each other, like music always: mysterious, moving, incalculable.

The Day Jimmy Leaves Me

1.
Dawn breaks through drawn shutters,
its light so pale a yellow it's almost
white. A deserted room perhaps,
its walls unadorned, a morning glow
to it, bedsheets golden, dust like dancers
swirling freely through the air, a host
of minute glittering jewels. A bird raps
on a window with its beak, seeking refuge from snow.

2.
Spring in an old growth forest,
dense brush, trees pocked with lichen,
moss-covered, thick canopy, dark
as night though it's noon, coldest
before sunrise, the smell of wet bark,
decay, Jim's betrayal, drawing me in.

The Return of the Prodigal Son

I was cleaning my hunting boots, old and creased and worn, the most comfortable I'd ever owned when Cindy opened the door to my shack. I'd fixed it up over the years since I'd been back from Iraq, painted the walls a nice bright blue and sanded and varnished the floors as best I could with the tools I could borrow. But the place still looked like a shack. A mess. A wreck. Cindy'd hated it. As recently as three months ago, we were still seeing each other on the sly. I needed the money. But it was no good. After four or five more tries, I gave up. I didn't have it in me anymore, if I ever did. She kept nagging me to better myself. I didn't want to better myself.

She unbuttoned her long red winter coat and flopped down in my one comfortable chair. I'd salvaged it from Sue Ellen Dial's place, up river about a half a mile from mine, before the auctioneer arrived after she'd died. I figured Sue Ellen owed me at least that much for favors rendered. It's not like I'd enjoyed it. It's the same with all my women. They bore me or they tire me out.

"I wish you'd get a phone," Cindy said. "That hike up here from the road wears on my stamina."

"You used to complain I wore you out, Cindy."

"Did I? I don't remember. That was much too long ago. For Christ's sake, Walt, you're twenty years younger than me."

"Twenty-four."

"All right, twenty-two. Don't you exaggerate, child, and I won't either." The last time I saw Cindy, Cynthia now, her hair had been gray. Now it was white. She wore it tucked into a kerchief that matched her red coat. She tugged off her mittens and stretched her fingers. "You been out hunting this morning, Walt?" When she smiled, she could still look right pretty, old pretty, but pretty nonetheless. The things you do for a twenty or two. I used to be worth lots more. "I detect a gamey smell in here."

"No'm. Just walking. Hiking up by the cut. Maybe I stepped on something."

"But you're o.k. Dried out? Not drinking?"

"Can't complain." I tried to distract her and me both from that topic by polishing another pair of boots. "How's Jamieson?" Jamieson was her second husband. Billy Lambert was her first. He died from forty years of three packs a day almost a decade ago when I was still in the Middle East.

"You know Jamieson. He won't ever change." I did know Jamieson. He'd been my boss for a while at the mill. I never did like him. Since she'd married him, Cindy painted her face, using too much powder and rouge. She'd look a lot finer, for a woman of sixty or so, I mean, if she'd quit messing up her face with cosmetics. She wore her keychain around her wrist so she wouldn't lose it just as Jamieson had ordered her to do. In the old days, she could grumble about me all she liked. But I never bossed her around. "Kenny's back," she said. "It's been a couple of days. I thought you should know."

"So I heard. Leastways, I'd heard he was on his way. Strange, though. Living in y'all's old home near the Route 4 bridge, out in the middle of nowhere, weak as I've heard tell he is."

"He's not doing so hot, Walt." She glanced out the window behind her. "With all those trees gone, you've got yourself a real nice view of the valley, Walton." She brushed her little girl bangs out of her eyes. They used to tickle my face. She'd complain I'd laugh at the most inappropriate times. But she wouldn't think to trim them. I had no feeling for women, not the kind they want you to have anyhow, but she never seemed to notice. Or, if she did, she didn't appear to mind. For me, it was just another job and mostly a whole lot less bother than those I'd managed to hold on to for a year or two. More work maybe, but less of a bother until I just couldn't anymore.

Two robins I'd carved from wood left over from the trees the last big storm had felled that I'd sold for their lumber sat perched on the window sill. "Those things give me the creeps," Cindy said. "They look too real. Only dead real. Like folks that've been embalmed." She shuddered. Cindy had always been terrified of death. I blamed her church. Our church, Brookside Baptist that is, the one my family used to go to together with the Dunns. They still do, those that are left. Only I'd quit it. And Ken. All that preaching about the end times. I could have told her something about those end times. But I wouldn't. I liked her too well. Besides, she was too easy to spook.

"You'd think, after all he's been through, Kenny would have changed some. But no," she said. "Just as stubborn and reckless as always. Mark my words, he'll fire anybody Jamieson or I or anybody else hires to help him out. You know he will. No one'll last longer than a day or two. I'd bet my reputation on it. Why did he move back? That's what I don't comprehend. He despises this place. And for lots of folks the feeling's mutual."

"You got me. Nowhere else to go?" I shook my head. "How should I know? I haven't seen him since he left for Afghanistan. At your granddad's funeral, remember? How long ago was that, Cindy?" There'd been letters exchanged between us, too, but I didn't want to tell her about those. I'm good at keeping secrets. I've had to be.

"Too long to think about. Put another log on the fire, Walt. I'm cold."

I was trying to husband my logs. The way the owls cried at night promised a long winter, well into what used to be called spring, the one season that seems to have quit on us for some reason. Winter summer fall. That's all we've got now. But I did what she'd asked. "You still stepping out, Cindy?"

"Don't be ridiculous." She lit a cigarette. She shrugged. "Maybe. Once in a while. Jamieson's not all that keen these days and nights. He says he's too busy with work. Men." She dragged on her cigarette. "You all sure have the wrong reputation for love making."

"That may be so, Cind. How are your kids? Doing o.k.? They sure married well, one and all."

"Still scattered all over the country. It's hard to keep track. I hear from Sarah once in a blue moon. She's got two boys in the service now. She tried to warn them about how the army never did anyone in her family any good. What can you do? Boys will be boys and boys will be soldiers." She winked at me. She'd never understood a thing about me. Winking at me, for Christ's sake, like she'd just made a joke only I'd understand. It rattled me when she acted like that. I never did follow what the point of it was.

My knees cracked when I bent to reach for another log. I liked to blame the V.A., for the way they'd treated me the six weeks I was in the hospital. But the truth was that I was forty-one. I was getting old. I could feel it. It was a long time coming, but I wasn't a kid anymore.

It wasn't regret for missed years I was suffering from but something more serious. I still loved the guy. Not just any guy. Kenny. I was almost a boy then, too, when it started, at least in what I understood about life, though the year on the calendar might not have agreed. It would have said I was ten years passed being young.

What could I tell her? That I owed him the only happiness I'd known in my life? It was my own fault it hadn't lasted. But I didn't want to talk about that. Not to anyone, not even myself. "Somebody's got to look after Ken," I said. "Full time."

"You're telling me. He's frail. He can barely walk." She crushed out her cigarette and put her mittens back on. "And you've just been elected by my unanimous vote." Her eyes were watering some. Maybe it was the cold. Maybe it was tears. Cindy was good at turning on the tap when she wanted to. She wiped under her eyes, smearing her mascara. "What happened to those cute curtains I sewed for you back when, Walt, love in every thread?" She gave me a look that meant to let me know she was just teasing. I wasn't so sure. I was still proud of my looks for no reason a mirror could validate as once they all had. Vanity. I could never figure out what Cindy's real affections toward me were until she'd hand me the cash.

"Had to toss them away. They wore out years ago, Cindy."

"Oh. Yes. I suppose they would have. Time flies and all that." She grimaced and pulled a piece of paper out of her purse. "Jamieson drew you a map."

"What for? I know where it is. I used to visit y'all nearly once a week. You remember, don't you? Your memory's not fraying is it, sweetheart?" Jamieson Allen thought me some kind of fool. An idiot. He always did. He hated my father, too. In his eyes, we were both no good. Trash. All of us, the whole McClendon clan, what was left of it. Dumb hicks. A map, for crying out loud. "Keep it," I told her.

She re-opened her purse and slipped it back in. "Don't blame me if you get lost, Walt."

"Damn it, woman. You know better than that. How could I? I know it's been a long, long time since I was last out there. But I have my reasons for recalling every inch of the way," I said. "Every sign. Every roadside tree. Every rock on the shoulders."

"Do you, Walt? Would one of those reasons be me?"

"I can't lie," I said and winked at her. Fair's fair, I thought, a wink for a wink. Pretense was everything in my former line of work. The old bible belt, God love it.

I walked her back to the trailhead and the mud road that led to where she'd left her car at the end of a winding paved road. She drove some big old hulking Buick if I was remembering right. It would have gotten stuck on its way up for sure. You'd have to have owned a four wheel, like me, if you wanted to drive around here where nobody but me and a few hillbillies lived. I liked it because it was peaceful most of the time. Peace was the hardest thing in the world to come by. Peace and quiet.

My clunky truck gave everybody fair warning I was coming, noisy as a bag of rocks rolling down a ramp. The loose springs in the seat hurt my butt. After I'd turned off the old Oak Ridge Road, I had to drive another couple of miles or so before I reached the long gravel driveway that led to Kenny's family's old cabin-sized cinder block house. I parked on a cement slab.

It looked like a lot of slabs, mostly stone, I'd seen fallen by the wayside outside Fallujah. Or Mosul. Or some other godforsaken desert city. Whenever my headaches came back, I'd mix up the names of those places pretty bad. Before you're in it, during it, after it, a war's nothing but chaos and confusion. I'd lost some pretty good friends in that one. The saddest thing was how the confusion stayed, like it was you're real home, not here. Something in me still clung to it, to the war, not letting me go, not letting me come back here and forget it even though here is the only place I'd ever truly wanted to be, hard as the living is, harder in some ways than fighting an enemy. I've never been able to figure out why.

Kenny was staring at me through the window. How long had it actually been since we'd seen each other? What I'd told Cindy, everyone about us those years ago was a necessary lie, of course.

It was too easy for me after it was over between us to lose track of the years. I kept excusing myself for this or that by trying to forget not him, but some of the details about him that drove me wildest, the way his eyes looked in the morning, how the water poured off him like light as he walked out of a lake, the left over smell of the leaves in his hair after a night in the woods. I never really could forget a single thing, a single time we were together, no matter how brief it was, even if the exact dates of when we'd met up escaped me.

We were both staring at each other, me at him through my windshield, him at me through the cracked panes of his cinder block house. The broken glass distorted his face. But I couldn't mistake that black black hair no matter how different he might have looked otherwise. Black and shiny as roofing tar, I used to tease him.

His house was surrounded by red clay mud everywhere except those spots that last week's snow had covered over. A drooping vine twisted around a tottering drainpipe. The stoop was missing its first step. The sump pump sat in a gaping hole. Old tires, rusty bumpers and hubcaps, tin basins, a broken washboard lay in a random pile threaded with kudzu and a kind of madcap ivy. Ken had reoccupied a house that the Dunns had abandoned when he left for his war a year after I'd flown off to mine. I opened the truck door and slid out. It was despair I was looking at, the house, the land around it. Maybe Ken.

When my youngest sister Patty was little, I gave her a doll that had wide blue eyes like Kenny's. They'd stare at you no matter where you stood. Ken used to stare at me like that. He still did, it seemed. Or I wished he could with its meaning the same as it once had. Before he'd gone. Before he'd met Sean. My fault, I knew, but still.

I walked up to a snap, a click, and a jangling chain. Why had he locked his door? What was he afraid of? He was miles from anyone. Maybe he was remembering how he'd been threatened if he hadn't taken off on the day he did, if he hadn't escaped. Who could blame him for being fearful? A lot of the good folks in this country were plain Christian hateful to him. I blamed myself, too, of course, for having stayed away, having kept a safe distance as his father and half-brothers shoved him out the door.

It swung open. With the help of two canes, he shuffled away from me. His hair was long and scraggly. He was bean-thin. Neither of us said hello. He appeared not to be surprised to see me. Not happy about it either. In no way pleased. His face looked the same as the faces of some wounded men I knew whose expression seemed to die before the rest of them did. I helped him sit in a wicker chair. I thought he might flinch from my assistance, but he didn't. The shaggy brown carpet stunk of rot.

"Cindy sent you?"

"Her and Jamieson. They're family, Ken. They're worried about you."

"Like shit. They want to send me to that rehab hell house in Mt. Tabor. To live like a caged beast, for fuck's sake, until I get better. If I do. Which I doubt. They told me so, as if it was a generous offer I'd be a complete fool not to take. I don't want any of Jamieson's money.

The idiot head of their lynch gang.”

“This is better?” I glanced around the near empty room. “This dungeon?”

“I’m dying anyway. This was once my home. I’ll make it do. I had to before. I don’t see how it’s different now. If you don’t have much left, you don’t want much more.”

“It’s seen happier days once upon a time.”

“Really? When? Maybe a few. ‘Once upon a time’ is right. In some fable. But not for me. Or you, Walt.” He pat my hand. “I’m glad you’re here. You look o.k. How are the knees?”

“Creaky,” I said. “You’re not dying, friend. I won’t let that happen. I’m going to live here for a while, Ken. With you. This has nothing to do with Cindy or Jamieson or anyone. It’s true she visited me earlier today. But I was on my way here anyways. She just delayed me some.”

“I’m a wreck. A human ruin. Look for yourself, buddy.”

“You haven’t changed that much. You’re five years younger than me before. You’re five years younger than me now.”

“I feel like I’m twenty years older than I was just a year ago. Thirty. I feel old. And tired. Really tired. As if I all I want to do is find some bed of leaves in the woods and lie down in it and let the earth take me back.” He gazed up at me sadly. “We should have told. We should never have kept us a secret.”

“What the devil are you suggesting, Ken? I would have been arrested back then if anyone had known. You barely fifteen, me twenty. Thrown in jail. Probably would still be there, breaking up rocks. Being some big bad dude’s bitch. Come on, Ken. Laugh. That’s funny. You look healthy enough to me,” I lied. “Too thin perhaps. Your legs obviously need some attention. Nothing that can’t be healed, right? What doctor told you were dying anyway?”

“I don’t need a doctor to know what I know.” His hands and arms were trembling worse than my grandma’s did near the end. “Since Sean died, I’ve been falling apart. I think it’s what I want. I sincerely believe that, Walton. I want to break into a thousand little pieces and be blown away like dust. I don’t like the world at all anymore. I’ve grown allergic to it. It’s killing me.”

“How did you hurt those fingers?”

“Burned them this morning on the stove.”

“I’ll get some bandages,” I said. My shack was too cramped for me and Kenny both, though it would have a cheerier place to live in together. Better light. Better air, for that matter. Nicer woods nearby. I'd brought everything I might need from my place to his in one load. My mattress was thick enough for me to sleep on with nothing else between me and the stinky, probably bug infested floor. I'd slept on worse in worse places. I wasn't complaining, not even to myself. I wasn't sacrificing myself either. It was just the truth. I didn't mind.

That night, I grilled us some fish I'd caught ice fishing the previous day and steamed some rice. He dropped bits of the food onto his lap. What was he so scared of? Death maybe. Maybe me. "There's nothing to do here," he said. "You'll get bored."

"I don't get bored that easy, Ken. If I did, I'd have checked out long ago. What do you do to pass the time?"

"Read some books my father failed to find and throw out. But it's hard for me to hold them with my hands shaking so bad. And this house is too dark most of the day. I manage. I dream a lot. Fantasize."

"About?"

"Sean, of course. Sean and me."

"I wish I'd met him," I said, though I was glad I hadn't. He was better than me. I didn't have to meet him to understand that. "I've brought a lamp with me. I'll read to you."

A bit of saliva slipped out from between his lips. I wiped it away with a clean rag I carried in my pocket. Since his friend, 'lover' was a word still tricky for me to say, all right, since his lover Sean had been killed about a year ago in an accident in upstate New York, he'd been living like a recluse in the big city. They'd been driving north on the turnpike for a little holiday out of town to celebrate Kenny's getting out of the army and home to their apartment. Unlike me, he'd returned stateside mostly safe and sound.

The blizzard that night was much worse than had been forecast. On a wide curve, Sean lost control of their car. It slid into a snow bank and hit a railing. A semi plowed into it, pressing the trunk and everything in it into the back seat. The roof bent and collapsed like tin on a barn in a ferocious storm. Sean was killed. Kenny suffered a concussion, a broken collarbone, several broken ribs, a collapsed lung, and two broken legs. It wasn't a war that had mangled his life so bad. That had nearly destroyed it. It was winter. It was snow. It was the unexpected severity of a solitary storm.

After he'd been released from the hospital, he wrote me again. After our first years apart, we weren't much for writing letters anymore. I was no good at it. Ken was ten times brighter than me. And the war, his, mine, well, I couldn't say much about it except that it was hell. But everyone knew that. Or should have known it. But it'd silenced us. I didn't know why. Or maybe I did. Some things that happen to you are too terrible to talk about. I saw what happened and I knew it was meaningless. Pointless. Senseless. All I could do was keep my mouth shut. Ken, too. So much for sharing war stories. We quit writing each other. And by then, of course, he'd fallen in love with Sean.

After he was let out of the hospitals, plural, Ken had returned to what he still called his home, by which he meant back to his and Sean's apartment. His life was over. That's what he said. He couldn't live without Sean. His legs ought to have, but for some reason didn't get stronger. Then he took sick. Viruses wouldn't leave his body. Colds. Flu. Pneumonia. He sold what little he had and, three days before, had bought a ticket to fly back here. To die, Cindy had said, repeating to me what Ken had told her, I reckoned. She thought it was nonsense. I wasn't so sure. He looked to me like a determined man.

She was his sister, his oldest sister. The only one who hadn't condemned him when, in anger at them, raging against their crazy ideas about God, at the mad, hate filled sermon he'd, we'd all had to listen to even though it was Easter, he'd let his guard down. His folks were poorer than mine were and had twice the brood to raise. Bible believers, they were, every last one of them, like mine, all of them, that is, except for me and Ken. He'd told them the truth about him, though not about us, and it hadn't set him free.

The house smelled of water left too long in a vase full of flowers. I needed to chop some more firewood. I'd brought my small TV. At least the house had sockets that worked I could plug it into. Sometime back in the fifties, it had been the office for a new development. Not a lot got sold. They'd erected all those poles, brought in wires for nothing. Ken's dad bought the place for not much more than the bills he carried in his wallet. Ken said that was all of theirs bad luck. He'd hated living in the middle of nowhere. He'd had to walk two miles and a half to catch the bus to school, no matter what the weather was like, pouring rain or crazy hot.

I'd left my ax in the truck. The field outside was stubble and ankle deep in mud. Through the window, I could see Kenny staring at the TV. He wasn't watching it. Just staring at it. Desperate for something to look at outside of himself, I guessed. I shouldn't have brought it. He'd always hated TV. The one thing Ken wanted most was to get away. He confided in me once that the three biggest liars he'd known in his life were his church, his family, and the damned TV.

We settled into a life together without too much trouble. He didn't talk much. Read. Gazed into space. Slept when and if he could. I tried to keep busy. During a string of warmer, thawing days in early February, I laid down some slate for a walkway out front and fixed the stoop. I cleared out the brush in back. I repaired the broken or cracked windows. I nailed some new shingles on the roof where it had leaked. I painted the bathroom and scrubbed the shower stall until it gleamed.

Every morning, every night, I had to help Kenny dress or undress. At first he'd resisted. It was too much like old times. His being stark naked in my sight. In my arms. I was the one who'd been too scared to keep it going, to keep us alive together. I was the one who'd broken it off. I was the coward. But I loved him.

I should have known better. I was the older one. The experienced one, I'd falsely claimed, though he was my first guy, too. We both laughed at that. He was much smarter about sex even, having learned by reading books he shouldn't have been able to find. And braver, more daring. And he got badly hurt for it.

Everyone in the county we knew except me and Cindy turned their backs on him and drove him away. He was a scapegoat, sure enough, just as he'd said. He had no money, no education after high school. What else could he do except sign up? They'd forced him all the way into a god-forsaken desert. Maybe some of them wanted him killed. I wouldn't have put it past them, not one of them, especially not his dad.

So we'd made a game of it, my helping him with his clothes, like a mother does with a troublesome little boy, appealing to and teasing him at the same time. It worked all right until he finally became more comfortable with it, being naked in front of me, it not meaning anything, not anymore, to either of us, or so I pretended, and I could quit the teasing and the cajoling.

I bought him a walker like my Aunt Ruth's. He refused to use it until one of his canes slipped out from under him. He hit the floor hard. He admitted it wasn't the first time. I believed him. His legs hadn't healed right. You can't walk right you might as well be in prison. I'd known a little about how he felt.

Whenever I watched TV, he'd sit in the same room with me and gaze at something else. Wherever he was looking, it was always at something I couldn't see. Something in his past. Something in his mind or his soul. Something I had no right to look into or ask about. Whatever he was seeing seemed to make him happier. The good times with Sean, I imagined. Not with me, that was for certain. We'd always had to be a secret. Furtive, he called it. Sean and him never had to hide a thing. That's how much Ken had changed. They'd met in Manhattan. DADT hadn't fazed Kenny one little bit in Afghanistan.

He didn't eat much. I was a lousy cook. He complained about a pain in his gut but swore he wouldn't see a doctor, not ever again. Quacks and crooks. He claimed he wasn't afraid. He didn't believe in an after life. In anything at all. But he wasn't afraid. I was for him, though. Scared senseless. I didn't want to lose him again, not even if this was all we could have or be ever again. Just looking after each other. Or me looking after him anyway. Yet that was what was so strange. He was caring for me, too.

Cindy invited us to her place for a Sunday dinner on a weekend when Jamieson was out of town on business. Ken swore he wouldn't go. He'd never let me drive him anywhere. That night, he was so stubborn I had to pick him up and carry him into my truck and then lift him out of it and practically haul him into her house. It felt good to hold him in my arms like that. It always had. It always would. I told him he could kick like a girl even with his bum legs. The crack just made him madder.

"I'm tired," he whispered to me after the apple pie. It was time to leave. We said our thanks to Cindy and took off. I helped him walk back to the truck. He'd been silent through most of the meal. Cindy had tried to pretend everything was o.k. between him and her even though it obviously wasn't. She'd never known about me and Ken. She never would, not if I could help it, whatever Ken might say by then. All through dinner, she wouldn't quit flirting with me.

After we'd driven off, Ken said, "Are you still sleeping with my sister?"

"No. Cynthia's a good girl now. So she says, though I don't buy it. I don't do that anymore, Kenny. Or I try not to."

"It didn't look like it."

"Jealous?"

"Don't be absurd, Walt."

"Her husband hates my guts."

"You needed the money," Ken said. "That's what you told me."

"I wasn't lying to myself, Ken. I know who I am. I know I'm a queer, as folks around here still seem to enjoy saying about those they disapprove of. But you bet I needed the money. My whole life, I'd have been nothing but a worthless fool to everyone if it hadn't been for my magic dick. I was good looking back then, wasn't I, babe? Not all that long ago either. My prick's still a thing of astonishing beauty, I'm proud to say. I don't mind a woman's using it for her own purposes now again. Share the wealth is my politics."

"Yep," Ken said. "Handsome. You sure were. Are," he quickly corrected without much conviction. I didn't care. 'Were' was the word time had written all over my face.

At an intersection just east of the old Perea highway, a deer dashed across the road, the fifth I'd seen that winter. I tooted my horn to warn the others to stay off the strip until I'd driven past.

"I don't feel good," Ken said when we'd reached Route 4. "I can't wait. Something I ate. It was too rich. It's rushed straight through me. I need to go to the bathroom now."

I pressed on the brakes. "Use the bushes. I'll help you."

"Hurry," he said.

But it was too late. He shat in his pants. As we bounced and rocked over the bumpy country road, the stench grew worse. I rolled down the window and stuck out my head.

"I'm so cold," he said. "Ashamed."

At his place, I carried him to the bathroom and slowly undressed him. His pants' legs, shoes, and socks were soaked with diarrhea. Shit coated his boxers like a baby's diaper. I lugged Ken into the shower stall, too small for both of us, but I squeezed in with him anyway. He grabbed the bar I'd screwed into the wall. I tossed his soiled clothes onto the frozen ground outside, stripped down to my briefs, and rejoined him in the shower, ready to scrub him clean, soap in one hand, washcloth in the other.

His body shook. Trembled. I started with his back and worked down. I washed his butt and the crack of his ass, his thighs, calves, and feet. "Turn around," I said. "Keep hold of that bar but turn around. Face me."

"I'll fall."

"If you do, I'll catch you. You won't fall."

"I can't. I'm too embarrassed."

"You think I haven't cleaned shit off a guy before, guys so scared they went in their pants? This is nothing, Ken."

"It's not that." He slowly, carefully shifted his body so I could wash his front. His cock was hard and red, throbbing like a teenager's.

What could I do? Nothing but wash him. Let the water run over him and wash him. Over and over wash him. Until he was clean. Until his skin shone. And he could lean on me and I could carry him to bed. And like the boys we'd long ago been we'd made no more than a hesitant kind of love.

"I'm sorry, Walt," he said afterward.

"For what? I enjoyed it too."

"It was like we were kids. Fumbling in the dark. Not knowing quite what to do. It can't happen again, Walt. I can't let it. I felt untrue."

My heart sank the way it would sink whenever a woman asked me why I'd been so cool to her. So needlessly rough. Only now I was the woman. "I know, kid," I said, clicking off the lamp in his bedroom. Well, not his bedroom exactly but the room with a bed in it that he tried to sleep in night after night.

I went for a drive. The night felt like some holiday I had forgotten about, like a Christmas without any decorations put up to remind you what day it was or was coming or was just over. Some celebration I'd missed completely.

I knew Cliff Ogden would be home and lonely and he never wanted me to spend the night. Never once asked me to. He was too scared someone might see me leaving in the morning or spot the truck where I'd parked it in the woods. I left it far enough away so no neighbors could spy it and walked across the river dividing him from me on the new, quieter plank bridge. When he opened the door at my knock, he was smiling as if I'd been expected. I can appreciate a man who smiles at me the way Cliff always did. He was nice looking too, though going seriously bald at only thirty-nine.

I stayed longer than I'd meant to. It had started snowing again, this time truly hard. As I drove back to Ken's in the middle of the night, fierce winds were blowing down from the mountains. It was hard for me to see through the windshield. Several inches had already settled around his house when I parked the truck. He was asleep, wrapped in the sheets and blankets I had tucked around him before I took off.

Why had I gone at all? Still horny, I guess, or something like that. It's strange how sometimes shooting off a load only makes me need it more right away. Like some drugs do, I'd been told. But it was wrong of me. I'd known that as I closed Cliff's door behind me. It was love I was looking for. It was what I had always been searching for. Love. I wasn't ashamed to say it. Not anymore. The lonesome word. What sex at its best meant inside you. What you think you know all about. But you don't. It comes like a revelation. What you see at the end, I'm told, if you've lived a good life.

I brought in a box of groceries I'd bought in a store that stays open all night next to Slim's Barbecue on Route 4. The storm hadn't closed it yet. Too bad Slim's wasn't open too. I always enjoyed a plate of pork barbecue and hushpuppies and slaw after a few hours at Cliff's. I fixed myself a cheese sandwich and watched late night TV, flipping channels. I was trying to make myself, the world, feel a little bit more normal.

The winds from the north blew fiercer and more cold. Ice coated the panes. I built up the fire and checked on the heater in Kenny's room. He was thirsty, he said, awfully thirsty. During the night he called for more water three or four times. He'd spilled the jug I left for him all over the floor.

At four in the morning, he was gushing sweat. His bedding was drenched. I felt his forehead. The thermometer read 103.2.

"I'm cold. Cold," he said, shaking terribly. "It's so cold, Sean."

"It's Walt, Ken," I said. "I got to get you to a doctor. To a hospital." He hadn't heard me. He was breathing crazily fast, taking too short breaths.

The lights in the hall and living room went out. The red coils of the heater in Ken's room dimmed to orange, then ashen black. In the kitchen, I picked up the phone. It was dead. I shoved on my galoshes and grabbed my coat and knit cap off the rack.

The fucking truck wouldn't start. It was too cold. Snow had piled around it in drifts high as dunes. I waded through them. If I could avoid the worst of the ice, I knew I could make it. I was strong. I was in pretty good shape despite my years, except for my knees. All I had to do was walk not quite three miles from Ken's to Route 4. Where it joined the old Oak Ridge Road, I might find a house with power and a phone. Or a cell phone. Or I could flag down a car or truck if any were still on the road. It didn't matter. I had to do something. Find a doctor. Call an ambulance. Anything. Only fast. Faster than I could move.

The snow had stopped falling at last. The clouds cleared. The moon was out, glittering on the ice and showing me the way. Pretend it's an adventure, I told myself. Pretend you're back in Iraq. Ignore the snow. Make believe it's the desert. But in lots of places the snow was deeper than I'd guessed. It was tough going, a slow slog. My knees cracked and hurt. I had to stop to catch my breath. Snow seeped into my galoshes and soaked my socks. The tip of my nose and my cheeks became numb. I tried to think about some sexy song I could sing but nothing came to my mind except for some old hymns. I hated hymns. But I sang a couple as lustily as I could, blaspheming, deliberately mangling the words and the sense, preserving just the lovely tunes.

Having reached the wide curve in the road around the frozen pond, I was halfway to my goal. The hill in front of me worried me some. The downward slope looked dangerous, steep, sheer, and slick. I'd already fallen several times before I reached it. The last time, when I shoved myself back up, I was panting hard.

I knew the road I wanted skirted the thickest woods. Route 4 bordered them half a mile closer. If I went in instead of around them, I could reach it faster. Moonlight helped me find an old hunter's path through it where the snow appeared to be less deep.

In the woods, though, I lost most of the moon's light. I had to feel my way. But walking was easier where the snow wasn't so heavy under the protection of big longleaf pine trees and the entwined limbs of tall oak. I picked up my pace.

I was happy. That was what was most puzzling to me. I felt really happy, proud of myself that I'd made the right decision for once in my life. It was going to work. I was going to find a car, a house, someone, anything that would help me save Ken. I was almost there, almost home free, I thought. Until I skidded badly on an ice slick and started to roll down a steep decline I hadn't noticed. I'd lost my footing. Toppling head first, I must have tried to grab a limb or a branch to check my fall. All I remember was rolling over and over on hard, stony ground while the underbrush whipped my face.

Cindy found him, worried after she'd heard on the radio how his quarter of the county had suffered a blackout overnight. It was Cindy, his oldest sister, who discovered Ken, almost dead, and saved him, not me. Using the phone in a gas station on the highway, she called for an ambulance. Cindy could drive like a stock car champion when she had to. On the way to the hospital, riding with her brother, she remembered me. The next call she placed was to the sheriff's office about nine hours too late.

Rescuers found my body only after most of the ice and snow had melted. It took a couple of days, off and on. One of them told a reporter from the local TV station that I must have bashed my skull on a boulder at the bottom of the ravine where they'd discovered me lying face down. The steady cold kept me in pretty decent shape. For a dead man, he'd meant, as good as if I'd been lying on a slab in the morgue.

I don't doubt most of what he'd told the reporter is true. All I recall is a quick strike to my head and a blinding clean flash, bright as what years before in Brookside Baptist Church I'd been promised would be how glory would appear to us all some day if we stayed righteous in our ways and walked with the Lord. And it does look like that. Like lightning. Or the flare of a match struck in the back of a cave blown out by a gust of wind from who knows where. Or the glare in your eyes after you've stared at the sun too long.

You see your whole life in a moment's illumination. And it is glorious, as splendid as the sun or full moon shining on snow. And it's love. I've no doubt of that. Then, as suddenly as it'd showed me the way, like a flare in the sky, my life was over.

And what am I now instead? Everything? Or nothing? I don't know which. What does it mean to be with God? Only that He's as dark forever as He was for that brief moment of my dying blindingly bright? The darkness seems to go on and on, as if it might last eternally, and I can't see through it to know whose night it is, mine or His.

Say this to Ken when you see him. I promise to get back home to take better care of him as quick as I can. I'm not certain how. I'm not sure it's even allowed. But he knows me. He knows I keep my promises. Or at least I try to.

Mallards

Early May was bright sycamore, oak,
maple, the dawn in pine,
birdsong, the chirping of crickets.

He'd left that and didn't go back.
Life follows no design,
no pattern. He misses the sunsets,

the boyhood pleasures that cling
to him still, visions of spring's
wild flowers on the hills where he lived,

the joys of a creek spilling
over a dam, the mallards' wings'
iris blue as they flew or dived,

their iridescent, velvety
green heads, their bodies' gray,
brown, and black feathers, white

on their chests. Reeds, ivy,
wild grass grew on the red clay
banks he lay on, sunlight

on his naked skin. Every season, the mallards would stay
on the lake, no southward flight

despite winter's ice. He's set
his eyes on dying, to go
for a walk round a lake, to be free

of anxiety, of fear for the net
that'd capture them, the mallards slowly drifting by, diving gracefully

for food, glistening and wet,
their feathers, beaks measuring what holiness means, the beauty

of earthly things: never to let
it leave his dreams, the allure
of the world, what it gave him to see.

A Pilgrim from the Land of Loss

Like an oil slick on asphalt, the sky was sleekly dark, the moon and a few stars haloed with translucent red and gold and blue. Moths whirled and flitted round the porch light like bees circling a hive. Locusts whirred and hummed. Leaving a trail of slime across the walk, a slug slithered into grass. A giant black ant was crawling toward a window pane. Dash leaned toward it, squashed it with his thumb, and flicked its mashed carcass into weeds.

If the porch light had been off, he'd have been able to see almost to the creek where it began its meandering way toward the lake far off near his father's farm, the lost good times, the old days that promised more than he's been offered or earned feeling almost close enough to walk to in what remained of the night.

One beetle clung to, another laboriously crawled over the screen door. He began to stroll toward a pond close by his home to look at the ducks where they bedded near lilies and watch the moonlight ripple in the water. A sweet breeze blew through the spindly dogwood and skinny pine trees in his yard. The perfumes of gardenia and japonica, too rich for him, tickled his nose. A bat swooped through the overlapping limbs of an ancient pin oak.

In less than thirty minutes, he strode into an open field. Patches of thistle, milkweed, sumac, and goldenrod grew hay-high across it. An old broken shingle farmhouse tilted perpetually near ruin at one corner of the woods.

A big rig skidded around the arc of the new highway that skirted what once had been an end zone where he'd scored his first touchdown. As the truck seemed to rush toward him, one section of the field shone from its headlights, the crabgrass and tall weeds that had claimed it bright and unreal as in a movie. Every detail looked uncannily clear and artificial, as if each twig or stalk or leaf emitted its color and form from within.

The crumpled damp earth beneath his feet smelled like the clods the gravediggers had shoveled up from his mother's plot at noon today. As he raced through the weeds toward an imaginary goal post, trying not to stumble on patches of clotted grass or trip on an unseen rock, he could hear his mother, his brother in the stands, cheering him on.

In the morning, brakes off, Dash glided down their drive toward the street while he watched Jennie working on her tulips, red and yellow rows of them blooming in front of carefully pruned pink and white azaleas. She'd tied a kerchief around her hair. Her loose blouse dangled over faded jeans.

She protected her hands with heavy cloth gloves. With a short hoe, she bent over to chop into the soil or to cut the roots off weeds before she tossed them into the folded rectangular fragment of an old sheet she used to haul the waste to the mulch pile in the rear of their yard, near the gully. She paused from her labor to glance at him as he left, wiping the back of her right glove across her sweating brow.

They had been high school sweethearts. To most of their friends, they were high school sweethearts still, still the couple who led the last dance at the last prom, circling the gym's floor while all the others stood staring at them, a little dazzled and in awe of the way the world worked to its perfection through them. Dash waved toward his wife. She looked away and did not wave back.

Perched on a bobbing stem that poked through the trellised honeysuckle, a purple finch closed its beak on a fat berry. Their bright feathers shining after an early morning shower, two male cardinals squabbled on a limb of a giant hickory.

In his youth, his father had been an itinerant preacher. After he'd returned home from the war, having been wounded in a skirmish with fascist partisans slightly north of Naples, he'd founded his own Pilgrims Blessed Church of God and assembled a congregation of nearly a hundred souls, families who would stay faithful to him and his visions of doom for all except the graciously saved through three generations until his mind began to slip and wander. From the lectern Penn had built himself, wanting no one's help, his former choir master, a gentler soul, now thrilled those who remained with visions of the joyous heaven awaiting them all.

Dash stepped onto the creaking back porch of the house he'd been raised in, knocked on the door, opened it, and stepped into the kitchen. A ripped baseball cap on his head, his father sat on a stool, his skin cracked and dirty yellow like a chicken's foot. Drool dribbled down his chin and long weasel neck, staining his undershirt. With a finger, he stirred the already soggy cereal into mush as he held the bowl with his trembling hand.

He glanced at his son. One eye twitched. "Praise the Lord."

"Praise him all ye people," Dash replied, feeling as he always seemed to around his father like a child. He removed the bowl from his father's tight grip on it and set it down in the sink. With a towel that drooped over the spigot, on his knees, he cleaned the spattered floor.

He stood up and tapped his father's shoulder. "Do you want to sit outside for a while, Pop? It's a nice sunny day."

His father needed to blow his nose. "Where's Elizabeth? Where's your mother?"

"With the Lord," Dash said. "Don't you remember yesterday at all, Pop? The service? The singing?" He wiped under his eyes with the corner of a paper napkin and guided him out to the wooden bench his old man had made for his wife more than forty years before, when Dash was a little boy. Where his father sat, a few of the tulip tree's flowers's petals dropped into his lap. His fingers played with them. Several times, he brought his hands to his nose to smell them, smiled, and sniffed again.

A maze of furniture cluttered the living room. Many of the pieces his father had built himself: cane chair, wicker rocker, pine hutch, knick-knack stands, and cupboard, cedar chest, and two lamps constructed out of green wine bottles. All were squeezed into the one small room and shoved together as if in preparation for a move.

Dash sat near the top of the stairway to the second floor and surveyed the goods, all these years, nearly a whole life, now waiting impatiently to be sold at an auction to which few had come and none had bought. He should return them to where they belonged in the rooms, but Penn wouldn't approve. He wanted the money. He needed the money, he'd said. But there was no money.

Back outside, he sat next to his father who was quietly babbling. He held him tight and let him rest his head on his shoulder. He was wheezing like one of his old asthmatic hounds. "I want to go back to bed," his father said. "Make your mother let me go back to bed. Why is she all the time treating me like this? Making me work so hard day after day? I'm tired."

"Are you, Pop? Me too, some days," Dash said. "Real tired."

"Restless, you are. I can sense it. Like your brother was. I don't understand it. You boys, always dissatisfied. Always grouching. Where's your mother gone off to?"

"I don't know, Pop," Dash said. "I wish I did." He squeezed his hand. "You going to be all right for a while?"

"Sure. I reckon so."

"I'll be back later."

"Bide your time."

"I'm trying to, Pop."

"Help me back to bed. I need to sleep. So bad." His father's eyes widened as he surveyed the sky and breathed in the sweet-smelling air as deeply as he could manage. "It's going to be a dandy day. Just dandy."

In the divider between the two lanes of Laurel Road, the dogwood bloomed profusely every spring, the air full of its woody scent. Red bud petals showered the road and curbs. As he drove into the Y's parking lot, Dash honked a greeting at the gardener who was watering the rhododendron that lined the brick wall. A butterfly landed on the windshield of his parked car and opened its blue satin wings to the sun.

The locker room was empty. Wearing only his jock, Dash examined himself in a mirror. Beneath the bright lights, his muscles gleamed. Like armor, Dash thought for a second before he laughed at himself. The numbers on the scale read exactly the same as they had when he'd turned twenty-five. He checked for dark splotches or growth, pulled on his tank top, and tugged on his gym shorts. He worked out in the noisy weight room for over an hour.

When he entered it, the sauna was empty except for Jack Whitaker. He'd been wounded at An Loc in Vietnam. His scars crisscrossed his gaunt, falcon-like face and turned his few attempts at smiles into sneers. Its effect on others seemed to please him.

Long ago, in their early twenties, they'd been rivals for Jennie. In his living room, Jack displayed a photograph of a late nineteenth-century German dueling society. His maternal grandfather stood in the back row, far right. It was Jack's idea of a joke to point him out, never minding how often he'd done so before. He was a born dueler, he was letting people know. Everything in life was a contest, a challenge, a moment to take charge and gain the victory. He'd never forgiven Dash for winning her.

Sweat dribbled down his cheek and off his chin. He blinked at Dash. "What are you doing here, Penry, the day after your mother's been laid to rest, bless her soul?"

Dash tightened the towel wrapped around his waist. "I'm o.k., Jack. Thanks."

"Make sense for once, Dash, will you? You should be at home. In mourning. Or putting your troubles aside for a while returning to work at your tire store. I heard it's not doing so good, now that that chain has moved in." Jack wiped his fingers on the towel that lay across his lap, put his glasses back on, and unfolded the business section of the morning paper. "Your precious mother's body has just been placed into the ground. Respect it, why don't you?"

"I've mourned my dead, Jack."

He glanced up, squinting at him. "Have you? Really? Good for you. Tim, too, I suppose." His lips smacked. "My lord, what an unquiet grave Tim's has got to be."

"What do you mean by that?"

"Oh, nothing. Just saying."

Dash's left cheek had begun to twitch. "I always have hated your smug ass, Jack. I know you think my family's trash. That Jennie married way beneath her. Go screw yourself."

"That's the best you've got? Well, well. So I've gotten under your skin, have I, Dash? It doesn't take much, does it, champ?"

Dash's right fist meant to land exactly on the bone of Jack Whitaker's left jaw, but it missed and knocked his glasses off his nose, flinging them into the air. They perched precariously on the back of a bench and fell to the floor just as Dash's second punch veered off Whitaker's right shoulder. The third and fourth connected with his belly. "You're in shitty shape, Jack. You've been drinking too much whiskey. Fight me. Why don't you fight back, asshole?"

A drop of blood trickled down Jack's chin, mixed with his sweat, and seeped into the towel that Whitaker wiped across his face and chest. "And risk having your blood gush all over me? How do I know you haven't caught that virus from your faggot brother? How does anyone? Get out of here, Penry. You'll pay for this, believe me. I'll make sure you do. It's pure assault is what it is. Don't think I won't report this. I mean to ruin you, you scum."

"I'm certain you'll try to. Fine, go ahead," Dash said, flinging his towel over his shoulder and heading for the showers. He was outside the gym, near his car, breathing almost normally again before he'd noticed the broken skin on his knuckles seeping red.

Sitting across from her husband at the supper table, their two girls in their rooms studying for school the next day, Jennie rested her hands on a paper place mat. She dug into the embossed design with a sharpened fingernail. "You were in another fight today. I saw your hand. You shouldn't still be fighting at your age. It isn't right."

He smiled wanly. "Isn't it? Why not?"

"It's undignified, Dash."

"Undignified? Maybe so It wasn't much of a fight. Jack wouldn't fight back."

"I don't understand. Either of you. I never did."

"You should have married Jack, Jennie. That's what he thinks."

"It's not what I think."

"What do you think, Jennie?"

"Oh, Dash. Not now. Why are you always so angry these days, Dash? Every time I look at you, your hands are clenched into a fist. It makes no sense to me."

"You're a woman. It wouldn't. Women are better than us. Nicer. More peaceable. That's what you keep telling me anyway."

"Let's not argue, Dash. It's too late for that. Too late in our lives."

"What's gone so wrong with mine, Jennie, that so many people think they have a right to despise me? Including you."

"I don't despite you," Jennie said, looking away, toward the bronze light of the sunset that filtered through the gauze curtains. "I admire you. I admire what you did for your brother. Bringing him home from Charleston. Back here to sleepy, peaceful, quiet, mean-spirited Cherith where you knew no one would understand or sympathize for a second. I just can't accept that it had to happen, you see. To us, to this family, to our daughters. All that fear we had to suffer from, too. It wasn't fair. The silent, unostentatious ostracism. The girls are just beginning to recover. Their boyfriends are back to calling them and walking beside them to classes, thank god."

The clock chimed six. The last of the sunlight poured into the fancy bottles that Jennie displayed along the window sills and flowed out onto the opposite walls where the colors blazed like stained glass. Starlings swarmed the birdbath in the backyard where a neighbor's near-feral cat prowled and hissed as they attacked it. A TV in the house next door shouted out a message for a snack Dash had never heard of while rap music thrummed loudly from a window in a house across the street. Its dog barked unstintingly.

"Are you afraid of me, too, Jennie?"

"Afraid of you? Yes." She wouldn't look at him. "Yes, I am. Very much."

"Why, Jennie?"

"Because I can't forget that day I walked into Tim's room at Penn's and saw you covered all over with his blood. All over, Dash. Skin. Clothes. Hair. It might have been your blood I was seeing, not Tim's. It terrified me. You terrify me."

"Why, Jennie? Tell me better why. Please."

"Because I don't love you. Because you don't love me. Because we never have loved each other. Not ever. Separate bedrooms for a decade bear witness to that, doesn't it?" She took a deep, almost sensual breath. "Because I don't want you here in this house anymore. I want you to leave, Dash. Because I don't know what you'll say or do when I tell you to go. When I say our twenty years together have all been an awful mistake."

"Like I said, you should have married Jack."

"That's a stupid remark, Dash. Unworthy of you. Please don't repeat it to me ever again," Jennie said. She gathered some plates and glasses from the table and left the room.

It was several hours after dark before he heard the locusts again. His wife's heels clicked down the uncarpeted hall. The air in the corridor was filled with her perfume. He wanted her next to him, lying next to him, holding him not as a lover but as a friend. He wanted to be able to confess his secrets to her, those he'd known all his life, those he only recently discovered he'd been keeping even from himself. Why did he learn so late in his life about his need for freedom? He'd been living his forty-four years, every day of them, in a land that felt to him now devoted solely to loss.

He wanted to be honest with her, but he didn't know how to be truthful, with her or himself or anyone. Whenever he'd offered her his hand for her to hold, she'd refused it. When he'd pressed the side of his head against her soft arm last night as they sat side by side on the couch, she let it stay there only until his silent crying had ceased.

While the girls were busily dressing for school and Jennie was scrambling eggs as she watched an early morning weather report, Dash left the house without saying good-bye. He already knew he wouldn't be back except to pick up some of his things and later, maybe, to visit his daughters for an hour or two every few weeks. Or months. Those would be Jennie's rules, harsh and unbreakable. He couldn't quarrel with them. She was probably right. He had no intention of staying, remaining behind, beyond what he had to.

Thin clouds coated the sky with a dappled gray as dull as the tarnish on chrome. As he walked the path toward his car, it was so quiet he could hear doves cooing in the ditch around back, their gentle gurgling as peaceful as the old fountain in the park where most of his life he'd enjoyed swapping sports stories with the old timers who whiled away their last days sitting on a cement bench under a big oak lamenting the loss of the old good righteous ways of doing things they'd known like the bible as boys or young men.

As he climbed the stairs to his father's room, Dash rehearsed what he would say, how he would tell him that he'd be living again in his father's home, taking care of him, of his father, the once popular fire and brimstone preacher Penry, in the same house where his brother had died, no one, no place else willing to take him in, the reason kept secret from Penn, the preacher, the holy man who wouldn't have stood for it, who couldn't have understood it, who believed to the end it was some sort of consumption Tim had contracted that had wasted him away and brought him so low as to spew blood out of his flesh corrupted body. Oh, Tim was a sinner. His father had no doubt about that. He just didn't know how far he'd fallen into the pit.

Dash moved as slowly as he used to when he was scared of being scolded or whipped. He hesitated outside the door, rapped, and twisted the knob. "Pop?"

"Who are you? What do you want?"

"It's Dash." He hesitated for a moment. "Your son."

"Dash, is it? Go away. I'm fine. I've got the Lord laying his hand on me."

"Unlock the door, Pop."

"Go back to town. You're nothing but bad luck."

"Pop."

The bed springs squeaked. The old man shuffled toward the door. A lock clicked. The door cracked open. The room smelled of greens and pork lard, an unfinished plate of them lying on the floor, and an old man's pee. He appeared less annoyed than puzzled. "Where's your mother? I've been looking all over the house. Out in the fields. I can't find her nowheres."

"She's dead, Pop. She's been dead a week."

He look bewildered. "A whole week?"

"Here. Let me help you back into bed. Your nose is runny as a sick dog's."

He slipped his hands under his father's armpits and guided him, light as one of his daughters, toward the mattress. His joints cracked like dry twigs. His eyes were possum red. Where they glistened from mucous and spit, Dash dabbed his father's lips with a tissue.

"She was just here a minute ago," his father said. "And then I couldn't find her again."

"It was a dream, Pop."

His father shook his head. "No, not a dream. She was here, real and alive as you are. She asked me what I wanted for supper. She said she'd cooked me whatever I liked. So I ate me some of those greens and fatback she prepared there, see?" His father's tongue clapped against the roof of his mouth and stuck there until he could moisten it again with the water Dash poured for him from a jug. "I've had a shock."

"I know, Pop."

"She was right here, standing about where you're standing now." His head fell back into a dent in the pillows. "Now you tell me she's dead."

"You'll see her again real soon, Pop. I promise."

"I will?" His father's eyes strained to open wider. "Of course I will, praise Jesus."

As soon as he'd found an old wire scrub brush, a bucket, and a hefty hunk of caustic soap under the kitchen sink, Dash went to work on the kitchen until it was almost spotless again, as it always was while Elizabeth was still strong enough to keep it as clean as she insisted it look, despite the many ailments and complaints of her later years, the arthritis, the angina, the weak heart. He slopped the black water out of the bucket onto a thick layer of pine needles near the woods. As the water seeped into the earth, the needles sieved out chunks of char and bits of old dried food.

Back in the house, he pressed an ear against his father's door. Penn wheezed and hissed as he slept. Dash tiptoed down the hall to the room which had been his and Tim's but which their mother had converted into her own private place after both boys had left home, first Dash to the army, then Tim to college. She preferred the view from it, she'd said, how it looked out on a new paved road rather than worn out, untilled fields, no use to anyone anymore, just dirt and weeds and a few harmless snakes.

"Explain to me," his mother had begged him there just last winter a few days after Tim had been quietly buried in Penn's church's crowded graveyard, twenty times more people in the ground along side him than those who'd attended, his parents, Dash and his family, three girls, now women, he'd known in high school, Cole Roberts who'd driven down from Richmond, Dash could only guess why or how he knew.

"Tell me. Where did Timothy go, Dash?" his mother had asked "He said he was a pilgrim. That was what he was, he said, a pilgrim in a new land. What did he mean, 'pilgrim'? The bible says the Lord will always bless his faithful. Stay here with me just a little longer, Son, I feel so bereft and lost. Let me feel through you how I am still so abundantly blessed."

His father, his upbringing, their church, school, most of his life had taught Dash that pilgrims were serious people in search of the Lord. Had his brother been serious? Was that what his mother had been asking him?

She was blessed by all of her children, his mother had said just minutes after Tim had died, a scene he'd failed to protect her from.

"I know," she'd confessed to him later through her tears. "I know he'd had to leave us. I know why."

Green was her favorite color, especially lime green. She'd decorated her room—the walls, the chintz pillows and cushion, the gauzelike frilly bedding—all in a green the frothy color of lime sherbet melting into ginger ale that was at weddings, other festive occasions a Baptist's sugary, unpalatable substitute for champagne. His mother's most treasured photographs sat on a swatch of apple-green lace spread out on her oak dresser, the only piece of furniture she had brought to this house from her childhood.

Dash's army picture was on the right, the same one he had given to Jennie Haynes before they were engaged. It still hung over her vanity, part of her tribute to her "hero," as Jennie used to say, teasing him. Tim's was on the left, snapped by Dash the day his brother had graduated from Chapel Hill, a peace symbol taped to his mortar board, long blond hair blowing in the wind as he smiled proudly, the first Penry to graduate from college, two fingers of his right hand forming a V.

Dash blew the dust off the glass and put it back on the dresser just as his father, startling him, grabbed the door handles to keep from falling. Dash eased him into a chair whose rockers where they had slid off the braided rug struck the floor like shoes dropping. Withe-thin and sun-splotched, his father's arms trembled where they rested on the chair.

222

His eyes darted about the room as if following a fly's trapped flight. "I thought she was calling for me. I thought I heard Elizabeth."

"No, Pop."

"She's out there hiding in the woods. She pretended to be strong as a man. But she wasn't. She took fright easy, your mother did." He tugged on the furry hair that grew out of his ears. "It broke her heart when Timothy went. She loved that boy so."

"You loved Timmy best, too, didn't you?"

"Didn't mean to."

"I know. It's all right, Pop."

"A strange boy, though, Tim." His father scratched his chin. "It looks like a fine night."

"Let's go sit on the porch. What do you say, Pop?"

Dash kept the porch swing stable while he helped his father sit in it. Squatting on the top step of the stoop, Dash rested his back on a splintering post that shifted slightly as the full weight of his body pressed against it. In the moonlight, the hydrangea looked like the paper bouquets his younger daughter would dip in blue ink to wear in her hair. Crickets chirped and twittered in unison.

His father sucked on his cheeks and spat in an arc toward the grass. "My mind's not right sometimes, Son. I wish you'd stay here. With me. I wish you could."

"I'm going to, Penn. I intend to. From now on."

"What good am I? I can't preach anymore." He scratched at an itch under his jeans. "You think I was serious about your taking care of me? I was just testing you."

"Like you always did."

"Darn right. What about your girls? What about Jennie? I got no life left to live, Dash, darn it all. I'm not much longer for this world. You imagine I don't know it? I like life. I'll miss it. But I'm glad of dying. I'm glad to be bound for paradise. But I worry about you. About your soul. About your family. Think of them, not me. The Lord's care is all I need."

"I do think of them, Pop. All the time. Let's not talk about it. Not now, please." Dash stretched his arms. Muscles twitched uncomfortably. "Not ever, Penn. I've got no choice. I'll be sleeping here from now on."

Penn spat over the porch railing. "Something good's gone badly wrong. Something's not right, not right at all." His father sat up straighter, tugging on a chain. "What are you trying to tell me? Don't disappoint me, Dash. Don't let me down like your brother. You want to take what little I've got left away from me? God gave you a wife and two fine, beautiful daughters. You're their breadwinner. You're their comfort and provider and solace. You go on home now, boy. I mean it. I'll be fine. I have my bad hours, some bad days, it seems like. But I can take care of myself and what I can't handle Jesus will."

"No, you can't, Pop. You never could."

"Yes, I can. I'm in the Lord's watchful eye. That's all that matters." His hands formed bony fists he pounded on his thighs. "People talk too much nonsense, stuff no man needs to hear. Your mother too, always restless, never satisfied with anything. I could hardly keep that woman's mouth shut once she started in on something." With enormous effort, his father pushed himself out of the swing and away from Dash, grabbed the door handle for support, and shuffled into the house. "Blabbing, going on and on," he muttered. "Dreams, she had, she said. Dreams." He spat. "Stuff and nonsense. You go back home where you belong and stay there. I don't need you. I never did. None of you."

"You needed us all, Pop. Still do. So hush." Dash took his father's left hand in his right and aided him up the stairs.

"Untie these boots for me," Penn said as he sat on the bed. The springs were so weak they sagged beneath his wasted body.

Dash set the shoes down in the opposite corner. "Your socks need washing. So do your feet. They stink."

"I know. I can't help it." His father lay back on the quilt and stared up at the ceiling, his eyes fixed on a light fixture filled with insect carcasses. "You know what I'd do if I wasn't a bible-believing Christian and a god-fearing man? I'd shoot myself."

"Don't talk crazy, Pop." Dash unfastened his father's pants and drew them off him harshly. "Your legs are covered with sores."

"You got rough hands, boy." His father struggled with his teeth and put them aside on the nightstand.

"Good night, Pop," Dash said as he switched off the lights.

"You mind me, boy. You mind what I said," Penn mumbled. "And you tell your mother to get in here. Tell her to hurry. I got a terrible pain in my legs."

Outside, as he sat on the stoop, all the lights inside turned off, something as sweet and sticky as the smell of honeysuckle clung to the locusts' drone and dizzied his senses like an intoxicant. The sweetness of it at once confused him and left him feeling for a moment elated. He abandoned the house and circled the little pine grove that bordered the tobacco field. When he felt the need to sob pierce his gut, he tightened his muscles against it. Not now, he warned himself, not here.

But instead of dying away the grief surged through his body as uncontrollably as an orgasm in the final moments of ecstasy. He grabbed an oak limb to keep from falling. The tree frogs' croaking throbbed like the pulse in his ears.

Lights from cars driving on the country road along the field illuminated the caterpillar tents in the trees and the thickets of plants that thrived in the gullies in what early last summer, after having taken what would prove to be his final walk outside, Tim had called a beautiful, tangled profusion. Wild roses, ivy, kudzu, blue grass, queen anne's lace, brome, chickweed, all rooted in the same soil, the same muddy gully, struggling for the same light that broke through the woods' canopy of sycamore and oak and hickory, all intertwined together.

"Life's excess," Tim had said a short time later as he steadied himself by holding on to the back of a chair in his room.

Had he meant he hated life now or was he still marveling at it? When Dash tried to coax him into bed, he wouldn't budge, but pointed out the windows. "Look at it all, Dash. Just look at it. Hard as you can. This is all of God's face we'll ever see. The uncanny, lovely earth we live on for so brief a while. The whole world's just like that gully we saw this morning, a beautiful, horrid mess all mixed up together, appalling and wonderful. That's all. That's all it will ever be, I promise, wherever you go, whatever new world it is you've told me since you were a kid you'd like to travel to some day. Just don't wait too long, Dash. You're almost old already. Or too soon will be. Like me, now."

Was it really all? Dash was trying to see for himself, to find some way of believing in a world that made sense to him, no matter how hard or far away or long he might have to search to discover it. What was he hoping to find? The more he noticed, the more he saw of it, the stranger life became.

What did he want? His father had preached that the sins of fallen mankind meant that those benighted fools who sought freedom from God found only more to mourn for, their lost souls most of all.

All right. Perhaps no one's ever completely free. To leave means to return, at least in your spirit. Every pilgrimage requires doing penance to whatever, whoever it is you've left behind, maybe abandoned, whether you meant to or not. That's what Tim had taught him without intending to, wasn't it? Or would Tim have laughed at him for believing it was true? That life was in part inevitably penitence, just as their father had claimed?

For a second or two, the sky was illuminated by another flash of sheet lightning. Thunder rumbled across the sky. Like his mother, Dash loved a good storm. Rain or, if he was lucky, maybe a roaring downpour would shower on him soon. No pestilence, no pebble-sized hail, but a cleansing he dearly sought.

Tomorrow, better weather permitting, he would start to work on the barn. That job done, there were shingles to paint and stairs and wiring to repair in the house. He could replant parts of the abandoned fields, fallow too long, where the soil was still almost fertile.

He'd need to keep busy. He didn't want to have to think. Not yet. There would be time for thinking later and for a different life, too, perhaps. By betraying his own life, he'd wounded the lives of Jennie and his daughters. Perhaps they might forgive him some day.

In the days ahead, he might begin to learn how to become the man he probably ought to have been from the start. He had much to discover. But for now, for a while longer, he must wait, wait and mourn. Nothing could change, not really, until after he'd known more grief, after his father had died and he'd sold, if he could, with pain in his heart, the last of his father's father's father's long-dying farm.

Freedom

Waste water run off, nearly black
from power company coal ash,
balls-shrinking cold from mountain
streams, an abandoned gravel
pit, hidden deep in back
woods, loosened stones splashing past the surface's pane-
like shine down a fathomless well.

And he, naked, uneasily balanced on a ledge
of the cliff, arms spread wide for a swan dive,
leaping off the edge toward the pool, not frightened, his dive like a kingfisher's after catch, plung-
ing in head first, his body ash-tarred but surviv-
ing the fall, lying on grass, reveling in sunlight.

Give Us Peace

A converted mansion, the Baptist Home was built on flat farmland: sparse windows, black oak molding, paneling, wainscoting, no carpets on hard floors, no flowers, no decorative pictures, no paintings allowed, all profane, worldly scenes forbidden. A black slate roof is capped by a bell tower that narrows to a steeple's sharp point. A curving thick brick wall borders a horseshoe drive. Each spring, when the grounds flood, debris dragged from ragged upriver farms litters the yard. During the storms, Ned hears the walls talk. Like an insomniac, he glares at bare boards and swears ghosts sigh through windy cracks or chinks in the chimney.

Next to Mrs. Kittle's office, in the break room, Jeremy clicks on the TV, prays the war won't last another month. For Jesse's sake, he stays vigilant, listens to reports of the battles fought, suicide bombings, roadside explosions in Iraq. Though he refuses to recall his dreams, they hurt him bad all day.

The rain has turned to sleet, the sleet to ice, buckling trees and bushes. Pole wires sag. He pronounces with the announcer Baghdad, Al Anbar, Fallujah, Samara. Then checks on Ned, gazing out the window, to him one season much the same as any other. The river rises or falls, the birds soar away or fly back, the brick wall crumbles more, an old cedar grows taller, its boldest limbs touching his sill with their fingers.

Jeremy undresses him, slips on his nightshirt, carries him, so light he might be his child, to bed. Ned vows he never sleeps, fearful of the little boy inside his head who begs to save him from the dark. Childless, he sometimes talks about his young grandson fighting in the Middle East.

"Peaceful," Jeremy says to comfort families when they ask how kin die in the Home. "Peaceful." But he knows, if Jesse has been killed since his last letter, he didn't die peacefully. Shock and awe. Few people ever do. Not even Jesus did. He tucks Ned into his unmade bed, begs him not to tell him his dreams again, leaving always unsaid Jeremy's fear of his own.

In the blank dark, Ned again watches his younger brothers run away, through with mucking barns, slopping hogs, spreading manure. In his store, he'd sold hard candy, chews, snuff tins, cotton bolts, jeans, shoes, boots, mugs, jugs, earthenware plates, hammers, saws, levels, ladders, bright glass beads, paper flowers, wax fruit, straw hats, their bands either yellow or red. In time, the aisles lengthened, narrowed, the store smelled musty as an attic, stinging noses like dust blown off a fallow pasture.

On his eightieth birthday, a preacher pinned a medal on his lapel because he'd never missed a Sunday service or a Wednesday night choir practice in over seventy years. Try as he might, he can't recall falling the next morning between a pile of tin buckets and a pot display, his scalp bleeding from a gash it took when it bashed the counter.

He feels sorry for the birds and squirrels whose nature compels them to live all winter in snow. In newspaper photos, soldiers march by ruined sand-colored buildings, their faces glassy with sweat. His room smells like the liver pills he'd sold. Lights on, Jeremy offers him a chew and wipes off a resin-colored crust that's formed round his nostrils and teary eyes. Ned lets him, though he's never cottoned to the idea of men replacing women as nurses.

Ned's favorite time of day is dawn, not for the sun it promises but the light it discreetly holds back while he's stripped, made to pee, sponge bathed, shaved, dressed, brushed, combed. His pants and shirt droop off him like a child playing in grown-up's clothes. Suddenly tired of it all, the time he spends each day and night uselessly dying, getting nowhere, he picks his walking sticks off the floor, sneaks down the hall past Jeremy who's distracted by the TV, and wanders out the door, unnoticed and free.

But his sticks crisscross on the sidewalk, his legs buckle. A hum like the river's sings in his head and curves lazily away, like a boy on his bike. The nurse's hands, picking him up, are so kind he sobs at his touch.

"You could have broken your hip," Mrs. Kittle scolds him back in his bed. He tugs on his thin white hair, purses his lips, despairs. Will he ever walk again, with sticks or without? Jeremy expresses no doubts and tells him again the story of how he and a friend, lost after running out of gas driving off the road the south slope of High Rock, had stumbled out of the woods into a moonlit clearing just after Jeremy had spent his last match.

Back from basic training, just before shipping out Jess had sung him a bawdy ballad while he tinkered with his truck. Jeremy sings it to Ned, humming the words to the dirtier parts, and delights as the old man smiles.

After lights out, Jeremy refolds Jesse's weeks old letter along its creases and tucks it into a back pocket of his uniform. The Home's perpetual dim light, like the last rays of twilight, frightens him some. Not even by day, after he's drawn back the curtains and lifted the shades, does the sun ever brighten its halls and rooms.

Once he's heard enough of the news on the TV, he moves from room to room, against the rules clicking some lamps back on, longing to be surprised by some attractive print hanging on a wall, a rug with an arresting pattern, flowers in a lovely vase. So much of the best of life is forbidden by religion. Him and Jess. Him and his God. The war must be over soon. It must. It makes no sense to fight for lies.

Outside, the lawn sparkles like salt. As a full moon lifts over the old oak grove, patches of the white world below gleam like his mother's porcelain set on her shiny, silver-threaded linen cloth—the one she promised his sister after her high school sweetheart finally proposed.

Anxious, drawn, Jeremy is spending too much of the morning in the break room, listening to new reports. Down the hall, Maud Swindle thumps her cane on the floor. Mrs. Kittle calls to Jeremy from her door to look in on Room 214 first. So weak he can no longer sit without support, Ned is staring out his window. Jeremy sneaks in and sits next to him to hold his hand. For the first time, Ned lets him.

Mrs. Kittle is standing outside, looking in. They could be two good children minding each other on a park bench or a pew in church. "The Lord shine his face on us," Ida Kittle murmurs, "and give us...." She couldn't finish.

Overcome, she retreats to her office. Sixty-six, yet she still misses the wrapped baubles her mother would leave at night on her chest of drawers, the hard candy treats her father brought her home from work, warm and sticky from his fist.

An Old Man's Prayer

Old age, like childhood, is a time for make believe, for reveries
in the fog by day, by the fire at night, any half-light
that allows you to recover the past, the truth, the clarities
bestowed on life as it slips through mist and out of sight.
Return to me, my friend, to the field where, before, I
patiently waited for you by a pine grove, high fences, black bulls
in a pasture, your clothes, face, hair drenched from rain,
boy's swings hanging by chains creaking in the storm, not a lie
I fantasize but a story from long ago I daydream of that lulls
me into believing for a while that both of us are young again,
you vivid in the back of the barn, not seen through the haze, the blur
of failing eyes, the two of us washing afterwards in the water
that soaks us as black clouds empty on us. My love, my last reality,
you're worth more than all the world I'm leaving. Do not forget me.

Acknowledgments

Movietone: Detour was first published in *Fourteen Hills* and also appeared in 'Prize Stories 1998,' *The O. Henry Awards*.

Return of the Fallen was first published in a radically different version as "Dying" in *Magazine*, a publication of San Francisco State University. It also appeared in *In a Time of Combat for the Angel* (Five Fingers Press). The two stories are so distinct in both substance and theme, however, as to constitute not different versions of one story but two distinct and separate stories. Many of the anecdotes about Earl Long and much of the attitude toward him in it are indebted to A. J. Liebling's *Earl of Louisiana*.

A Pilgrim from the Land of Loss was first published as "Pilgrimage" in the *Harrington Literary Quarterly*. It, too, has been significantly revised since its first publication.

Give Us Peace appeared first in *Prick of the Spindle* where it had been awarded the Grand Prize for prose. The version of the story in this book has been updated from World War Two to the Second Iraq War.

Dedications

The Return of What's Been Lost is for Clarinda Harriss.

The Wild Waters in This Roar is for Susan and Sam Crowl.

Movietone: Detour is dedicated to the memory of George Stambolian.

Missa is for John Nichols.

Whose Woods, Their Silence is for Forrest Gander.

Gift Givers is for Jon O'Bergh.

Return of the Fallen is dedicated to the memory of Michael Rubin.

My Father is for Kevin Dyer.

Heavy Fog on an Early Morning in Late July is for Robert Mohr.

Snow Cover is dedicated to the memory of John Arthur Pettet.

When Summers Were Younger is dedicated to the memory of Jay Hayes.

A Story of Love and the Sea is dedicated to the memory of Gerry Colletti.

Laguna Beach is for Mary Walshok.

Morning Light at Sunset is for Elizabeth Spinner.

The Schlieffen Plan is for David Bjork.

The Return of the Prodigal Son is for L.D. Siedler.

Mallards is for Helen and Jack Alford.

A Pilgrim from the Land of Loss is dedicated to the memory of W.S.F.

Freedom is for David Morris.

Give Us Peace is for Lindley Young.

Many thanks to Galen Garwood for his constant support and contributions, beyond measuring, to this book.

Peter Weltner has published five previous books of fiction, including *The Risk of His Music* and *How the Body Prays*, five poetry chapbooks, among them *The One-Winged Body* and *Water's Eye* (both in collaboration with the artist Galen Garwood), and six full length collections of poetry, *News from the World at My Birth: A History*, *The Outerlands*, *To the Final Cinder*, *Stone Altars*, *Late Summer Storm in Early Winter* (with photographs and paintings by Galen Garwood), and most recently *The Light of the Sun Become Sea*. He and his husband live in San Francisco by the ocean.